THE PRINCE'S PILOT

SHELLEY ADINA
R.E. SCOTT

Moonshell
Books

© 2022 Shelley Adina Bates and Regina Lundgren

License Note

This eBook is licensed for your personal enjoyment only. It may not be resold or given away to other people unless it is part of a lending program. If you're reading this book and did not purchase it, or it was not purchased for lending, please delete it from your device and purchase your own copy. Thank you for respecting the authors' work and livelihood.

This is a work of fiction. Names, characters, places, and incidents are a product of the authors' imaginations. Locales and public names are sometimes used for atmospheric purposes. Any resemblance to actual people, living or dead, or to businesses, companies, events, institutions, or locales is completely coincidental.

Cover design by Tugboat Design. Images used by permission.

The Prince's Pilot / Shelley Adina and R.E. Scott—1st ed.

ISBN 978-1-950854-45-5

R100822

❀ Created with Vellum

PRAISE

"Adina and Scott launch their Regent's Devices series with a witty and whimsical flight of fancy in a subgenre they call *Prinnypunk* (Regency-era steampunk); it plays out as a delightfully fun mash-up of Jane Austen and Jules Verne, right down to the hint of sweet romance and the array of ingenious inventions."

— BOOKLIST ON *THE EMPEROR'S AERONAUT*

"I recommend this series for readers who enjoy adventure, subterfuge, and a realistic plot line that will hold their attention and never insult their intelligence. Steampunk, historical fiction, and the wits of two amazing authors blend seamlessly to give readers an adventure that will long linger in their minds."

— HUNTRESS REVIEWS ON *THE PRINCE'S PILOT*

FIND MORE DARING ADVENTURE TO LOVE

Sign up for Shelley Adina's mailing list and begin the adventure with "The Abduction of Lord Will."

Sign up for Regina Scott's mailing list and learn what happened in France while Celeste was in England.

Don't miss out!

~

IN THIS SERIES

The Emperor's Aeronaut
The Prince's Pilot
The Lady's Triumph

To friends near and far.
What would we do without you?

THE PRINCE'S PILOT

CHAPTER 1

TRURO, CORNWALL

Late August 1819

"Is there anything else I might do to assist you, Loveday?"

Such a civil inquiry to be made in such a roar, but this was red-bearded, irascible Thomas Trevithick, who had probably proposed to his wife at the same volume.

"Thank you, Thomas, but no," Loveday Penhale said over the ringing of Rudolph Clement's hammer as he battled a sheet of copper. "This small boiler is even better than our last one, thanks to you and your men here. Now that we have installed it in the gondola, I believe we may call it complete."

What a change three months had wrought—free rein at the steam works for herself and her friend Celeste Blanchard, actual civilities falling from Thomas's lips instead of criticisms, and tolerance of their presence that was now almost cordial.

It was as great a miracle as finding lifting gas in the depths of the Cornish bedrock.

"Aye, it's a fine bit of work," he agreed. "Better this be done in the full light of day, and not cobbled together with bits and bobs and hope."

"We still have hope," she reminded him with a grin. *"That* did not wind up in the sea in the spring, at any rate."

He hesitated, his ham-sized hands pushed into the pockets of his leather apron. "Tez glad I am, Loveday, that you made landfall on your own doorstep. It would have been a sad loss to us all if you'd gone down with your air ship." His face turned even more scarlet than usual. It looked almost painful.

She resisted the urge to pat his shoulder, for that would have embarrassed them both to no end. "We will not distress ourselves with the might-have-beens," she said bracingly. "Come, tell me what you think of my work on this narrow-gauge copper piping."

Relieved, he bent to inspect it, and they returned to a congenial discussion of hydraulics and pressure. Celeste sent her a commiserating smile from where she was inspecting the installation of the steam engine.

Yes, how far they had come in every part of their lives since May! For once the original *Lark* had been launched and her remains subsequently washed ashore near the St Mawes harbor—truly, there must be some reason why the tides so consistently brought in large floating objects that she and Celeste had misplaced—there was no keeping secret any longer what the two of them meant to do.

Compete for the Prince's prize. And win.

She and Celeste were young and unmarried. Neither of them were permitted to attend a university to take a degree in engineering, like Emory Thorndyke over there at the metal forge. Neither possessed the means to build an air ship, only the imagination and the will.

And yet they had done it.

They'd built it, and flown it nearly to France and back, and lived to tell the tale.

Now, as though the district had been shaken awake by the novelty and sheer nerve of such an endeavor, Loveday and Celeste were suddenly—well, perhaps not the belles of the ball, but certainly the apple of their neighbors' eyes. Why, even Sir Robert Jermyn, the terribly severe magistrate for Truro who used to frighten Loveday half to death as a child with his beetling eyebrows and abrupt manner, had stopped his landau in the street two days ago to greet her and Celeste as they walked back from visiting their friend, the elderly émigré Madame Racine.

"Good day, Miss Penhale, Miss Aventure," he had said, lifting his hat.

Loveday curtsied and hoped the two seconds with her head bowed would be enough to wipe the astonishment from her face. And for Celeste to remember she still went by an alias.

"How is that flying vessel of yours coming along?" he boomed.

A pair of women with baskets over their arms had slowed to hear the reply.

"Very well, sir," Celeste had answered when Loveday could not find her tongue. "We obtained the silk for the new envelope for a very good price, since we could not use the old after its second sea-bathe. Thank you for recommending that mill in Bristol."

He looked pleased, though the silk was such a revolting shade of brown it was no wonder no lady had wanted to purchase it. They'd had all the bolts for next to nothing, for they could not be particular at this late date.

"And we have had a new gondola built to specifications and have not had to importune our neighbors for their old carriages to be cut up for the purpose," Celeste went on.

"Capital," he had said, his face creaking into a smile. "We'll have that prize, won't we?"

"I certainly hope so, Sir Robert," Loveday finally managed. "Though it seems the high-pressure pump built for the mines by the Trevithick Steam Works may give us a run for our money."

He had nodded sagely. "You have the right of it, Miss Penhale. Either way, we'll put Cornwall on the map."

"We will indeed, sir."

And he had tapped the floor of his landau with his cane to signal his coachman and rolled away, leaving that little word ringing in Loveday's ears.

We.

Oh, dear. If something went wrong, it would no longer simply reflect badly on her and Celeste. Or even Emory, who had perfected his pump at last.

Their failure would reflect badly on all the county.

But she must not think of that. She had spent far too many hours of her life feeling like a failure. A failure to be graceful and accomplished. A failure to be a good marital prospect. She and Celeste were something else now. Something England had all too rarely seen.

They were aeronauts.

A glow of happiness suffused her that had nothing to do with the sun pouring in the isinglass windows of the workshop. She and Celeste were *aeronauts*. What other young lady in the country could say the same?

"Miss Penhale, Miss Aventure," Colin Treloar called from the big double doors of the workshop that faced the street. "The wain's come for your flying boat."

"It's come early! Celeste, we shall have to finish installing the pipes at home." Thomas and Rudolph were already rolling the overhead pulleys into place to hoist the gondola into the wagon behind the Puffing Jenny.

While Celeste rolled up the pipes in canvas, Loveday hurried over to Colin. "Have them back the wain up to the turntable and we shall have our Jenny deliver it directly."

"Tisn't any old *them*, miss. It's Captain Trevelyan from Gwynn Place and your Mr Pascoe."

She tilted her head back as Pascoe, the Penhale stable master, backed the big Percheron borrowed from one of the Jermyn farms so that the wain could receive the gondola. "Captain Trevelyan, I did not expect you today."

Arthur Trevelyan dismounted a little awkwardly from the vehicle's bench and bowed once he had reached the ground. "It has been some years since I rode in a wain, I must admit. But the excitement of collecting the gondola was too much to resist."

"What, no racing curricle?"

"And be thought of as an obstruction in the road compared to the triumphant progress of the new and improved *Lark Deux*? I think not." His hazel eyes twinkled, and not for the first time, she marveled at his utter lack of pretension or self-importance. Instead, he entered into the spirit of the thing with the gravity of a man and the enthusiasm of a boy.

The sound of rapid footsteps made them turn.

"Vite, Loveday!" Celeste cried, her arms full of canvas-wrapped piping. "Stand aside or you will be run over."

To put punctuation to her words, the Puffing Jenny let off a gout of steam with a whistling sound that pierced the ears. And here she came, the tiny locomotive engine with the tall stack, stronger than a brace of oxen. She ran back and forth on her track in the workshop to take heavy equipment to the street. Coupled to her was a flat-bed wagon, on which the gondola had been roped. Their Puffing Jenny was very similar to Richard Trevithick's original engine, the *Catch Me Who Can*, built right here in this shop by the great man.

"Oh, but this is exciting," Celeste whispered. "I can scarcely breathe."

After all their work, all their revised plans, their dreams were now coming to fruition. No more cut-up carriages for them—the new gondola had been financed by Mr Trevelyan and Loveday's father, in a humbling show of confidence in their abilities.

Loveday took her arm. "Isn't it marvelous? Careful, now, the turntable is about to move."

The Puffing Jenny rolled onto the turntable, and with a jerk and a puff of steam from the engine below the floor, it began to move. When it locked into place, the Jenny now faced back the way it had come, the wagon neatly lined up with the rear of the wain. The pulleys and winch rolled down their track to the door, and their new gondola was lifted onto the wain, to be cradled in a generous bed of straw. How lovely it was—as smooth and sleek as a seashell, its wooden curves gleaming in the sunlight.

Celeste gave a sigh of happiness.

"It is a lovely sight," Emory said as he walked up, his gaze resting warmly upon her friend.

"It is," Arthur agreed. "Pascoe, are you sure you trust me with this great beast?"

"His name is Hugo, Sir Robert's man tells me. It is more a matter of his trusting you, sir, and I believe our journey here made it clear he does. Now, Miss Celeste, if you will step up, I will go back and tie down your vessel."

With a smile of thanks, Celeste laid the bundle of pipes in the straw and held out her hand to Emory so he might help her up. "We must not keep the captain waiting any longer."

Pascoe made short work of the ropes, ensuring the gondola would not fall over or suffer any damage on the way, though goodness knew the apparatus was sturdy enough that it would take more than a pothole in the road to move it. Sturdy, but light, its form would sail through air more easily than a ship through water. As easily as the lark for which it was named.

Not for nothing had they taken two weeks of unrelenting work to create a scale model of the *Lark Deux*, right to the silk envelope with its internal corset made of wicker and a second, more durable bladder of treated canvas inside the corset to hold the lifting gas. Each pipe, each tiny control, was created from clock parts and scraps of copper and tin. Even the vanes operated, to control direction and altitude. Loveday had built an engine no bigger than her clenched fist, and when the whole was assembled, Loveday's family had joined her and Celeste on the lawn to test it.

And it had flown, on the end of an entire spool of Mama's silk thread, which Loveday subsequently had to spend the evening rewinding. The landing was not quite as successful as they had hoped, and had broken both the bow vanes, but she and Celeste had soon made an adjustment to their placement. When she came in at full size, nothing on the hull would interfere with the ability of *Lark Deux* to moor or launch, including their mount and dismount.

"Miss Penhale, may I assist you up?" Arthur held out a hand.

Oh, that rascal Pascoe! He had engineered it on purpose so that Celeste would sit on the outside and she in the middle, next to Arthur. But she kept her head high. "Thank you, Captain." She waved to Thomas and Emory, and they were off.

Somehow, though they had told no one that the gondola would be going home today, word had got out. People stopped in the streets to cheer, and children came to their garden gates to wave as they went by. Even Hugo, Loveday was quite certain, had a livelier step as he pulled a wain as full of hope as it was of their invention through town and out onto the road that led to their village and home.

"I wonder if the Tinkering Prince himself will have such a reception when he rides through town." Arthur's voice held laughter.

"I should hope he would have quite a lot more." Loveday turned to face the front after checking that all was well with Pascoe in the bed of the wain. "I feel equal parts proud and dismayed."

"What do you mean?" Celeste asked. "For me, it felt quite

like old times, when my mother would be cheered in the streets for her latest ascension."

"But did Madame Blanchard have quite so much riding on her shoulders as we do?"

"Before my flight, she did," Celeste said soberly. "Every bit as much, and perhaps more. For the villagers and townsfolk here do not have the power to have us imprisoned or even executed for our failure to perform."

That certainly put her worries in perspective and shrank them to the size of their scale model in comparison.

"Surely you are not losing your nerve now," Arthur said, glancing at her.

"No indeed. But what if something goes wrong?" Loveday asked. "It was bad enough when our hopes went to the bottom of the bay. It seems infinitely worse to think of the hopes of the entire district doing so as well."

Celeste regarded her, concern in her dark eyes. "This is not like you. What has happened?"

Loveday straightened her shoulders and sat up taller. "Nothing. Perhaps I am simply weary of always hearing that the Prince Regent will come and never actually seeing him arrive."

"Have you heard nothing, Captain?" Celeste asked, squeezing Loveday's hand in a gesture of comfort.

"Not a word," Arthur said. "Not since he was sighted in Lyme Regis earlier in the summer, and we thought he might come to the Midsummer Ball. After that, not a whisper or even a rumor. I suspect he has been called back to London."

"Perhaps the King has taken a turn for the worse," Loveday suggested. "Or he must deal with some fresh scandal of the Princess of Wales."

"It is a shame, whatever the cause," Arthur went on. "Here is Emory's steam engine and pump working as well as they are designed to do, emptying the mines of water. Even if powered flight were to come to nothing, at least the mines will be fully operational again by Michaelmas. To the miners, that is worth more than any royal recognition."

"But the gas must still be removed," Celeste said. "I hear in a number of drawing rooms much speculation about the mysterious warehouse built by your fathers in St Mawes and the barrels being filled with the gas and stored."

"The fishermen and miners must think us mad," he said with a laugh.

"Mama still thinks so," Loveday said. "She will not even let us say the words *lifting gas*. Which is difficult, since we must fill our lovely envelope with it, and there it will be, staring her out of countenance upon the lawn."

"She will change her mind soon enough," Celeste said. "When we win the Prince's prize and Mr Penhale, Mr Thorndyke, and Mr Trevelyan become the richest men on the Cornish coast."

Hale Head came into view, the promontory that resembled a crouching lion thrusting out into the Channel that had given her family its name, and soon they were turning off on the road that led home.

It was no easy feat lifting the gondola from its comfortable bed and into the place cleared for it in the carriage house. The hay hook was dragooned into bearing pulleys and winch, and with the help of Pascoe and the stable boys, the gondola was guided to its place, where it was held upright with triangle-shaped blocks.

After Arthur had called at the house to give his regards to

her parents and then departed, Papa had come out to watch the operation as Loveday and Celeste directed their crew. At length it was completed, and the wain taken back to the Jermyn farm with a promise that Hugo would get an extra ration of oats for his unusual duties that afternoon.

"Thank you for allowing us to complete the final steps in the carriage house, Papa," Loveday said. "I know it is an inconvenience."

"I am committed to the project now," he said with gruff affection. "Besides, with your grandfather's old coach out of the way, there is plenty of room for it. When do you propose to take her up?"

"Well," Celeste said, "we must fit the pipes and be sure the engine performs as well as it did in the steam works, and the vanes react as they did in our model. Then we must rig it, fill the gas bags, and finally fit the envelope over all."

"So, by Christmas, then?" Papa said with a smile.

"No indeed," Loveday told him, tilting her chin. "Two weeks at most."

"So soon?" Had he been the sort to wear a pince-nez, it would have fallen off his nose.

"No need to look so amazed—the most difficult parts are complete. Oh, Papa," she said, clasping her hands in delight, "the boatwright has done a masterful job, has he not? Have you ever seen anything so lovely?"

Her father contemplated the gleaming gondola. "Not in the realm of mechanical devices," he said at last. "But see here, Loveday. This is more important than I think you realize. I believe that if your project is to be taken seriously, it must be witnessed and documented."

"Our journals have documented each step, sir, down to the

screws and nails," Celeste assured him. "And your entire family witnessed our last ascension."

"That is not what I mean," he said. He motioned toward the double doors, and they followed him outside into the sunshine. "I believe that in order for this air ship to be taken as seriously as it deserves, you ought to have someone with you as witness. Like Captain Trevelyan or Mr Thorndyke. Or both, for that matter, unless this marvelous craft won't hold more than two."

"Of course it will," Loveday blurted, stunned. "But that is not the point! Papa, surely you do not mean we must have an audience."

"Is our word not enough?" Celeste added. "Why must a gentleman's observations carry so much more weight than our own?"

"You mistake me, my dears," Papa said. "No one contests your observations and achievements. In fact, it is all I hear of when I go into the village. But this is your home, where you are known and respected. If these same achievements are recounted in London, it is a simple fact that they will be discounted on hearing, simply because you are young and female."

Celeste said something in French that Loveday was quite certain should never be expressed in polite company. Whatever it was, it could not do justice to her own feelings at this moment. It was a very lucky thing that the crowbar was inside the carriage house, for she wanted to hit something—or at the very least, throw it.

"I can see you boiling over, maidey, like your own steam engine," her father said mildly. "But apply that brain of yours to what I have said, and you will see the truth of it, right or wrong. I shall call on the captain and Mr Thorndyke with all dispatch. I would trust none other but those two with such a challenge—and such a privilege. For the ship will carry precious cargo indeed." With a smile, he left them simmering.

CHAPTER 2

*C*eleste glanced at Loveday as they trudged back into the workshop, Mr Penhale's edict still ringing in their ears.

"Can we reason with him further?" she asked as Loveday paused at the gate to the orchard, where the contented hens clucked as they pecked in the grass, enjoying the first windfalls.

"Never," Loveday said. "Much as my father has been willing to support us in this endeavor, I am afraid he is right that others will view our work more favorably if we have the endorsement of the gentlemen."

Celeste's sigh mirrored her friend's as they walked on. "Still, Emory will agree to come. He is fascinated by our work. And others will listen to his opinions. After his success with the mine pumps, all of Truro looks on him as a hero."

"Well," Loveday allowed, swinging open the door to the workshop and letting out the welcome scent of oil and metal, "he did solve a major problem for most mine owners. Now not only can they keep the mines from flooding, but they harvest lifting gas with each rise of the piston. It is ingenious, really."

"It is," Celeste agreed. "And it fits with our plans nicely, for we have no need to worry about the source of gas for the air ship. But to bring him and Arthur along on the voyage like two maiden aunts to chaperone? Can you bear it?"

Loveday wandered over to the plans spread out on the worktable. "You needn't worry. Arthur will refuse to allow us to take so much as the smallest risk."

And then where would they be? Risk was where discoveries were made.

Celeste shook herself and ventured closer to her friend, lifting her white muslin skirts to avoid picking up odd pieces of metal shavings. A shame she couldn't wear her flying costume, but she hadn't managed to convince Loveday's mother that the fitted redingote and wide-legged *pantalons* fastened at the ankle were a suitable outfit for a lady.

"He still considers flying dangerous," she said, tracing a circle on the plans with one finger.

"He considers flying too dangerous for any lady of his acquaintance," Loveday amended, gaze on her latest journal. "He may very well suggest that he and Emory take the air ship out themselves while we wait safely on shore, fluttering our handkerchiefs. *Grr.*" She slammed shut the cover.

Celeste understood. Even in France, where women were more likely to be applauded for being of a mechanical mind, some still thought a woman's place should be more limited. Thank goodness her mother had never subscribed to such views.

The thought of her mother could only sober her further. Though she had visited Madame Racine at least every other week over the last month and more, the older émigré had been unable to provide any news of France than what could be had in the newspapers.

"Our letters move by happenstance," she'd commiserated as Celeste and Loveday sat in her cozy sitting room overlooking the Trevithick Steam Works and the Truro harbor. "By the hand of this smuggler, that sailor. We do not even know if the notes have reached your mother yet."

Celeste had led Madame Racine to believe her mother had connections with l'École des Aéronautes in Paris. Which was mostly true. Sophie and Jean-Pierre Blanchard had founded the school and trained most of its illustrious graduates themselves. After Celeste's father had died following a fall from a balloon, her mother had gone on to greater glory as the Emperor's Chief Air Minister, destined to plan the great invasion of England. But she had not been able to find a way to fulfill Napoleon's grand dream… and so had fallen from favor.

Though her mother had long since given up the feat as impossible because of the contrary winds on the Channel, Celeste had been undaunted. Her arrival in England proved it could be done. That news alone should have served to elevate her mother into Napoleon's good graces once more. Yet, if the news of Celeste's success had reached her mother, why hadn't she written back?

If she was still furious with Celeste for running away and refusing the marriage the Emperor had sought for her, might not Celeste's friends, Amélie and Josephine Aventure or Marcel Delaguard, have answered instead? Were the messages not getting through? Or did her mother and friends no longer care about her?

Loveday cared. So did her family. Her mother, father, and

sisters seemed genuinely happy to have Celeste living with them, for they had made no more inquiries as to when she might leave. In fact, Loveday's two younger sisters, Rosalind and Gwendolyn, cared more about asking Celeste's advice on fashion. Mrs Penhale seemed glad Loveday had someone to befriend her, though she remained a bit mystified as to why young ladies would prefer to spend time in a former tack room instead of making calls upon the neighbors or attending card parties and assemblies.

Not that Celeste and Loveday avoided such things. Celeste had been introduced to all the families with whom the Penhales dined in the area. They seemed kind, considerate people, even if some viewed mechanization as a foreign concept.

Funny, but she wouldn't have put Arthur Trevelyan in that category. He'd sincerely appreciated the gift of a far-scope Loveday had invented and put it to good use, sitting upon his rock on the cliffs of his family estate and staring out toward the Channel as if intent on stealing France's secrets through the lenses. But he had other, more concrete methods. He had confessed to Loveday, who had told Celeste, that he worked with smugglers to gather intelligence for England.

Of course, expectations were growing that he would offer for Loveday, but so far, his visits had been no warmer than those of any other member of the gentry. Her friend seemed both relieved and annoyed by the fact. Mrs Penhale seemed to think Emory had similar intentions toward Celeste, but she could not be sure of him. Loveday was probably right that Arthur would refuse Mr Penhale's request to evaluate the launch of the air ship.

But it seemed Loveday's father had wasted no time in

asking, for both Emory and Arthur came calling the next afternoon.

At least they had sent word ahead, for Mrs Penhale had warned both Celeste and Loveday as soon as they came down to breakfast to be on their best behavior.

"It's not often we have two such presentable gentlemen in our sitting room," she said, spreading marmalade on her toast. "Rosalind and Gwendolyn, I will excuse you from this visit. I'm sure your sister and Celeste will have much to tell you afterward."

As Gwen sagged with obvious disappointment, Celeste exchanged glances with Loveday, whose brows had risen.

"I doubt this visit is all that formal, Mama," her friend tried, her spoon paused over her coddled eggs. "I believe Father arranged it." She looked to her father at the end of the table.

Mr Penhale set down his napkin. "I did, but you never know what young gentlemen have on their minds unless you ask."

"Just so," Mrs Penhale said complacently. "Loveday, you will stay away from that workshop this morning. I will not have you smelling of oil. Please wear your new promenade gown with the pink trim. Celeste, the white muslin will likely do."

That was the only problem with living on kindness. Little of what Celeste had brought with her from France had made it ashore. She had no income of her own. She was merely grateful that she was of a similar size to Loveday's sister Gwen and so could gladly accept her castoffs.

"She thinks they've both come to offer," Loveday murmured as she and Celeste made their way to the rear terrace, beyond which stretched the lawns overlooking the sea. "She will persist in thinking that, with no basis for it at all." At least the day was pleasant. Clouds the size of her balloon floated along as if they had no better place to be. Celeste and Loveday could take their journals with them and note new ideas, even if they could not work on them.

"Perhaps when they do not offer, she will cease nudging," Celeste suggested, going to sit on the chaise longue overlooking the lawns.

"Doubtful." Loveday dropped onto another chair and began scribbling notes.

Mrs Penhale herself came to fetch them when the gentlemen arrived. "Head high, Loveday," she said as they all started for the sitting room. "Celeste, the ribbon in your hair has come loose. Stop a moment."

Celeste paused in the entry hall and allowed the lady to tie the blue satin ribbon through her curls. They had been mercifully short when she'd arrived, but the months in England had seen them grow until they reached nearly to her shoulders.

"There." Loveday's mother stepped back and gazed at them both, eyes tearing. "Remember this day, my dears. It may well be the start of a new life."

"Only if Arthur says yes," Celeste whispered to Loveday as they followed her mother into the room.

One look at the two men who stood up on their entry, and she almost thought Mrs Penhale might be right. Emory was wearing a coat of navy superfine far better than what he generally wore at the steam works, and Arthur had decked himself out in a bottle-green coat that nicely showed off his shoulders. He had even eschewed a cane as an aid to his injured leg. Both their visitors bowed at the sight of her and Loveday. Celeste and her friend curtsied in return.

Mrs Penhale went to join her husband on chairs near the hearth, leaving the spot on the sofa beside Arthur empty. Loveday marched to the chair farthest from him. Celeste sat closer to Emory, who smiled at her, and a battalion of the Emperor's balloons took flight inside her.

"Good of you to come," Mr Penhale told their visitors. "I assume you have considered my request."

Mrs Penhale glanced his way, frown gathering, but she did not refute him.

Emory looked to Arthur, then focused on Loveday's father. "I have, sir. I'd be delighted to watch the air ship rise for the first time. I'm eager to see how it performs and will be happy to evaluate it formally, as a trained engineer."

Mrs Penhale's hand went to her throat, as if she were suddenly having trouble breathing—or wanted to burst out in protest.

"And you, Captain Trevelyan?" Loveday challenged.

He looked more solemn, firm lips tight together and eyes narrowed ever so slightly. Everyone in the room seemed to be holding their breath.

"I would enjoy that as well," he said. "My focus will be on its potential for use by the War Office. When do you plan to lift?"

One week later

Arthur Trevelyan shook the far-scope out of the velvet bag in which it had been presented to him and considered it. She'd told him that it was only a prototype, and that he was to tell her what improvements might be made to it, but that might mean her taking it away from him. Taking it apart.

That he could never permit. Not when it was the only thing Loveday Penhale had ever given him. The fact that it worked brilliantly was a bonus.

The case looked as though it had come from a country far away, perhaps on a tea clipper and meant to be a pipe or instrument of some kind, for it was inlaid with woods that did not grow in England. But whatever it had contained before, now it held lenses, and a kind of gearworks, and three wheels spaced along its exterior that brought the view in close... closer... closest. So close that he could see the glint in the eye of a gull a quarter of a mile off.

Now he sat upon the rock where most of his convalescence had taken place, scanning the sea with the far-scope. Its only limit seemed to be the curvature of the earth, beyond which no one could see—though he had no doubt Loveday lay awake at night trying to figure out how to overcome that, too. He put the device to one eye and adjusted the wheels, keeping the horizon in view. At least one of the lenses had been treated in some way so that the glare of the sun on the water was eliminated. It made the colors of the sea more intense and varied somehow—not only blue or grey, but green, aquamarine, cerulean. In truth, he hadn't known the ocean could convey so much color until the first time he'd used the far-scope.

They were out there, he knew it.

The French *sous-marins*.

This scheme of Mr Penhale's, while laudable in its concern for the young ladies' reputations among those who would judge them, had another purpose. Arthur had every intention of bringing the far-scope with him in order to see as far as he could beneath the waves. See what the French were up to.

His meeting this afternoon would, he hoped, be just as illuminating.

At the scrape of boots on the cliff path, he slid the far-scope into its bag and tucked it into the pocket of his coat. When his guest appeared at the top of the cliff, he slid to one side on the rock to make room for him.

"Morning, Captain," Robbie Pendragon said, seating himself.

"Mr Pendragon," Arthur greeted him. "I hope your mother continues well after the sad loss of your father."

"She does. She wished me to convey her thanks for the basket your family sent for Saint James's Day. And for the coin."

"No thanks are necessary. I owe it to Barnabas Pendragon to take an interest in all of you. If I had not arranged to go out that night—"

"He'd have gone anyway, sir. Tez what he did, and a happy man he was to tweak the noses of the revenue men. He understood the price he might pay. I told you afore, no sense in your paying it."

Arthur was silent a moment. He was incapable of not paying his debt to the drowned man, now that his wife was left alone with children still at her knee, and only seventeen-year-old Robbie and his next youngest brother to provide for them. "And now you are carrying on his trade, I hear."

"Aye. I'm mate aboard a vessel for now, until I c'n afford my own." The young man looked out to sea, his hair as black and his eyes as dark as his father's. As those of the Spanish sailors who had washed ashore after the Armada had sunk and been taken in by Cornish families. "We came in on the tide last night."

"I hope you had good hunting. Did you spot any prey that might interest me?"

Robbie smiled, the smile of a pirate. "I might have noticed a thing or two swimming about under the sea."

"Only a thing or two?"

"Between Jersey and the coast, at least fifteen. Something's set the hake among the pilchards, sir, and that you can tie to."

"I see." He hated the French *sous-marins*, those slippery, impossible-to-fight underwater vessels that harried the shipping lanes, looking for English and Spanish ships to sink. Even the presence of Old Job's Pisky—the marvelous device that looked like a mantel clock and had the curious ability to maze the navigation of the *sous-marins*—aboard the smugglers' vessels had not prevented attacks upon them. What a shame he hadn't been able to save the one aboard Barnabas's ship. Nor could he speak of it now, even to the latter's son, having been sworn to secrecy.

But no point crying over spilt milk. He must consider the questions that lay before him now. Had the *sous-marins* been called in to school along the coast? And if so, for what purpose?

"Any word of the *sous-marins* in the streets and warehouses?" he asked.

"A lot of talk and gossip," Robbie said. "Most of it we've heard before, but some was odd. *Charles-rue* was a word I hadn't heard before."

Charles-rue? Arthur's mind repeated it, and he sat up. "Do you mean *Karlsruhe?*"

"Aye, that's it. Care for a drop?" He slid a silver flask from his pocket. "What's that, sir? This Karlsruhe?"

"Thank you." Arthur took a sip, and the fine French brandy filled his mouth with its bouquet and warmed his belly. "The Karlsruhe Confederacy lies along the French border to the east. It is a consortium of nations—Prussia, Bavaria, and the *Öst Reich*, the East Kingdom—determined to stop Napoleon's march into their lands. The War Office is doing its best to make allies of them, but so far we are like a pair of matrons who took offense twenty years ago and have not yet made up our quarrel. We simply sit, waiting for the other to make the first move."

"P'raps they've accepted an offer to dance."

"Let us hope not." That would be the worst of several terrible scenarios, all of which ended with England as a vassal of a more powerful entity. The current fragile balance was not because wiser heads had prevailed. No, it was simply that whoever made the first move—Napoleon, Karl Caesar, King George, Tsar Alexander—would plunge all of Europe into a war from which it might never recover.

Europe teetered on the blade of a sword. The smallest event could push them over into bloodshed.

Was the massing of the *sous-marins* a sign of such an event?

He thanked Robbie Pendragon for his information, pressed half a crown into his hand, and limped slowly up the slope to the house.

There was no way to know if this were a sign or not, but he would send a letter to the War Office all the same.

CHAPTER 3

Five days later

That's it," Loveday called to Arthur, whose turn it was to man the pump connected to the barrel of lifting gas. From the other side ran copper tubing into the valve of the second gas bag. "Just a little more, and she will lift. Carefully—carefully— There!"

Lark Deux seemed to shake herself, like a carriage horse preparing for the harness, and with a creak of her glossy hull against the support blocks, she rose off them. The mooring ropes snapped taut, and she was aloft in the glow of the dawn sky!

A foot in the air counted as aloft, didn't it?

"*Magnifique,*" Celeste said on a sigh of happiness.

"I've never seen anything so thrilling." Loveday clapped her hands in delight, then pulled her friend in by the waist and danced her over the lawn, laughing. "She's aloft!"

The words had hardly left her tongue when a strong arm slipped about her own waist, and she was being danced awkwardly back in the other direction by Arthur. His hat flew off, the tails of his coat blew open, and joy lit his eyes as he whooped like a schoolboy. He released her when they reached *Lark Deux*, and breathless, she saw Emory waltzing across the grass with Celeste as though he had chosen that moment to ask for a lesson.

The stable boys applauded until Pascoe shushed them, but he was smiling, too.

"Aye, maidey, I'd take a turn about the lawn with you myself," Papa said, fitting his hat back upon his head and handing Arthur's to him, "if I did not fear falling upon my face. Captain, it seems your leg is healing in leaps and bounds."

"Literally," Arthur said with a chuckle. "I was transported by joy at our contestants' success."

"Shall we take her out on her maiden voyage, then?" Emory asked. "I have brought a notebook, compasses, and a warmer coat, just in case."

The smile faded from Loveday's face. "A warmer coat? But you do not intend to fly with us. You are simply to be witnesses of the test. From the ground."

"Yes, we will perform several tests at the ends of the ropes," Celeste said.

Arthur shook his head. "I am afraid there is a mistake in our definition of the word *witness*." He smiled, but Loveday could not yet return it. "I feel we ought to test her in a proper flight. I am, after all, compiling a formal report for my superiors in London."

"And the sooner that is done, the sooner you may inform the Prince of your official entry," Emory put in. "Many of our observations will be at your service for that purpose."

This put a whole new complexion upon the matter. For of course they would have to include scientific observations of the flight in their application.

"I agree," Loveday said, her spirits returning. Bob about at the ends of ropes? Indeed not. "As we predicted, conditions are perfect—a slight breeze from the west to blow us up the Channel while the propellers guide us south."

"Clear skies," added Arthur, scanning them with the eyes of experience. "The barometer is holding."

"Then you have nothing to wait for," Papa said with a smile, "except for Mrs Kerrow to bring out the hamper of food."

"Papa, she shall do no such thing," Loveday objected. "We are only going out a few miles. We will be back in time for breakfast."

"*Au contraire,*" Celeste said with a twinkle. "Flying is hungry work. Imagine having a picnic in the skies!"

Well, put like that…

"Very well." Loveday sent one of the boys scampering to the kitchen door to alert the cook. Celeste followed him and returned wearing the green watered-silk redingote and *pantalons* that she used in the skies. Emory gaped and hurriedly found something else to occupy him while they waited for the hamper.

When it arrived, Loveday stowed it in the compartment under the aft seat so considerately built by the boatwright at Mevagissey. "Who would have expected that cupboards would be necessary in an air ship?"

"And yet we have already proved they are," Celeste said. "Though it was not in our plans. The boatwright has taken a liberty—but at least it is a useful one. Not a handsbreadth of space is wasted."

Arthur saluted smartly. "Ready for duty, Captain," he said. "As soon as you tell us what it is."

She indicated the seats set in each side of the vessel. "Along with your weight keeping us in trim and your astute observations, we shall ask each of you to control a set of vanes, which act as rudders do in a sailing boat, only here we are using the wind. Celeste will attend to the instruments in the stern and give us instructions to adjust our speed and altitude. My task amidships is to keep the fire and water at the correct levels in the boiler to power the hydraulics and propellers."

"Since no flame is ever exposed on a powered air ship," Celeste added. "The steam is carried entirely in the pipes."

"So who is actually in charge of this voyage?" Emory asked.

Celeste and Loveday looked at one another with a smile. Trust a man to want to know that.

"We did not ask ourselves such a question last time," Loveday said. "There was too much to do. We simply worked together. But in my mind, everything depends on the instruments. They tell us what we must do. So in that sense, along with her greater experience, I suppose that makes Celeste the person to whom you must salute."

Emory and Arthur promptly snapped salutes, though Arthur's was by far the neater.

Celeste laughed and motioned them into their places on each gunwale, then climbed in to make a final check of her instruments. Loveday jumped down, and pulled on her warmest wool pelisse with the military-style frog closures across the front. It didn't look in the least like Celeste's redingote, but it would do to keep out the cold air at altitude.

Then she turned and kissed her father. "We hope to be back within two hours, Papa."

"And if you are not?" His gaze was sober. Behind him, she could see her mother standing on the terrace, her hands clasped under her chin. Clearly she had not been able to resist watching the ascension, despite her feelings about it.

"If we are not, wait until sunset. If a squall comes up, as it did last time, we may have to land to wait it out."

"And what am I to do at sunset?" Her father was beginning to look worried now.

Loveday touched his cheek. "Try not to worry. We will return, even if we have to swim."

She climbed back into the gondola and ignited the engine, then sent the first load of coal into the firebox. Within minutes the pressure gauges had begun to respond, and moments later the pistons began to move.

"Ready, crew?" she asked, hardly able to keep her voice level from excitement.

"Ready!" they cried.

Oh, what was one to say at such a momentous juncture? *Take up the air ship.* That was it. But what came out was, "Up ship!"

The stable boys let go of the ropes, and *Lark Deux* fell up into the sky.

Arthur let out a whoop, and Emory grabbed for his hat as the wind seized it. Truly, they must turn their attention to some more practical headgear when they returned. But then all of Loveday's thoughts were consumed by the engine and what it needed to give them the best performance.

"Set vanes horizontal," Celeste called. "We have reached five hundred feet, wind from the west at five knots. Our target speed is seventeen knots."

"I have never gone so fast in my life," Arthur gasped, pushing on the levers to extend the vanes. "Not even on a pirate sloop." The wind snapped out the vanes, filling them like the sails of a tea clipper while the fuselage pushed through the currents of air. Slowly they rose higher above the sea.

As she worked, Loveday could see the two men experimenting with the vanes, testing them, seeing what would happen if one man did this and the other that. It was all well and good; they must report on every moving part, every response of the air ship. Perhaps it was just as well they had two extra pairs of hands aboard—she and Celeste would have had a merry dance to keep everything in order had they been alone.

They could have done it, mind you. This was simply more efficient.

"Porthkarrek Light to port," she called.

"I see it." The sextant was steady in Celeste's hands. "Twelve hundred feet. Let us level out and put her through her paces."

"Speed first?" Loveday suggested.

"By all means."

They had laid in extra coal for just such a test, so Loveday scooped it into the firebox for the simple joy of watching the pressure and heat gauges respond, leaping to attention and then leaning over to the right. Then she engaged the propellers.

"Twenty-five knots, flat out!" she cried.

Emory's mouth moved, but no words came out at first. The gondola was snugged up under the envelope, but still the air flowed in over the top, whistling through the rigging with a voice all its own. He managed, "It is unbelievable that this little vessel should attain four times the speed of Admiral Nelson's, on his voyage to the West Indies."

Laughter bubbled from Loveday at the thought of such a comparison. "You have hit on it, Emory—we are a little vessel. And we have not the drag of water to slow us down. In fact, one cannot compare sailing vessels to flying ones at all—it is like comparing a bucket to a soup tureen. Just because they are the same shape does not mean their materials and purpose must also be the same. And one is certainly more elegant than the other."

"You are quite right," he said, giving up on his hat completely and handing it to Celeste to stow with the food hamper. "I shall record that very statement in my notes."

"I declare the speed test a wild success," Celeste said. "What next?"

Next came turns—to port, to starboard, and in a full circle. Loveday seized the wheel that caused the rudder and hull vanes to turn this way and that, and when the gentlemen sensed the change in direction, they engaged the horizontal set of vanes to assist.

Arthur glanced over his shoulder at Loveday. "A horse may win a race in a burst of speed, and make the turns in the track, too, but can it go the distance? I say we test her ability to maintain altitude at cruising speed."

"Very well. How far out are we, Celeste?"

"Ten miles, I think. Not far. Our circles have brought us rather closer to England than not."

"And how far is it to France?" Arthur asked.

"Over a hundred miles."

"Shall we go halfway?"

Celeste smiled. *"Certainement."*

Except they did not. At the halfway point, somehow Arthur managed to egg them on another ten miles, and another, and in the heat of the moment Loveday found herself unable to resist his repeated challenges, the cocky rascal. The sun slid higher in the sky until it looked for all the world as though it meant to meet them in Bretagne.

"Good heavens, Celeste, we must turn back," she finally said, breathless with what they had accomplished. "Papa will be worried. I told him we would be back for breakfast—and now we have missed luncheon."

"We have luncheon with us," Emory pointed out. "Just a little farther?"

"No need for that," Arthur said. He pointed over the bow. "I believe we have arrived."

France

Celeste's spirits soared as the coast of France reared up in the distance: green fields stretching out toward the Channel, waves lapping at the shingled shore. Here and there, white marked the lines of stone fences, farmhouses, and outbuildings. Once this had been home, where she had been born, where she had learned to fly, where her *cher papa* had breathed his last. But she had to remember it was home no more. If she set foot on French soil, she might well be branded a traitor. And traitors did not fare well in Napoleon's court.

Something flashed below the waves, and she spotted ripples in the water, parallel to the shore. What was that?

She glanced at the others. Loveday had her hands on the wheel, and Emory had practically become one with the vane levers. Arthur had the far-scope to his eye and was gazing out the way she'd been looking.

"Are those *sous-marins*?" she asked.

He jerked and nearly dropped the far-scope before catching himself. Now Loveday and Emory were looking at him, too.

"Perhaps," he allowed. "I imagine they could leave that sort of wake at the surface."

Emory leaned over the glossy gunwale to peer into the water as well. "There! That silver shape like an elongated bubble. That cannot be a whale."

"Another here," Loveday reported, shifting her focus a moment to glance out the starboard side.

Now Celeste could spot the outlines as well. "Four, five, seven. Why are they gathering?"

"That," Arthur said, returning the far-scope to his eye, "is what I want to know."

A chill ran through her. Napoleon could have only one reason to bring together so many of his prized underwater machines.

He was planning an offensive against the English.

Emory must have thought so too, for he was shaking his head. "He cannot invade with them. They hold too few troops. We've proven that. He would need thousands of them to make a landing."

"He does not have thousands," Celeste said. "Not even fifty."

"When you left France," Loveday pointed out, gaze veering back to her steam gauges.

"I have been gone no more than four months," Celeste protested. "How could he have multiplied the number so soon? Surely your spies would have noticed."

Arthur turned away from her as if uncomfortable with the direction of the conversation.

"An assault on British shipping, then?" Emory mused.

"He has had no trouble in that area," Arthur said glumly. "No, this is something else. Loveday, can we go a little lower?"

Loveday's mouth settled into a tight line. "Certainly we *can*. The question is whether we *should*. Very likely there are shore defenses along here."

"Cherbourg is a military port," Celeste confirmed. "The Emperor has a manufactory for behemoths there. But if we stay to the west, we should be able to avoid the battery." She went to lay her hand on her friend's arm. "If there are this many off Bretagne, how many must there be off Normandie, where the Channel is narrower? Your country could be in danger. Cornwall could be in danger."

Loveday narrowed her eyes. "Hang on to something. Gentlemen, vanes vertical, please."

Celeste stepped back and clung to the closest shroud. Emory gripped the levers on his side. Arthur operated his vanes with one hand and kept the far-scope to his eye with the other. The air ship swung lower.

"They seem to be heading for Cherbourg," Arthur reported. "They might only be returning to home port, but they may also be gathering a fleet to attack Poole, the Isle of Wight, or Portsmouth."

"Portsmouth?" Emory put in. "Where His Highness is building his own steamships?"

"The very one," Arthur agreed. "This could be a preemptive strike."

Outside came a whistle, quickly approaching, then shooting past.

"What was that?" Emory demanded.

Celeste knew. She leaned out over the railing to eye the walls of the fortress at Cherbourg in the distance. Who would have thought the creamy stone hid such dark weapons?

"That was a cannonbomb," she told them all. "I heard the same sounds when the shore batteries at Le Tréport fired on me by mistake when I was coming over."

"They're firing on us?" Emory turned white.

Arthur lowered the far-scope and straightened. "Loveday, evasive maneuvers. At once."

She eyed him. "In the first place, do not presume to order our air ship, sir."

Another cannonbomb whizzed past. This time Celeste saw it go, iron-grey and heavy. If that hit the envelope…

"And in the second," Loveday continued, "you saw what it takes to turn. Give me a moment."

She cranked the wheel, the gentlemen deployed the vanes, and the air ship began its turn to the east.

Arthur lurched to her side and grasped the iron ring. "Turn away from the battery, not toward it!"

"We must take advantage of the winds," Loveday informed him, hands locked on the wheel. "They are running from the west at the moment. We'll use up too much fuel if we turn in that direction. We won't have enough to get home."

"Better that than being hit."

Too late. The battery must have taken their measure at last, for the shrill whistle sounded overhead a moment before the air ship shuddered.

The gondola swung, and Celeste tumbled into Emory. She had only a moment to register his arms around her before the air ship's bow tilted for the sea.

CHAPTER 4

Vanes horizontal!" Loveday shouted, the wheel hard over. "As tight a circle as we can! We must slow our descent."

Heaven must be watching over them, for despite the cannonbomb's damage to the aft shrouds that had all but detached the stern of the gondola from the silk-covered corset, the pressure had failed to trigger the bomb to explode. Further, it appeared they would not ditch in the sea. The breeze pushed them eastward, and the land caught up to them as they descended.

"St Malo!" Celeste exclaimed as they passed over the medieval city. It was nearly square, its winding river and harbor practically making it an island.

"How clear the water is from here," Arthur marveled. "I can see all the way to the bottom—and not a *sous-marin* in sight." Then Loveday saw his gaze catch on something else. "Jupiter aloft, are those forts, there on those islands?"

"Yes," Celeste told him. She had managed to disentangle herself from Emory and was once more at the instruments.

"They protect the harbor, not for the Emperor's navy, but for the pirates. They have no interest in us. Loveday, lower the steam pressure, if you please."

Pirates? Might Arthur know someone in a pirate port? For it was clear they were going to need a rescue. "Celeste, if these are pirates, we might be able to ask them for help," Loveday said, venting steam. "We must land somewhere close enough to walk to St Malo. We must try for those grassy fields, do you see? Just this side of that belt of trees, where there are no stone walls to cause more damage."

"I see it. Vanes vertical," she commanded. "We are setting down."

Going down was more to the point, but nobody corrected her. The air ship came out of its corkscrew descent and leveled out. Loveday cut off the steam pressure and cried, "Brace yourselves!"

The air ship floated down like a gull with one broken wing. *Oh, please let the gondola stand up to the landing—*

They bounced once. Again. Slid along the grass. The wheels caught. Rolled.

And came to a stop, the breeze tugging at the silk. Hop-skip. Jump.

"We will be dragged if we do not moor her," Emory said, leaping over the gunwale.

"Emory!" Celeste cried out, leaning over. "For heaven's sake, we have a door. Are you all right?"

"Perfectly." He shook out his left foot. "An awkward landing, but no harm done."

They disembarked through the gate, jumping lightly to the ground rather than risking the five-foot drop Emory had made. Had this been England and they'd made such a poor landing on their return, Loveday might have fallen to her knees and given thanks that they were alive. But they were not in England. They were more than a mile behind enemy lines. Oh, why had she allowed herself to be caught up in Arthur's ridiculous challenges? She, who prided herself on her logical mind! Accepting such a challenge had to be the most featherbrained thing she'd ever done. Challenges got men killed in curricle races to Brighton, for goodness sake.

They were much farther from home than Brighton. And in even more danger to life and limb.

"We cannot leave the air ship here," Celeste said, her voice trembling. "If anyone sees it, they will report it at once to the *préfecture*, who will be obliged to report it to the Ministry of War. Napoleon must not be permitted to know of our design. *Lark Deux* must stay hidden at all costs."

"Come, then," Arthur said at once. "It is only a few hundred yards to those trees. *Lark Deux* must roost under their branches for the time being, out of sight."

Sweat trickling down her back to wet her chemise, Celeste collapsed on the ground beside the air ship. Loveday and Arthur came around the gondola to fall beside her. Emory was the only one who wasn't panting. He was, however, standing bent over and red-faced.

"Very wise of you to put those wheels on the bottom of the gondola," he said, hands braced on his knees and his gaze on the iron wheels now embedded in the needle-strewn ground. "Still, the ship doesn't move easily."

"She has never been a carriage," Loveday reminded him.

"She wasn't designed to run along the ground." Her hair had come free of its pins and was tumbling down her back, and the seam holding her sleeve to her pelisse was pulling apart with her efforts.

"All the more reason to return her to the skies as soon as possible," Arthur agreed.

Loveday grimaced. "Have you seen the size of the hole in the second gas bag? I shudder to think how many of the ribs are broken in the corset, not to mention the lines that have snapped or frayed. And what of the strain on the engine? I can't make such repairs, not in the middle of the woods."

"Copse," Emory informed her. "I believe this is merely a small group of pine trees. Not a woods *per se*."

Leave it to him to be precise. Celeste shook her head.

Loveday glared at him. "Acres or feet, it matters not. I cannot repair her with what I have on board. And we'll need to take on more water and coal for the return flight."

"Perhaps the battery at Cherbourg," Arthur ventured, wiping perspiration from his face with the back of one hand.

"We undershot Cherbourg," Celeste explained. "From what I can tell, the closest non-military fort is Mont St Michel."

"Le Havre," he suggested. "They must have supplies to repair balloons there."

Celeste's throat was tight. "Le Havre is nearly two hundred miles from here. And you will not wander into the Aeronautical Supply Station without your papers or at least a uniform."

"A manufactory, then," he insisted. "The French are harvesting lifting gas from the ground around Rouen."

Emory dropped his arms and straightened. "How do you know that?"

Arthur colored. "It was in the *London Times*."

Somehow, she doubted that. "Then *The Times* is misinformed. Lifting gas comes from here in Bretagne, with some in Normandie, but we cannot very well mine it ourselves. There is only one place where we can find all we need—l'École des Aeronautes in Paris."

"No," Arthur said. "Too dangerous. And too far."

Loveday climbed to her feet. "I have had just about all I can take of your arrogance, sir. Whatever you think you know about France is obviously in error. And you certainly know nothing about air ships."

He rose as well, one hand on the gondola as if to steady himself. "I may be mistaken in some things, Miss Penhale, but I am sure of one. I would be no kind of man if I let you and Mademoiselle Blanchard wander loose in enemy territory."

Celeste looked away from their tense faces, up into the sky, barely visible through the trees. "We will not be wandering anywhere, loose or otherwise, for now. It will be dark in an hour or two. We must spend the night here."

Loveday shivered, as if she felt the coolness in the pine-scented air already. Though the day had been warm, temperatures would drop at night with the moisture-laden wind off the sea.

"I suppose a fire is out of the question," she said.

Arthur unbent enough to nod. "As Celeste feared, some may have seen us come down. Soldiers could be looking even now. Best to give them nothing to trace."

Loveday sighed, but she didn't argue this time.

In the end, they huddled inside the gondola and opened Mrs Kerrow's hamper. "We must save half for morning," Arthur said, his voice hinting at grateful amazement as he surveyed the small wheel of cheese, the pasties wrapped in cloth, the loaf of bread, the apples, and the cake. There were two bottles of lemonade, too, and a flask of cold water. "This is a feast."

Celeste was hungry enough to eat the clover growing in the field, but she could not argue with the wisdom of conserving their meager supplies. By the time they had finished their repast, darkness had fallen, and they faced the unhappy prospect of sleeping on the narrow deck of the gondola. Better that, she supposed, than lying in the pine needles listening to nocturnal creatures hunting prey... or investigating their sleeping selves.

Arthur suggested they mount a guard as soon as the quarter moon rose. They had brought no weapons with them, but he hoped a warning from the guard would at least give them time to hide in the trees if French troops approached. The former soldier tried to divide the watch between him and Emory, but Loveday and Celeste insisted on each of them taking a turn. That brought on another argument which was only settled when Celeste pointed out that they would need him and Emory to be rested enough to take on whatever they would face the next day.

At least they had water, and when that was gone, they might siphon enough from the boiler into the empty lemonade bottle for everyone to have a sip. But when the food was gone...

"We will seek more food tomorrow," Arthur promised them all. "Perhaps a farmer hereabouts has crops ready for harvest and will not miss a few."

Perhaps.

He took the first watch. Emory, Celeste, and Loveday sat

on the plank deck of the gondola and braced their backs against the bulwarks. Emory's legs stretched from one side of the craft nearly to the other. Celeste couldn't help bumping against them as she smoothed the fabric of her *pantalons*. Such muscled strength. Her shiver had nothing to do with the temperature.

"I banked the fire," Loveday reported, settling beside her. "It should give off no smoke, but we shouldn't feed it. We will need all the remaining coal and quite a bit more to return home."

Celeste was just glad for the warmth that trickled into the space from the cooling boiler. "You have made it cozy. *Merci.*"

"I believe that means thank you," Emory said across from them.

"Very good," Celeste said. "You are learning."

"I have come to realize both you and Loveday can teach me much," he said. "If anyone can derive a solution to our current problem, I would be willing to wager on the two of you."

A rare declaration indeed. Celeste grew warmer still. "Thank you. Good night, Emory. Wake me when it's my turn."

"I will. Sleep well."

She wasn't sure she would sleep at all. She knew what must be done. The leg injury that had sent Arthur home from the front had healed a great deal in recent months, but it was unlikely he could walk to Paris. Emory tried to hide it, but it was clear that jump from the gondola had resulted in a twist to his ankle. They might stumble upon someone willing to give all four of them a ride, but she could not count on such good fortune. For one word from Emory's mouth would instantly brand him an Englishman, and the enemy.

The prefect in St Malo would turn him over instantly, and he would be shot as a spy.

The best thing for all was if Arthur and Emory remained behind to guard the air ship and attempt some form of repair while she and Loveday made their way to Paris. The torn aft gas bag must be mended and filled with lifting gas.

Paris. She hadn't thought to set foot in the sweeping metropolis again. Would her mother agree to see her? Had she reported Celeste a traitor? Were they walking into a trap?

Obtaining supplies from the school had seemed so logical. But it would not be as easy as she'd made it sound.

CHAPTER 5

$\mathcal{E}$mory's interesting dream of discovering a hitherto unknown metal that was as malleable as gold and stronger than steel was interrupted by a shake of his shoulder. Opening his eyes, he saw Arthur bending over him in the dim light of the moon. With a nod, he scrambled to his feet, careful not to bump Celeste and Loveday across from him. Celeste's dark head had fallen onto her friend's shoulder, and one arm hugged her waist, as if she were fending off a chill. He shrugged out of his jacket and draped it over her. Then he followed Arthur outside.

He couldn't spot the quarter moon through the trees, but enough light trickled down through the stiff pine branches that he could make out their surroundings.

"Anything unusual?" he asked Arthur, who showed no sign of being willing to take his own rest.

"No," his friend murmured. "Though you may wish for your coat."

He felt the cool breeze as well. "I have never been bothered by changes in temperature."

"I remember," Arthur said, smile in his voice. "You'd be the first on the cricket pitch and the last to leave. But this—this is something else entirely."

Emory positioned himself with his back to a tree, where he had a view to either side of the air ship, and slid down onto the needle-strewn ground. "You've been behind enemy lines before."

"But I've generally only had the safety of myself or perhaps an English sympathizer to consider," Arthur said. "This time, I have something far more precious."

"The air ship," Emory surmised, wiggling to settle himself between the tree roots.

Arthur hesitated, and for a moment Emory thought he would contradict him.

"Celeste is right. The air ship cannot fall into Napoleon's hands," he finally agreed, pacing the length of the gondola and back. "Neither can Loveday Penhale. Can you imagine what he could do if she were to be coerced into using that inventive mind on his behalf?"

"She would refuse," Emory said, leaning his head back against the bark. "She is a lady of uncommon character and strength. So is Celeste."

"You will get no argument from me, my friend. But I fear Napoleon takes a dim view of refusal, as Celeste has told us."

"So do you," Emory told him. "Is that why you haven't offered for Loveday yet? You think she might refuse you?"

Arthur jerked to a stop, and Emory shook his head.

"I may not always understand how others think, but it's clear her parents and yours are eager for the match," he explained. "And just as clear that you admire her."

"Too much to saddle her with an encumbrance," Arthur

muttered, pressing a hand against the hull as if he needed its support.

Emory frowned. "Encumbrance? Do you mean your leg? Surely that is nearly mended."

"It grows stronger," he allowed. "Let us merely say that I am working to be worthy of such a bride. But I am not the only one smitten. Why haven't you offered for Celeste?"

Emory chuckled. "A fair question. In truth, I have been too busy working on the high-pressure engine and refining the mine pump to consider courting. And there is my family."

"Ah." Arthur shifted as if his leg was beginning to protest the cool air and prolonged use. "Your father has been vocal in his condemnation of all things French."

"He has been vocal on any number of matters. I have had to stand my ground with him and my older sisters for years—on leaving Truro to attend Eton and Oxford, on pursuing my engineering work instead of managing Wheal Thorne." He sighed. "I wonder if I have the fortitude to continue fighting the rest of my life for a wife they may not be able to respect. In short, Celeste deserves better."

"It seems we are in similar circumstances," Arthur said. "And I cannot help thinking that my foolishness in being the cause of this crash will only make matters more challenging."

Loveday could only gape and admire Celeste's *sangfroid* as she negotiated with the farmer who had caught up to them on the road. He agreed to convey them as far as Caen. From there, he assured Celeste, his cousin would be able to take them in to Paris, as he traveled there every week with a load of furniture to be sold at Les Halles, the great central market in the city.

"I was training this sorry cadet when my balloon went down," Celeste said to him, somehow managing to look both authoritative and annoyed, "so I cannot complete my mission. I left the balloon with a unit of the corps in Bretagne, but they can spare no one to return us to Paris or even supply us with proper uniforms. L'Ecole des Aéronautes is indebted to you for your assistance."

Loveday closed her mouth at this information. An excellent idea, to masquerade as an aeronaut and her chastised cadet. Loveday spoke quite good French, thanks to Madame Racine's tutelage, but it would not be long before any conversation would progress into dangerous waters. Better that she curtsey and smile, and keep her mouth firmly closed.

They had left Arthur and Emory early this morning, the knowledge lying heavily upon them that they had no time to waste if the gentlemen and *Lark Deux* were to be kept safe. Loveday, who had spent five or six days together without so much as a glimpse of Arthur without a qualm, now felt as though her stomach might betray her at the thought of being separated for even an hour.

Naturally, she was concerned about his safety. Emory's, too, of course. But setting off across half the length of France, leaving him behind, gave her cold chills.

She could do nothing to change their situation. Making herself sick with worry would improve it not one whit. So she must keep herself distracted by evaluating and documenting the many modes of transportation that met their eyes on their journey.

She might fill her notebook by the time she reached Paris.

How had she not known how technologically advanced were the French? Arthur had fought here—why had he not told her?

In England their tenants worked with horses and wains and wagons. And there were plenty of the same here, visible even now on the gentle swells and valleys of the land. But even the vehicle upon which they rode—a farm vehicle, for heaven's sake—put Thomas's Puffing Jenny, of which he was so proud, to shame. Its engine worked very much like that of their air ship, only to a different purpose. It traveled along the graveled main road at a speed that kept their hair out of their faces most efficiently, so fast it was. As fast as a good horse could gallop, and certainly faster than the post chaise between Falmouth and Exeter.

She held the pages of her notebook open with one hand and sketched as quickly as she was able between bumps in the road. And before she could even complete one sketch another marvel overtook them.

"Celeste," she hissed as it passed by on the outside. "What is that?"

"It is a *chaise roulante*," she whispered back. "Its wheels are so large for speed, and the engine that powers it is necessarily very small, for weight. This one has only one pilot, but the chaise can seat two comfortably."

The man in the chaise rolled past them at twice their speed, only visible through a flashing blur of spokes.

"Imagine our going in to Truro on such a thing," Loveday said, sketching furiously as the chaise disappeared over a hill. "Why, we would arrive five minutes after we left."

"And cause such a scandal we would never be able to show our faces again," Celeste said with a laugh. "Even in France, ladies do not ride the *chaise roulante*. At such speeds, one cannot control one's skirts."

"But the *pantalons*—why would a lady not wear an ensemble such as yours?"

Celeste shrugged, one hand gripping the wooden side of the vehicle in which they rode. "It is one of those mysteries of fashion, like your custom of putting the fichu in the neckline in the afternoon, to conceal a figure it is perfectly appropriate to reveal in the evening."

Loveday had to concede the point. But regardless of fashion, she must sketch these wonders while she could. And pray she would be able to explore these marvelous concepts further, if only they could reach home.

CHAPTER 6

$\mathcal{I}$t took longer to convince Emory that he must stay with the ship than it would to walk the two miles across country to St Malo. In the end Arthur was forced to blunt speech with his friend.

"I must let them know at home where we are," he said, "or when we get back our families will be wearing black crepe for us. I speak French with greater fluency—"

"That is an understatement," Emory said, frowning, unwilling to concede that they should not either stay or go together.

"—and you must prevent *Lark Deux* from being discovered at all costs."

"Do you suggest I murder anyone who comes within sight?" Emory's eyes held shock.

"Certainly not," Arthur said. "I trust that you will provide enough distraction that they will not come close enough to distinguish the envelope from a rock."

"It is a shade so revolting I do not blame the manufacturer for being anxious to get rid of it. It looks like a rock."

"All the better for purposes of concealment," Arthur had told him. "I will return by midafternoon."

He had set out on foot, walking through fields thigh-high in hay grass and flowers, climbing over stiles quarried from the local white limestone. The stone through which the lifting gas percolated. Even now his nose was tickled with the occasional faint whiff of lavender, though none grew near here.

Close to the walled city of St Malo, he changed direction so that he met the road as it joined the causeway. Clearly it was a market day, and foot traffic as well as a jaw-dropping array of vehicles flowed into the town. Fishing boats had moored, their captains selling everything from fresh-caught hake to bushel baskets filled with pink and white scallops. The tide was going out, revealing a stretch of golden sands beyond the city.

How different it was from the wild coast of Cornwall, and only a hundred miles away as the crow—or the lark—flew!

At the very end of the harbor, closest to the sea, lay moorage for a different kind of vessel. Here there was no sign of fish, but men stood in clusters on the docks or on the decks of their sloops and brigantines. It was clear that the harbor had been excavated to form a pool where the deeper-hulled ships might float unaffected by the tide, and a deep channel dug to give them safe passage to open water. The pirates might prey on vessels in the shipping lanes, but no one should prey on them in their own territory. No wonder St Malo was so prosperous.

The waterfront bustled with commercial traffic, both legal and not, and a babel of several different languages made him breathe easier. His French was as good as fighting a war and sailing with Barnabas Pendragon could make it, but he was not fluent by any means. Here, among men of many tongues and faraway homes, it would not be nearly so easily remarked upon.

Within the ramparts of the city walls overlooking the pirates' pool, he chose a likely-looking inn solely because of its whitewashed walls and its name—Auberge Mouette. A wooden board swinging on an iron pole above the door sported a carving of a gull with a fish in its mouth. From the fish's mouth peeped a ring of gold.

If that was not a signal that smugglers and pirates were welcome here—and probably owned the establishment—he couldn't imagine what was.

The public room smelled of rosemary and hot oil, and old wood and the sweat of hardworking men. At the bar, he ordered an ale and breakfast, and retreated to a corner by the window where he could watch the street and listen to the conversations all around him. It might be only midmorning, but these men could have been out all night. His breakfast came, the same as everyone else's—broiled fish and cut-up potatoes fried in oil. Thick tomatoes swimming in their own juice completed the meal.

Nothing had ever tasted so good.

Arthur couldn't regret the sacrifice of the piece of silver such a feast had cost him. He had pressed his portion of the remaining food in the hamper upon Emory and the young ladies this morning, so he was ravenous.

He was mopping up his plate with a piece of bread in one hand when a growling voice stopped the mug of ale in the other halfway to his mouth.

"Here's a pretty face I didn't expect to see."

He looked up to see the mate from one of the vessels he'd

helped to load on Jersey earlier in the summer. His form did not fit his voice, being rather slender, but his hands were sinewy and strong, and Arthur had seen him lay a man out with one punch.

"Louen." He nodded to the chair opposite, and his unexpected companion seated himself.

Louen addressed his meal with gusto. "Seems strange to see you in the daylight."

"Seems strange to be here." Louen didn't care that Arthur's French was too careful, that he paused slightly to translate in his head after the man spoke. "Are you just returned?"

He shook his head. "Too many *sous-marins* about. Spent a week with the wife. Sailing on the tide, though."

"The *sous-marins* give you trouble? But you're French. And do you not have one of those devices—Old Job's Pisky?"

"Not we smaller enterprises," Louen said, to Arthur's disappointment. He very much regretted the one that had gone down with Pendragon's ship. What were the odds of finding one here, if his friend could not lay hands upon one? He would give quite a lot for Loveday and Celeste to examine it.

But Louen was still fulminating. "We have to watch for the blind beasts with our own eyes. All they see is a hull coming from England. A pox on 'em—if our captain were tempted to take a prize, he couldn't. The *sous-marin* would interrupt and sink us both before we could get the cargo off."

"I did notice a number of them off the coasts to the west," he said carefully. "Deeper water. What's afoot?"

Louen shrugged. "Rumor has it the Emperor is up to something."

"An invasion? That would put paid to the free trade, *n'est-*

ce pas?" It would hardly be lucrative if France and England were unwillingly united and the taxes paid to Paris instead of London.

Louen snorted and laid down his fork on his empty plate. He took a long swig of ale. *"Oui.* But I'll believe it when I'm pressed into service on his ships. Or his *sous-marins.* The ship-yard at Saint-Nazaire has been boiling like my wife's stewpot lately."

The contented feeling in Arthur's belly seemed to chill. "Building *sous-marins?"*

"That is so, it seems. Bigger ones. Fitted with new equipment a man can't make head nor tail of. Still, many of our men have given up the free trade and taken employment there. It's only a day's journey southwest on a steam wagon."

Saint-Nazaire was the largest shipbuilding port in France, its massive harbor facing out on the Atlantic and defended by both cannon emplacements and navy patrols. So had Celeste been wrong? In only four months, had something prodded Napoleon out of his preoccupation with an invasion by air and brought his attention to the sea? Or was the buildup to be on both fronts, using two technologies the English did not possess?

In either case, he needed to inform the War Office immediately.

"You said you were going out on the tide," he said, signaling for more ale. "Would you take two messages for me?"

"We're bound for Penzance. That close enough?"

"Oui, bien sûr. Give them to the innkeeper at the Cormorant, fronting Penzance harbor. He'll see them safely on."

Arthur bought two pieces of paper and borrowed a pencil from the innkeeper. The first he addressed to the War Office, care of his father. The second was to Mr Penhale.

Sir,

We were shot down near St Malo. Be assured all aboard are unharmed and repairs are in progress. We will let no harm come to those who are precious to us both.

A.T.

Louen stuffed the tightly folded notes and the silver coin that accompanied them into the pocket of his coat. He knocked back the last of his ale and nodded a farewell to Arthur. After that, there was nothing else to be done but to face the return journey to the air ship. His leg ached, and the stabbing pain in his knee that often resulted when he had overworked it had returned with a vengeance. But it could not be helped.

It was a stroke of luck when a pair of washer-women offered him a ride on the gate of their wagon, filled with baskets of shirts and sheets. As they rolled down the road, Arthur clung to the side and gazed out at the sea.

The tide would turn in a couple of hours.

Silently, he wished the two fragile but vital pieces of paper a safe journey.

IT WOULD TAKE every bit of two days to reach the outskirts of Paris. Loveday and Celeste reached the prosperous-looking house of Monsieur Charpentier, the kind farmer's cousin in Caen, that evening. The farmer explained their plight and along with him, they were invited to stay rather than taking lodgings at a hotel. But no amount of gentle, ladylike probing on Celeste's part could produce much news of the war, or whether Napoleon had made any announcements concerning powered flight. Not even a whisper of *La Blanchard* was to be had. Clearly this was a family who preferred the quiet of the country in which to work with their hands, not machines. Hardly better informed at bedtime than they had been when they arrived, they were shown upstairs to the bed of their host's daughter, who was awestruck at the sight of Celeste's flying costume.

"We will not be able to keep your identity a secret for much longer," Loveday whispered the next morning, as they climbed up on a high-walled wagon pulled by a larger version of the Puffing Jenny. "She will talk of nothing else with her acquaintance, I am certain."

"I wish I had thought to pack a valise containing a week's worth of ensemble changes for our two-hour flight," Celeste replied dryly. "We must do our best to maintain our false identities for as long as possible. Oh, Loveday, look at the *monoroue!*"

The slower steam wagon on which they rode with an assortment of chests and chairs and beautifully carved bedsteads was passed by a wondrous device, its pilot giving them a cheerful wave.

"Ohhh," Loveday moaned as she hunted about her. "Where is my pencil?"

The pilot actually sat within the wheel, which rotated around him powered by an engine in the rear, conveying him at a breakneck pace down the road. A ribbon of steam left behind gradually dissipated in the warm air.

"How beautifully made it is," she muttered to herself. "These arabesques both support the structure and make it a pleasure to look at when it is not in motion. Oh, how I wish our countries were not at war. If these wonders are on the roads, what must there be in people's houses?"

The furniture maker took leave of them at Les Halles in the late afternoon, and now they must ride shank's mare to l'Ecole des Aéronautes like anyone else. Loveday had been as far as Exeter and considered it a splendid city. But it looked like a village compared to Paris. The shadows between the tall buildings with their curved mansard roofs made the streets seem dark and cavernous, and she could hardly imagine how luxurious they must be inside.

"Is it far?" Loveday did her best not to stare like a child at the activity in the streets, the clothes of the ladies finishing up their shopping, the soldiers—

Oh, dear.

She cast her gaze on the cobblestones before her and tried to mimic the posture and attitude of a humble cadet, obediently following at her captain's elbow.

"Not far," Celeste assured her. "It is off the Rue de Renard, on the Rue des Aéronautes."

Half an hour's walk brought them to the stone walls of the building of whose name every man or woman interested in flight had heard. Never in Loveday's wildest imaginings would she have thought that she would be standing outside these walls. With the daughter of Sophie Blanchard, no less. What wonders would she see within?

Celeste grasped the round handle of the elegant front

door. "Welcome to l'Ecole des Aéronautes," she said with a smile over her shoulder.

The handle would not turn. The door would not budge.

"Why is it locked?" Celeste rattled it, then gave up in disgust.

It seemed no one was there. Only the doves on the roof next door, cooing in their dovecote as they settled for the evening.

"What has happened since I have been gone?" Celeste looked up toward the doves, as though they held the answer.

Neither they nor Loveday had a single word to offer in reply.

CHAPTER 7

PARIS

Celeste took a step back from the front door to stare at the rugged façade of the school. Not a light showed in any window, even though darkness was gathering once more. Though she could hear the clop and rattle of a horse and wagon passing, no voices called from within.

Where was everyone? Josie, Amélie, Marcel. Even her mother still visited the school on occasion, if only to make sure she had sufficient supplies for her next ascension.

"The rear door," she told Loveday, desperation making her voice sharp. "It opens onto the workshop. Someone may be there."

She walked around the building into the alley, so narrow that if she had been wearing a Lunardi hat, the brim would have brushed it on both sides. At the rear was a service track where supplies came in on wagons, as well as a single door into the workshop. Wooden planks had been nailed crosswise over the wider door, but the smaller door sported not even a padlock. Unfortunately, it too refused to budge.

Dread building inside her, Celeste knocked and waited.

Nothing. Who would have boarded up the bigger doors? Her mother needed them to move out her baskets and envelope for ascensions. She gazed up in case someone might have poked her head out a window.

"Josie?" she called. Were they even inside? "Amélie, *êtes-vous là?*"

A bat flew overhead, black against the deep purple of the sky. She shivered.

"Amélie!" she called through the portal. "Josephine! *C'est moi,* Celeste. *Ouvrez la porte!*"

The door remained shut.

Loveday put a hand on her arm, but Celeste shook her off. She fisted her hand and pounded on the unyielding wood. "Marcel! *Reponds à moi!* Answer me!"

This time, Loveday took her hand to pull her back. "Celeste. You will injure yourself. They are gone."

They could not be gone. They lived here. They had nowhere else to go. Neither did she. So many hours spent here, with friends, her mother, her father. It could not be empty.

And yet it was. As empty as she felt herself.

Something cracked, then whooshed, and Josie's head poked out of the window on the next floor. "Celeste! *C'est toi? Est-ce possible?*"

She sagged. "Yes, yes, it's me! Quick, let us in."

"The doors have been nailed shut inside," Josie explained in French, gaze drifting with a frown to Loveday. "By order of the Emperor. We hid and watched them leave through the workshop. We thought it safer not to remove the barriers."

Nailed shut?

"Here." Amélie's head appeared out of a window on the

other side of the entrance, and a moment later, a rope ladder descended to the alley. "Climb up, and we will tell you everything."

It took a little doing, especially with Loveday's skirts, but Celeste and she managed to climb up the ladder and into the school to tumble into what had been the girls' dormitory. Iron bedsteads, empty of mattress and occupant, marched away into the gathering darkness. Every movement echoed.

Amélie hugged Celeste tight even as Josie came to join them from the other side of the corridor. Over their shoulders, Celeste saw Loveday reeling in the ladder and lowering the window sash.

"You're here, you're here," Josie babbled, tears running down her cheeks. Her curls, usually so golden and springy, hung in limp brackets around her face, and her dress no longer fit her thinning frame.

"Of course she's here," Amélie, ever the literal, said. She too looked as if she'd lost weight, her blue eyes huge in her pale face. "Anyone can see that. And she's brought someone with her."

Both sisters turned to eye Loveday.

"Josephine and Amélie Aventure," Celeste said, "allow me to present Loveday Penhale, inventor extraordinaire."

Loveday inclined her head. "Miss Aventure. Miss Amélie."

Her French was good, but not good enough. Josie sucked in a breath. "She's English."

"She is," Celeste agreed, "and my very good friend. She's been protecting me all this time."

Amélie's eyes widened. "Then you did it! You made it to England, truly?"

Celeste nodded. "The design worked, until I hit a squall.

The balloon went down. Loveday rescued me from the waves, or I might have drowned."

Josie put a hand to her chest. "Thank God for His help."

Amélie stepped closer. "We have news as well."

Josie grabbed her arm as if to prevent her from speaking. "Later."

Celeste glanced between the two of them. Shoulders had tightened in their wrinkled blue chambray gowns, bodies tensed. "What's wrong?" she asked. "Why did the Emperor lock the school? Has he given up on Mother at last?"

They exchanged glances, then Josie squared her shoulders and took a deep breath. "He had to give up on her, Celeste. *La Blanchard* is dead."

She hadn't realized she'd swayed until Loveday put an arm around her waist to steady her.

"What happened?" her friend asked as Celeste struggled with her voice, her thoughts. Marie Madeline-Sophie Blanchard, the Queen of the Heavens, dead? How could it be?

Both Josie and Amélie began talking, and Celeste could barely make sense of them.

"The Emperor ordered her to perform," Amélie said. "She didn't like it."

"She never liked it," Josie agreed. "Such a waste of her talents!"

"But she promised to go up," Amélie said, "with explosives."

Celeste clutched Loveday's hand. "The little bombs?"

"Bigger," Josie said, voice haunted.

"We practiced with them," Amélie said as if begging Celeste to understand. "Everything went as planned. But when she ascended..." She shuddered.

"The balloon caught fire," Josie said. "She fell to the pavement."

"From five hundred feet," Amélie said. "I was calculating the rise."

Her sister rounded on her. "She doesn't need to know how high! Isn't it bad enough to know she lost her mother?"

Amélie bowed her head, her hands clasping each other tightly.

"It's all right," Celeste heard herself say as if from a long distance. "I want to know. Did she regain consciousness? Did she speak?"

Josie shook her head.

Celeste drew in a shuddering breath. "I cannot believe it! She was magnificent, determined. She cannot be gone. One may as well say the Louvre is gone, or Notre Dame."

"There is more," Amélie ventured with a look at her sister.

Josie waved a hand, as if giving up on holding anything back, and Celeste steeled herself.

"Dupont has been drafted into the army," Amélie said, lips beginning to tremble. "The Emperor assigned her to the front, along the border with the Karlsruhe Confederacy. We have not heard from her in some time."

Celeste had to sit down, landing with a thump on the flat frame of the closest bedstead. Dupont too, the woman who had all but raised her? Was there no one left to help them?

Loveday put a hand on her shoulder in wordless comfort.

"Worse," Josie said, taking up the tale, "there was reason to believe *La Blanchard's* death was not an accident. The Imperial Guard themselves came to arrest the accused."

Celeste rallied. She was finding it difficult to breathe. "Good. At least justice will be done."

"Justice?" Josie shook her head. "Celeste, they arrested *Marcel* for the crime."

"What!" Anger pushed her to her feet again. "*Non!* Not Marcel! He would never harm my mother."

"So we told them," Amélie said, chin up.

"Repeatedly," Josie added. "But they wouldn't listen."

"Is he…?" Celeste couldn't form the word.

"He is in prison, in the Tuileries," Amélie reported. "We have not been allowed to see him."

"We have not allowed anyone to know we are still in the school," Josie explained. "We were told to leave, but how could we?" She spread her hands. "This is home."

Her home, too, more than the houses her parents had leased, the hotels where Dupont had cared for her while her parents made their daring ascents. But without Marcel, without her mother, it felt like another cold, quiet ruin.

"We have plans," Amélie said softly into the stretching silence. "Perhaps a way to free Marcel and escape France. We thought we could go to Marcel's brother, Captain Delaguard, the smuggler."

Etienne Delaguard's ship plied the waters between Calais and Dover as he carried secrets for Napoleon among his illicit cargo. Above anyone else, he would know how to evade the authorities and keep her friends safe.

"What we need," Josie said, her gaze landing heavily on Celeste, "is help. Your help."

Of course. Immediately. Except—

Celeste glanced at Loveday. Her friend stood more still than a boiler left to cool, but her gaze was sharp, as if she had already calculated the odds of success. Easy for Celeste to say she would help Amélie and Josie, but she owed a far greater debt to her English friend. She could not abandon Loveday, Emory, or Arthur behind enemy lines.

And what of the air ship? It must be returned to England to protect it from Napoleon. They might be able to use it to carry Josie, Amélie, and Marcel, if they could find a way to free him. But it barely fit four, not seven. How would they counteract the weight?

As if she understood, Loveday met Celeste's gaze and nodded. Then she turned to face Josie and Amélie. "What can we do?" she asked.

WHAT, Loveday wondered, had l'Ecole des Aéronautes been like in the heyday of *La Blanchard*'s fame? With every step she took that evening, she saw the remains of what had been, not what was—the way fallen brown leaves reveal what a tree has been in the full glory of summer. Josie and Amélie had unearthed pallets for them to put on two of the iron bedsteads, and a blanket for warmth, but that only made her imagine the marching rows of empty bedsteads full of students, talking and laughing when they were supposed to be asleep. In the refectory, long tables still stood, dust covering them the way a tablecloth might have, but she saw every bench filled, the tables spread with food. Now Josie and Amélie ate in the kitchen, their pitiful dinner of bread and cheese divided among four when it was hardly enough for two. They stayed out of love, these girls. They must, for who could bear to be in these vast echoing halls and courtyards, hearing whispers of the past even more loudly than the present?

"Along with more food, we need a plan," Celeste told them. At least the water from the well in the front courtyard was cold and plentiful. She drank straight from the pitcher, as there did not seem to be cups.

"To free Marcel, we will need more than a plan," Josie said ruefully. "We will need money enough to bribe the guards."

"No," Loveday said, her mind flicking through possibilities the way her sister Gwen flicked through playing cards. "We must look higher. What solution will encompass both Marcel's freedom and the repairs to *Lark Deux?*"

For of course they had told Celeste's closest friends about the success of both versions of their air ship. For the first time, Loveday had seen the two young women the way they could have been, illuminated with joy at their friend's success, in the light of the single lantern upon the table.

"We must look higher even than that," Celeste said thoughtfully. "What solution could result in the reopening of the school as well?"

"I only know of one," Amélie said slowly, her gaze not leaving Celeste. "But failure will mean death."

"And success will mean all of our lives saved, and our ship, too," Celeste told her. "Is it not worth the risk?"

"Is it not worth *what* risk, exactly?" Loveday felt her breath slow.

Celeste paused, and in that moment Loveday could practically see the pistons in her brain begin to rise and fall. "I must return." She was still for a moment, her gaze seeing something far grander than the stone walls and bare shelves of the kitchen, before nodding as though the pistons were picking up speed. "I must return to court in the full glory of my mother's achievements," she said, and her voice became more certain. "I have been on a voyage at her command. A secret voyage, known only to we two."

"In a new prototype," Josie suggested.

"Which sadly went down… where?"

"England?" Loveday said.

"No, we must go as far from the truth as possible."

"Switzerland," Amélie said. "Lots of mountains. It took a long time to find your way back, to say nothing of getting through the front lines."

"Perfect." Celeste beamed at her. "And with whom have I returned? For I cannot take either of you—you are known to many in my mother's old circles. And Loveday cannot be English."

"I am not certain I can be Swiss, either." Loveday looked from one face to the next. "But it would explain my accented French." She thought a moment. "I know! I shall be the brave woman who dragged you from the wreckage, then guided you out of the mountains and could not bear to leave you."

"Oh, *bonne idée!*" Amélie nodded. "But have you ever been to Switzerland?"

"Of course not." Loveday laughed and wondered when the kitchen had last heard such a sound. "The closest I have come to mountains is engravings in magazines. And the memoirs in the circulating library—of gentlemen making their Grand Tour."

"That is more than I have seen," Josie said. "It will have to do." Her gaze fell upon their clothes. "But will you go to court looking as though you have crossed the Channel and ridden to Paris in a furniture cart?"

"We will go looking as though we had fought our way through armies of soldiers and walked for days through mountain passes," Loveday said. "Why, we have come as soon as we could to give our report to the Emperor."

"We will not have much work to do to convince him," Celeste said, plucking at one leg of her *pantalons*, which sadly had come out on the losing side of its journey up the rope ladder. She looked up. "But until I am revealed tomorrow, and find out whether I can reopen the school, you two must continue to come and go in deepest secrecy."

How wonderful it was to talk with these women! Women like Celeste and herself, who applied their minds to a problem until the solution was revealed. In the time it took to consume a few pieces of bread and cheese, they had a plan. Breathtaking in its daring, risky in every particular, but a plan nonetheless.

And they would set it in motion tomorrow.

CHAPTER 8

ST MALO

The cool night air, damp with spindrift from the sea, lay upon the back of his coat and breathed down his neck. Seated in the dark on the deck of the gondola, Arthur Trevelyan moved a little closer to the firebox and inserted a handful of coal as reluctantly as a miser giving alms.

"Careful with that," Emory said quietly. "If we are discovered by the army, we must keep just enough on hand to allow us to ignite the boiler and lift."

"I know," Arthur said. "I have been calculating the cost versus the risk, believe me. Do you think our repairs will hold?"

Emory gazed upward into the rigging, though they could not see much. Around their little clearing, the trees obscured most of the moonlight, which Arthur supposed was a benefit rather than a drawback. "I hope so," he said at last. "With your greater experience serving aboard smuggling vessels, you are better at knots than I am."

"You did your best."

"I am confident she will lift, even with only one gas bag remaining."

When Arthur had returned from St Malo with food and news, he had found Emory repairing the damage where the cannonbomb had torn through the rigging and destroyed the aft gas bag. Already he had removed the smashed wicker of the corset and left the gas bag exposed in hopes of its eventual repair. When Arthur had come through the woods into the clearing, careful not to be spotted, he had come upon Emory, knotting the severed ropes together in a different pattern so that they would bear the weight of the gondola.

"The trouble is," Arthur mused, "even if we did lift, a company of soldiers could simply take aim and shoot the remaining gas bag to bits."

"At least after its fall we would not be alive to be captured, and the ship would be destroyed."

If this were Emory's idea of a bright side, Arthur wondered what the more pessimistic view looked like.

But his point was well taken. "Emory, I have been thinking. It is inevitable that we will be discovered. It is only a matter of time. Do you not think that we ought to destroy the vessel in any case? If it falls into Napoleon's hands…"

"You do not need to remind me," Emory said. "I have turned over in my mind every possible plan of action. Even attempting a return flight."

Shock brought Arthur upright. "Without Loveday and Celeste? Are you mad?"

"I sincerely believe not," Emory said mildly. "Lower your hackles. One must think of every possibility, and if *Lark Deux* bears only two, not four, having one gas bag, not two, she just might come within sight of English shores again."

"And what of our friends?"

"Celeste is French," Emory said, as if this were an end to the matter.

Arthur had never been so shocked in his life—not even when the shrapnel from the exploding behemoth had torn into his leg. It had been bad enough to watch Loveday Penhale walk away through the trees. They had no choice but to split up and make the best of a terrible situation. But for Emory to suggest *choosing* to leave them here? Defenseless and alone? French or not, Celeste's mother had been in disgrace with the Emperor. Who was to say he would not take out his disappointment with the mother upon the daughter? And where would that leave Loveday?

"Unthinkable." He could go no further.

"Not unthinkable," Emory said. "I had to think of it. And subsequently, of course, to discard it as ridiculous."

It took a moment for Arthur's breath to come back.

"If any two people were to be sent back to England on a crippled air ship," Emory went on, "it would be you and Loveday. Celeste and I could remain here, where at least I could pose as her speechless manservant and protect her physically. If your smuggler friends were not inclined to offer us passage, she could talk our way to the border with the Karlsruhe Confederacy. In Flanders we might find passage back to England. Eventually."

These views were marginally better, though still so dangerous Arthur could hardly form an opinion as to their likelihood of success. "But these possibilities depend upon a flightworthy *Lark Deux*," he finally said, now that his heart had left his throat and descended to its habitual location. "What are our options without a vessel at all, if we were to destroy her? My thoughts have mostly been occupied on that side of the discussion. As you say, we might find a berth aboard a smuggler's vessel, once Loveday and Celeste return. It would only be a matter of concealing ourselves until then. We are more easily tucked into a hatch or a barn loft than an air ship."

"True," Emory conceded. "But have you considered Loveday's feelings should they return with supplies for repair and find we have used her beautiful gondola for firewood, and made silk sheets for ourselves from the envelope?"

"That would indeed be a sorry scene," Arthur said, gazing outward and imagining it. "We would be right back where we began, and neither lady would ever forgive us. To be honest, we might simply—" He stopped. "What was that?"

Emory looked about him. "What? An animal?"

"No, above us. I'll wager a gold guinea it was not a shooting star." His gaze still searching the starry sky above the black shapes of the hills, he went to the gunwale. "Come."

Emory, man of sense that he was, did not hesitate. Together, they slipped through the trees until they reached the fringes of the copse. Arthur crouched in the inky darkness of a small pine's shadow and pointed.

"Watch the sky. Tell me what you see."

There it was again. A flash of blue light in the fields. More than one. Then—a wash of silver in the moonlight. And another.

"Air ships," Emory whispered as two of them flew overhead. "Not balloons. These are powered ships, using lifting gas and an engine."

Another passed over their heads, so low that if it had been daylight, the pilot would have seen *Lark Deux*'s envelope in the clearing behind them. The thing imprinted itself in Arthur's brain, like an engraving.

"What on earth?" Emory said in a wondering tone. "That looks exactly like…" His voice trailed away, as though even he could not believe his own words.

Arthur supplied them. "*Lark*. The first one. Only a little less like a cut-up coach."

"How can that be?"

There went another, and another, heading from east to west, in the direction of the area where the *sous-marins* had been massing.

"I don't understand, either," Arthur said. "Surely they can't have been built from the same set of plans. That would mean—"

"—that Celeste had sent the plans here. Go ahead and say it, Arthur. I know you are thinking it."

Arthur did not remind him that *he* had thought of leaving both girls behind. "I cannot think it," he said. "I will not."

"Once again unthinkable, but possible." Emory seemed to be having as much trouble breathing as Arthur had had only minutes ago. "But no. I cannot believe she would have done such a thing. Not Celeste. She once accused me of stealing her plans for my own purposes. I will not do the same to her."

Arthur nodded, stunned brain beginning to work. "I'd forgotten. Someone did steal the plans for the first *Lark* and attempt to foil its maiden flight. That person must have sent the plans to France. It does not seem reasonable that two engineers would have had the same idea at roughly the same time in two separate countries."

"It has happened," Emory said. "French and English inventors have fought for supremacy in ballooning for decades, each claiming to have discovered a new facet first."

"But this is advanced technology," Arthur protested. Another ship passed over their heads. "Emory, that one was a landau in its former life, I am certain of it. They are all the same."

"What are the odds that they are coming from Cherbourg?" Emory wondered aloud. "Celeste said it was where the behemoths are manufactured. Why not air ships? And another thing—there is something very strange about the way they fly. Straight along the course of those lights. They are set on the tops of the hills, like the one above us. Do they form some kind of guidance system? Why are the pilots not using instruments?"

Arthur had no reply, not being an engineer, but a spy who used blue lights himself, to guide a vessel in to a safe harbor. "And where are they headed, if not the same destination as those *sous-marins?*"

"I thought your friend Louen said they were being built at Saint-Nazaire. We saw them gathering closer to St Malo."

"They are being built in the west, and in great numbers, from what I understand. But that does not explain these flying coaches. Or the lights. Or the pilots. They look singular. Stiff. And their heads do not move. We were in almost constant motion in *Lark Deux*. It doesn't make sense."

"None of this makes sense," Emory agreed. "What it makes me is uneasy. Very much so."

Arthur could only agree. But at least they were no longer talking about leaving defenseless young ladies behind in a country at war.

Not for the first time since the girls had departed, he

wished he could hear Loveday's voice again. More than that, he wished he could talk over these strange sights with her. She might be able to make sense of it all—or at the very least, her mind might rub up against those of Emory and Celeste, forming a spark of an idea that would lead to a discovery.

But for now, that was merely a dream. They could do nothing more tonight but return to the meager comfort of *Lark Deux*'s deck. Curl up close to the firebox. And hope for a little sleep in which he might dream of Loveday's smile, of kissing those tiny dimples on either side of her mouth, once more.

PARIS

The first thing Celeste observed at the Tuileries were the guards patrolling along the iron fences flanking l'Arc de Triomphe du Carousel. She and Loveday could not sneak in—they must be escorted, and not like supplicants or prisoners, either. She might be dressed in torn clothing, but Celeste had not forgotten *La Blanchard*'s way of looking imperious while at the same time charming. Two of the younger guards agreed to escort them—reluctantly enough, but Celeste did not care. As long as they were escorted with the dignity to which her mother had been entitled, she would ask no more.

Breathing slightly more easily at this leaping of the first hurdle, Celeste followed the guards through the massive stone arch, across the graveled parade ground, and into the tall doors to the palace. She could only take comfort in Loveday at her back, following two steps behind as befitted her rescuer—now assistant. And she needed that comfort. Thank goodness she had not forgotten the Emperor's love of ostentation and ornamentation. The contrast with their appearance would make their story completely believable. Even here in the entry hall, polished ebony adorned the lower portions of the walls, while the upper portions were eclipsed by massive paintings celebrating Napoleon's many victories. Their footfalls echoed against the patterned marble as they crossed the space, but another sound caught her attention—a soft clicking, like clockwork.

A small, gilded creature moved slowly along the wall on the opposite side of the entry hall. It reminded Celeste of a sheep, with a fluffy head, long back covered in lambswool, and short tail of feathers that was in constant movement along the wall. Dust motes danced in the sunlight as it passed. Similar creatures moved along rails set into the cornices, tails sweeping over the paintings that covered the ceiling.

Either Celeste had slowed too much, or Loveday was walking too quickly, for her friend bumped into her. Instead of apologizing, however, Loveday muttered, *"Automoutons."*

Celeste stifled a giggle at the silly pun on the French word for *sheep*. Then she sobered. *Automoutons* were all well and good, but here? When had this happened?

She wasn't sure whether the guard would take her to the Emperor or one of his many functionaries. As it was, they marched her and Loveday up the grand stone staircase into the *Pavilon de l'Horloge* with its great bronze clock ticking off the seconds since the day Napoleon had been crowned, and finally along the Gallery of Diana, with its heavy crystal chandeliers disappearing into the distance. A clerk of the court in an old-fashioned bag wig and long, embroidered waistcoat sat in state behind a gilded desk that had been positioned to partly block one of the tall paneled doors.

"Mademoiselle Blanchard has requested to meet with His Imperial Majesty," one of the guards told him.

The clerk blinked behind thick spectacles, looked her up and down in what could have been either affront or amazement, then turned and motioned to one of the footmen standing along the wall. "Take these women to the Sèvres Salon," he instructed.

Without another look at Celeste, her erstwhile escort pivoted on their heels and marched off.

The footman turned toward another of the tall doors, its panels gilded. Her heart pressed against her throat, Celeste followed, Loveday right behind. They stepped into another salon, this one floored with a fine Aubusson carpet patterned in gold and rose. Sèvres porcelain in royal blue, emerald green, and pearl glowed from glass-fronted cabinets along the walls. There was not a chair in sight.

"He likes to keep his courtiers uncomfortable," Loveday whispered in French to Celeste as the footman went to speak to another man in a long tailcoat, who stood near the door in the wall on their right.

"He likes to keep everyone uncomfortable," Celeste whispered back.

The footman bowed and took himself off. The new courtier, with powdered hair and large gold buttons on his coat, came forward, parchment in hand. "I do not see you on the list, Mademoiselle Blanchard."

Celeste gave him her prettiest smile. "But of course not, Lord Chamberlain. I have only just returned to Paris, and I did not want to keep His Imperial Majesty waiting a single instant for my report." She spread her hands to indicate the state of her dress.

He raised his dark brows. "You believe the Emperor hangs on your every word?"

Only a fool would make such a claim. Or ask such a question.

"Never," Celeste vowed, head high. "But I promised *La Blanchard*, my celebrated mother, that I would tell the Emperor of my flight. Do you think I would do less with her gone?"

She kept up her haughty pose while one of the porcelain clocks ticked off the moments.

He held out a gloved hand. "Your card?"

She refused to sag with relief. "Alas, all were burned in the fire when my balloon went down in Switzerland, and I have not had time to have more made."

"Excuse me." He stalked to the far door and disappeared inside.

"Is it always like this?" Loveday murmured.

"Napoleon likes a certain amount of ceremony," Celeste murmured back. "But this is worse than I remember."

The door opened, and the Lord Chamberlain swept in, at a far faster pace than when he had departed.

"Highly irregular," he said with a frown. "But I suppose we cannot deny the Emperor his least wish. You may go in." He glanced at Loveday. "You will wait here."

Meet the Emperor alone? Oh, no. That she was not willing to do.

"Impossible," Celeste told the courtier. "My assistant and guide must accompany me."

His heavy brows crashed down on his pointed nose. "I have not been instructed to allow anyone but you to enter."

Celeste's heart might be hammering harder than Loveday

at a sheet of copper, but she would not allow him to know that. "Then will you be administering my smelling salts?" she demanded.

He blinked. "Smelling salts?"

"*Oui*, when my nerves are overcome by meeting our most glorious Emperor. Or do you wish me to faint onto the carpet at his feet like a punctured balloon?"

His color washed out. "You may bring your assistant."

Celeste kept her smile hidden as she walked past him, nose in the air. She heard Loveday's skirts swish against the carpet as she followed.

The courtier minced to the door and held it open. "His Imperial Majesty will see you now."

Celeste drew in a breath. Whatever awaited her on the other side of that door—commendation, accusation, a demand to marry against her wishes—she must show no weakness. She was, above all, the daughter of *La Blanchard*. She would do her mother proud.

She sashayed through the door, then dropped a deep curtsey. "Your Imperial Majesty, you honor me."

Rising, she dared to look at the man who ruled France and a good portion of the Continent with an iron hand. At least he had changed little in the time she had been gone. The ladies of France extolled that chestnut hair, cut short except for a few locks that fell over his forehead and tempted a forbidden touch. The long nose pointed to lips that had been described as cruel by their enemies. He clasped his hands behind his back and thrust out his chest as he eyed her.

And he was not alone. Standing on either side were men she knew, men who had been entertained in her mother's home. Men who had once owed their living to her mother's genius.

The two captains of the Aeronautical Corps.

Like the Emperor, they were looking her up and down, as though they could see her fears, her inadequacies. The golden-haired La Croix, the youngest of the pair, went so far as to wrinkle his nose as if she smelled of day-old cabbage. The darker-haired Toussaint raised a brow as if prepared to question her parentage, or her sanity.

Napoleon, however, smiled. "Welcome home, *ma petite elfe*. Much has changed since you left us."

Celeste inclined her head. "But never my loyalty to you, Your Majesty."

He allowed his hands to fall. "You were told about your mother?"

She nodded, unable yet to speak the words.

"A tragedy," the Emperor assured her. "There are none like her. Do you not agree, Captain La Croix?"

"A loss for the nation," La Croix offered. "But I am persuaded we will yet prevail under Your Imperial Majesty's leadership."

Napoleon spread his hands. "Always it falls to me. And what of you, Toussaint? Are you not pleased to see Mademoiselle Blanchard returned to us?"

"A miracle," Toussaint drawled, long black mustache bristling where he could not. "You must tell us how you managed to survive, mademoiselle. We were given to understand you traveled to England."

Perhaps she would need those smelling salts after all. She could almost feel Loveday tensing behind her.

"England?" Celeste said airily. "Why would I go to

England? I was in Switzerland on a mission for my mother, to test a prototype for a new balloon. Unfortunately, it went down and was destroyed. I barely threaded my way through the lines to return home."

"With a companion, it seems," Toussaint said, tipping his head to look at Loveday.

She had wondered when one of them would notice. Apparently, the novelty of having the daughter of *La Blanchard* reappear from the dead had kept them focused on her.

"Your Majesty, may I present Mademoiselle Jourdamour, a brave gentlewoman who guided me through terrifying mountain passes and begged to accompany me to Paris," Celeste said. "For who would choose the provinces when she might breathe the same air as our glorious Emperor?"

Loveday curtsied to the floor.

"Who indeed," Napoleon allowed, indicating she might rise. He leaned forward. "And now that you are returned? What will you do?"

Celeste dipped another curtsey. "Like my mother, I live to serve. I am at your disposal." She said a quick prayer that he would not trot out the Comte d'Angeline, whom he had once determined she must marry.

He straightened. "*Bon.* Your arrival could not be better timed. I have been on a tour of the battlefields, but I called our valiant captains here today to determine who will lead my Aeronautical Corps as Chief Air Minister."

Was he trying to decide which to promote? Did he want her opinion of his candidates? Celeste glanced at the two men who had been both comrades with and conspirators against her mother. They had lifted their heads and squared their shoulders, each the epitome of capability.

She looked back at the Emperor to find he had narrowed his blue-grey eyes at her, and one foot tapped against the carpet as if keeping time with his thoughts.

Not marriage. Not now!

"You have been trained since birth by *La Blanchard* herself," he said at last. "*You* must be my new Chief Air Minister."

La Croix started, and Toussaint glowered.

She was young enough to be their daughter. They had barely listened to her mother. They would never listen to her.

Celeste fought through her shock and aversion to look at the benefits. For if she took the position, she could direct everything about the Aeronautical Corps and solve their difficulties in one stroke. She could reopen the school, send supplies to Amélie and Josie, find a way to restore the air ship, and rescue Emory and Arthur. She would be in a position to do England and Loveday the most good—until they escaped France once more.

She lifted her arm and saluted the Emperor. "I am honored to serve."

Even if the people she would be serving were not in the French court.

"*INCROYABLE,*" La Croix muttered as he and Toussaint followed Celeste and Loveday from the Emperor's presence. "How can we be expected to follow the lead of a girl?"

Celeste had her own doubts on that score, but she wasn't about to let the two captains know it. She turned on them as they entered the Gallery of Diana, their reflections glimmering from the two-story-high mirrors along the back wall.

"You will recall that this *girl* is an aeronaut with more time spent in the study of ballooning—and in the skies—than both of you combined," she informed them.

"An aeronaut who has been gone from France these many months," Toussaint allowed, one finger stroking his sleek mustache. "As His Imperial Majesty noted, much has changed."

La Croix flashed him a look, but clamped his mouth shut.

"You will need to explain the current situation, then," Celeste said. "Is the Corps still headquartered on the Place des Victoires Nationaux?"

"The aeronauts have barracks closer to Les Invalides," La Croix allowed. "But your mother had an office here in the palace she used on occasion."

Toussaint's smile was cool. "And I am certain His Imperial Majesty will want you that close. We will arrange for a suite of rooms for you and your assistant here as well. You are, after all, a national treasure, like your dear mother."

A national treasure. Once it had been an honor bestowed on her mother. Now Celeste recognized it for the prison it was. How could she and Loveday possibly repair the air ship or help free Marcel if they were confined to the Tuileries under the watchful eyes of a dozen of Napoleon's agents?

"We will return to my mother's house," Celeste informed them. "*La Blanchard* led you from there. I see no reason why I cannot do the same."

Toussaint took her elbow as if about to propel her through the windows opposite. "The house is in other hands, now."

Before she could insist, he went on, "And we could not possibly have you so far away in these trying times. Perhaps you have not been informed, Chief Air Minister, but your mother was murdered."

The words sent a shiver up her spine. "I was told. Marcel Delaguard was detained for the crime."

La Croix snorted. "Fool! He sought to profit from her death."

Celeste cocked her head as she allowed Toussaint to tow her toward the far end of the gallery, Loveday following. "And how would the death of *La Blanchard* profit one of her students?"

"Is it not clear?" Toussaint said impatiently. "He hoped to be raised in her place. And we cannot be certain others do not harbor the same ambitions."

She was fairly sure the two most likely to harbor such ambitions were at this moment standing far too close to her.

"No," Toussaint continued as a footman helpfully opened the door onto a long corridor lined with other doors, "we cannot chance losing another Air Minister so soon. Think how it would dishearten the Corps. How it would dishearten the people. You must be protected, Chief Air Minister Blan-chard. Leave it to us. We will find you appropriate lodging and supply you with a bodyguard."

La Croix brightened at last. "A bodyguard? Excellent idea. I know just the woman. She recently joined us from the front."

"Perfect," Toussaint said. "We will attend you to your new office, Chief Air Minister, and return for you when we have everything else arranged."

She could do little to argue, and she was eager to address all the questions she saw shining in Loveday's eyes, so she agreed with the plan. She expected them to stop at any one of the doors along the corridor, but they took her to the nearest stairway and guided her down to the ground floor, then along another corridor.

Perhaps she should not have worried. The Emperor would have quite a walk to find her.

Finally they stopped, and she could only guess they were at the very back corner of the Tuileries.

As if heralding her arrival, bells began to ring—echoing even here. What, was every clock in the palace chiming?

"Your office, Chief Air Minister," Toussaint said with a smirk that told her she should expect no more than a dingy, cramped space behind the gilded door. She could only hope the office held a window that looked out on the gardens. At least then she might catch glimpses of the sky.

He threw open the door, and Celeste walked into a long, high-ceilinged room, every wall covered with the stuff of which dreams were made. The far wall groaned with racks overflowing with materials—wood and iron, brass and copper, silk and cotton. The wall to her right was one solid bookcase, with leather-bound volumes crowding next to rolls of plans and maps. Opposite her, a multi-paned window flooded light into the space. A sturdy worktable ran along the wall closest to the door, with every tool imaginable hanging in easy reach—turnscrews and hammers and rules—gleaming with brass and polished wood. The lion-footed desk in the center looked oddly out of place.

An exhale of breath behind her told her Loveday was trying hard not to squeal.

Celeste lifted her chin. "I suppose this will do. You may go."

The two captains bowed and left her. She waited only until the door closed behind them before turning to Loveday.

Her friend's eyes were round, and Celeste could almost see the designs flashing in their blue depths. "Oh, Celeste," she breathed. "What we could do here."

"First, we must make sure we are safe," Celeste told her. She nodded toward the door. "Does it lock?"

Loveday studied the panel. "Not at the moment, but I could rig something for you. I could rig anything with all this." She shook herself as if trying not to get lost in their good fortune. "But Celeste—Chief Air Minister?"

Celeste shrugged. "Argue with the Emperor, and I would likely end up as Marcel's neighbor in the dungeon." She seized one of the lengths of copper tubing standing next to the worktable and dragged it over to the door, where she propped it under the latch, which was gilded, of course. "There. That ought to give us a little privacy for the moment. And to ensure it, you check that wall, and I will check this one."

Loveday frowned but ventured to the wall of bookshelves. "What am I seeking among the wealth of ages?"

"A hidden panel," Celeste advised, going to tug at the iron racks along the opposite wall. "It might only be used by the servants, but it might also allow someone to listen in on our conversations or even lie in wait for us. Ah." One of the racks felt less solid than the others. She pressed on it, and it swung outward to reveal a dark corridor behind. She squinted down its length but could not see the end.

Loveday joined her. "Where does it lead?"

"We must discover that another time." She closed the door. "Help me."

Together, they dragged a barrel of lifting gas across it, wedging it shut.

"Oh, for your articulated sideboard," Celeste said with a sigh, dropping into one of the chairs near the desk.

"Your Emperor certainly has his own set of automatons," Loveday allowed, taking a seat on the other chair. "Besides those sheep devices, I spotted any number of clockwork time-pieces, bronze statues or busts on gears so that they rotate to catch the light, and odd little boxes that tick." She lifted a foot and rubbed her ankle. "A shame they haven't devised a method to move from one end of the palace to the other. This place is huge!"

"My mother used to say they added another suite of rooms every month," Celeste said with a grimace. "But as my assistant, at least you should be able to order a carriage to come and go to the school."

Loveday waved a hand. "Once Josie and Amélie are supplied with food, I have every reason to spend time in here with you for the moment. I can accompany you nearly every-where, and, since I am deemed of so little importance, I will be able to go places you cannot."

"We may have reason to be thankful for that," Celeste said. "For if they assign me this bodyguard they spoke of, you can be sure her duties will include spying on my every move."

CHAPTER 10

The sound of booted feet marching down the corridor alerted Loveday just in time. She whipped the copper tube out from under the latch and crossed the office to the rack from whence it had come. As she turned, La Croix and Toussaint gave a peremptory knock and entered without invitation.

So much for privacy, to say nothing of respect.

"Your quarters have been assigned, Chief Air Minister." La Croix said Celeste's new title as though trying to expel it from his mouth, like a sour plum. "If you will come with us."

Not *Perhaps you would like to see them.* Or *Would this be a convenient time?*

Celeste inclined her head as though the man had said either of those things, glanced at Loveday to make sure she was coming, too, and followed them out.

It would have been faster simply to scale the wall outside, for it turned out their new apartments were directly above the office. However, to get there they once again had to walk down a long corridor, climb two flights of stairs with lovely carved bannisters, and walk back along the corridor two floors above.

Loveday would have given anything to have whispered, "We shall have to see about a secret staircase" to Celeste, but with La Croix at her elbow and Toussaint at Loveday's own, it was not possible. Did these men think they planned to cut and run, now that the Emperor had welcomed them so warmly? This close guard was beginning to wear on her, and they had only been in the palace two hours.

Another prettily painted door—in robin's egg blue and white this time—was opened with a flourish, and they stepped into a sitting room. Loveday struggled for a moment, dislike of their escorts paired with appreciation for the sheer comfort and elegance of the apartment they had located. Then she decided the former must be disregarded while the latter was enjoyed to the full. The Turkish carpet was enormous and covered nearly the whole floor, so soft under her feet it was like walking on a cloud. The sofa and wing chairs were upholstered in a sky blue and cream stripe, and the drapes framing the two windows in graceful swags were a matching blue velvet.

On the left was a bedroom and dressing room clearly meant for Celeste, with a single window framed in fabric to match the spread. On the right was a smaller room containing two beds and a wardrobe, also elegantly appointed.

"Two beds, messieurs?" Loveday blurted in French.

"Your grasp of French may be exemplary in your country," La Croix said, "but it has not served you well here. You recall our mention of a bodyguard for Mademoiselle Blanchard."

Loveday choked back an unladylike remark and did her best to reply with nothing more than a withering glare. The bodyguard was to sleep here, too? With Loveday? Was she to be with them day and night?

A tap came upon the door, and La Croix crossed the room with a smile. "Ah, here she is."

He ushered in a woman who looked like an illustration of a Valkyrie Loveday had once seen in a book of Norse tales. She could not help but stare. The bodyguard's posture was military straight, and over an impressive bosom was fastened a redingote similar to the one Celeste owned, in cerulean blue over a grey linen dress. Her white-blond hair was dressed simply, in a braided crown, with not so much as a ribbon threaded through it, and a smart cap to match the redingote upon it. She must have been in her late forties and had a kind of icy beauty that some might admire, but the sternness of her gaze made all Loveday's admiration drain away.

This, then, was their gaoler.

"Chief Air Minister, may I present *Gardien* Julia Wintzen, who will consider your safety her first priority, above and beyond her own life. *Gardien* Wintzen, this is Celeste Blanchard, daughter of the late celebrated aeronaut Sophie Blanchard." He paused for a beat. "And her assistant, Mademoiselle Jourdamour, from Switzerland."

The Valkyrie's attention swung to Loveday. *"Sprechen Sie Deutsch oder Französisch?"* she demanded.

Loveday very nearly said *Französisch*, which would have cemented her as a German speaker, which would have been disastrous. *"Je parle Français, Gardien."*

Wintzen expelled a brief huff of breath that might pass for a sigh. "Pity." Her gaze turned back to Celeste. "I am honored to serve," she said, unconsciously echoing what Celeste had said to the Emperor. Or perhaps not so unconsciously. For all

Loveday knew, Wintzen could have been within earshot behind a secret panel.

"Alors, we will leave you," Toussaint said, and without even a bow of farewell to the woman who now outranked him, both he and La Croix vanished.

The three women gazed at one another in an expectant silence. Then Loveday decided that perhaps they ought to behave as though Wintzen were standing as silently by the door as any suit of armor in a medieval castle. "Perhaps we might return to the office and begin an inventory of its contents."

"Oh, yes—" Celeste began.

"Have you a schedule?" Wintzen interrupted.

"A schedule of what?" Loveday said.

"The order of the day." Wintzen spoke as though to a dense child. "The palace runs like the clockwork of which the Emperor is so fond. Every hour is scheduled at his pleasure."

"Not *my* hours," Celeste told her, a frown forming between her brows. "I must work. In my office and at l'Ecole des Aéronautes. With my assistant." She nodded to Loveday.

Wintzen glanced about and finally located a card lying upon the low table standing between the sofa and the two chairs. *"Voilà."*

Order of the Day
August 26, 1819
7:00 Rise
8:00 Breakfast
10:00 His Imperial Majesty receives dignitaries
1:00 Luncheon
2:00 His Imperial Majesty receives his ministers and officials

4:00 His Imperial Majesty takes exercise
7:00 Dinner in the Salle des Fonctionnaires
10:00 Retire

Loveday was at an utter loss for words. So was Celeste, it seemed, for she finally asked, "And what has this to do with us? Surely *we* are not dining with the Emperor."

Loveday could not imagine anything more dreadful—except possibly being thrown in gaol by the Emperor.

Wintzen, instead of rolling her eyes, merely shook her head. "As one of his ministers, the only things that apply to you are meals and his two o'clock salon, should you wish to bring a matter to his attention as you did today. Breakfast may be taken in your chamber, and lunch in your office with your assistant and me, but dinner is required. All His Imperial Majesty's officials dine together each evening, so that they may exchange information of state."

How appalling. Loveday's gaze caught that of Celeste.

"Every day?" Celeste asked. "Surely we are permitted to dine out. And what of those with families and social expectations in society?"

"You see how early dinner is scheduled," Wintzen said. "Once completed, one may of course be conveyed to one's evening engagements. And most of your fellow ministers have homes in the city. You are one of the few housed here."

Yes, unfortunately. Well, if they needed to go out without discovery, they could simply say they were going to a card party, bribe the coachman, and be conveyed to l'Ecole instead.

"And what of my expenses?" Celeste asked. "I wish to reopen l'Ecole des Aéronautes. It must be cleaned. Supplied and outfitted. Made fit for students once again. I shall be spending a good deal of time there, naturally. From where is this purse to come?"

"You will have to take that up with the Chancellor of the Exchequer," Wintzen said, "for such matters are outside my remit."

"Where does *your* salary come from, *Gardien*?" Loveday asked her.

"I am paid a wage monthly," she said with some dignity. "A good wage. They do not stint with the Aeronautical Corps, even when one is seconded to duty under the palace guard as the Chief Air Minister's protection. Both are under the command of the Minister of War."

So, she had been seconded to the palace guard, had she? She was not a prisoner of war dragooned into bodyguard work. That meant she might know where all the secret passages and unused rooms were. Which could be both good and bad, Loveday thought. An attempt to hide in the secret corridor behind the rack in the office would not last long if Wintzen could appear behind them at any moment and report their least expressions to Captain La Croix.

She glanced at the clock upon the mantel over the unlit fire. Twenty past six.

"Are we expected to go down this evening?" she asked, spreading her stained skirts with both hands. "I am afraid I am unprepared."

Wintzen's blond eyebrows rose. "You, mademoiselle, will never appear in the *Salle des Fonctionnaires*. That is the place for ministers and high-ranking officials of the Emperor, along with their bodyguards. You will take your meals with the palace staff."

"Oh," Loveday said faintly. Thank goodness. Think of all she could learn below stairs!

"But to answer the spirit of your question, the Chief Air Minister will not be expected to appear this evening. You will fetch a tray for her, after which you will go down for your own meal."

"What about you?" Loveday asked. "Shall I fetch a tray for you, too?"

Wintzen sighed, as if she had had enough of impertinent questions. "Under normal circumstances, I would take my meals in the officers' mess, save for lunch, which is at the Chief Air Minister's pleasure. But this evening, no one expects us. If you will fetch trays for the minister and me, then you may join the others below stairs."

Were they not to have a single moment without this woman watching and listening? Is this how the mouse felt, knowing that the cat waited outside and could hear every breath, every pad of a foot on the boards?

Loveday inclined her head, then glanced at herself in the massive mirror between the two windows in their salon. Her appearance could not be helped. "I won't be long," she promised.

Wintzen gave her directions to the staff quarters, and for the first time in many weeks, she and Celeste separated. Fortunately, the kitchen was in the throes of preparations for the ministers' meal, so it was only a matter of looking businesslike and announcing which minister she served, and two trays were laid instantly with linen, china, and silver, and poached salmon with dill sauce and vegetables covered with a *cloche* of silver laid in the middle. A footman was summoned to carry the second tray, and once they were delivered, Loveday was free to follow him back downstairs.

She would remember the route from sheer repetition. And become very slender from all the walking.

The madhouse of effort to get the ministers' food up to the *Salle des Fonctionnaires* had settled down slightly by the time she reached the staff dining room. She was able to slip into an empty chair just in time to receive her own helping of poached salmon, this one with a lemon sauce, vegetables, and a compôte of something she had never seen before.

"Excusez-moi," she said shyly to the woman next to her, "but what is this?"

"Have you never had red rice?" The woman smiled when Loveday shook her head. "I hear in your voice that you are foreign, so I will tell you. This comes from the Camargue region, in the south. I am from Arles, so I have grown up on it."

Loveday tasted it. "It is delicious. How fortunate you are, to have known of it."

"We enjoy it down here in the staff dining room," she said complacently. "They consider it for peasants above stairs. Little do they know."

Loveday could only agree. She introduced herself to the servants closest to her as Aimée Jourdamour. The young man opposite looked surprised. "You work for the Chief Air Minister? But I thought she was dead."

"It is her daughter, returned from a test flight that went down in Switzerland. I was able to guide her out of the mountains and through the lines at the front. We only reached Paris this morning."

He gazed at her, his eyes narrowing with suspicion. "I

don't believe it. Two women, crossing the front? What, did you sell your bodies for passage?"

"Jean-Claude!" snapped the woman next to her. "Hold your tongue! Don't you see how she is dressed, despite the evidence of travel? She is clearly a gentlewoman."

"We had an audience this afternoon with His Imperial Majesty," Loveday said modestly. "His courtesy knows no bounds—he did not so much as remark upon my shabbiness."

"You," Jean-Claude said in flat tones of disbelief. "Had an audience with the Emperor. This afternoon."

"No need to repeat her words like a parrot, Jean-Claude," said the man at the head of the table, clearly the *maître*. "Forgive him, Mademoiselle Jourdamour. He is an uneducated buffoon who will be returning to his father's farm sooner rather than later, if this keeps up."

Loveday inclined her head and reflected that perhaps she might put off the humble posture of the cadet and become more like herself, a gentlewoman of some assurance. One who had saved the life of the Emperor's most valued minister.

"But what brought you all the way to Paris?" the woman next to her asked. They had the attention of the whole table now. "Surely your family would have objected?"

"Oh, they did," Loveday said with a smile, remembering Mama on the terrace, her hands clasped under her chin. "But even they had to admit that my attending *La Blanchard's* daughter to Paris is a wonderful opportunity. Truly, I look forward to studying with her, and learning how to be an aeronaut myself."

"Goodness," the woman said. "Let us hope you are not conscripted, then. It is lucky that Switzerland is not part of the Karlsruhe Confederacy, or you may have been shot on principle when you arrived."

"I am thankful for that, too," Loveday said. "Is there news from that quarter?"

"I thought you said you came through the front lines," Jean-Claude said. "You should be giving us news, not the other way around."

Loveday shook her head. "We were trying not to be killed or mistaken for camp followers, monsieur. There was hardly time to stop in the commanders' lodgings and inquire after battle positions and armaments."

A chuckle went around the table, and Jean-Claude flushed with vexation.

Stupid boy. The *maître* was right. He would be dismissed before long, with a tongue more active than his brain.

"I have news," said a thin, grey gentleman two places down from Jean-Claude. The chatter at the table quietened, telling Loveday that either the man elicited respect, or his master did.

"That is Monsieur Lafarge," the woman next to Loveday whispered. "He is a secretary to the Minister of War."

A tingle ran over Loveday's skin, and she gave him her complete attention while doing her best to look merely polite and interested.

"I believe the Chief Air Minister will find my information useful," Monsieur Lafarge said in a tone slightly above a whisper. "We have heard that the manufactory at Cherbourg has been successful in its test flights."

"And what are they testing?" Loveday asked, when it seemed evident she was expected to respond.

"Unmanned balloons," he said. "According to the new design."

"Unmanned?" she repeated, hoping she did not sound in the least like Jean-Claude. "How can that be? How are they controlled?"

He smiled, a crescent of lip that showed no teeth. "Our new Chief Air Minister is in need of a briefing, it seems. Perhaps I may schedule it at a time convenient?"

"*Certainement,*" Loveday said. "The sooner the better. *Merci,* Monsieur Lafarge."

"You are quite welcome," he said. Then his gaze became more intent. "I understand the Chief Air Minister is a young woman as yet untried in matters of state, or the management of men."

"I would not say so, sir," she said, hoping he would not mind a gentle contradiction. "She, after all, managed the students at l'Ecole des Aéronautes and was her celebrated mother's confidante in all matters after the death of Monsieur Blanchard."

"But students are not the same as full-grown, experienced aeronauts," someone else said, farther down the table. "Being the daughter of *La Blanchard* will not gain her any credit among the men and women of the Corps, it is certain."

"Can you be more explicit, sir?" Loveday asked. "What do you mean?"

"Only that there is a lot of resentment in the ranks, mademoiselle. Of the attention the Emperor paid to *La Blanchard,* the grandeur of her ascensions, all at the expense of the rank and file."

"But surely she cannot be blamed for His Imperial Majesty's decisions and preferences?"

"We do not permit questioning of our Emperor's decisions here," the *maître* said in a warning tone, though Loveday did not know whether it was directed at the other man or herself. "It seems that a word in the wrong ear can lead to instant dismissal."

"Dismissal," the woman next to her said. "Disappearance, more like. What happened to the Minister of Public Works? Here one day, gone the next. And for what? Did he plant a rose in the wrong color? Forget to send someone to unclog a *vicomte*'s drain?"

"That is cause for some dismay," Monsieur Lafarge admitted. "He had an appointment with one of our functionaries who oversees the barracks and did not appear, nor did he send an apology. And speaking of that, has anyone heard news of the Emperor's Grand Inventor? He has not been seen in a week, and I have not one, but two requests from the Minister of War to present himself at the earliest opportunity."

"Grand Inventor?" Loveday whispered to the woman on her left.

"Yes, Monsieur Patenaude, the man responsible for creating many of the helpful devices here in the palace and outside it. Like the *boîtes d'alerte* and the sheeplike creatures used for cleaning."

"The *automoutons?*" Loveday asked with a smile.

"*Automoutons!*" The *maître* slapped the table and gave a bark of laughter, and even Monsieur Lafarge's smile widened enough to show the edge of a tooth.

There being no news of the Grand Inventor, and with the sudden lightening of the mood, the conversation turned to other matters, and then dessert was served. Tempting as the glazed cakes were, Loveday took only another cup of *chocolat chaud,* nodded to those remaining at table, and hurried back along the corridors.

Unmanned flight. Disappearing officials. A missing Grand Inventor.

She must get Celeste alone and tell her all. Even if she had to lock Wintzen in the Necessary first.

CHAPTER 11

She was trapped.

The thought hovered in Celeste's mind like a second-year student's model balloon as she finished her dinner. Wintzen did not appear to be inclined to let Celeste out of her sight, except to visit the Necessary, and even then she waited outside the door of the little chamber as if ready to pounce. At least she'd had the good sense to check all the walls of the suite, which, mercifully, did not appear to hide secret passages or spy holes.

Still, Celeste would have liked nothing better than to share a long coze with Loveday over the dilled salmon that her friend had brought up on the dinner trays. She would have given a great deal to learn what was going through that inventive mind. But she dared not speak about anything of substance in front of the bodyguard. La Croix had hired her. The bodyguard would most likely be loyal to him rather than Celeste.

Wintzen was mopping up the last of the dill sauce on her silver-edged plate with a slice of crusty bread when Loveday came in with a bowl of *chocolat chaud*. Her friend looked as though she might burst with the need to speak, but she buried her nose in the large cup instead.

Wintzen waited for her to seat herself before she finally spoke. "What routine do you intend to follow?"

A reasonable question. Celeste thought back to her mother's schedule, and the card upon her own table. "I will spend my mornings in the office, if possible. I expect Captains La Croix and Toussaint to meet with me soon. And I must review the Corps at the barracks. Once I know more about the current state of the Corps, I will be better able to plan my time."

Wintzen nodded. "Very well. Unless there is a court entertainment, you will be in bed by ten and rise by seven. I will remain awake for a full hour after you lie down and will rise an hour before you." She speared Loveday with a look. "See that you wake me in time."

Loveday's jaw hardened, but she lowered her gaze to her bowl of hot chocolate. "I would be delighted to help, *Gardien* Wintzen, but I have no timepiece."

A dry rattle of a chuckle came from the bodyguard. "You will not need one. The Emperor's clocks will ring out every hour of every day. But if you can sleep through the noise, ask the Steward of the House for a *boîte d'alerte*."

"*Boîte d'alerte?*" Celeste asked.

"The little time boxes that ring to keep you on schedule," Wintzen supplied. "One of the winders, the footmen assigned to keep the clockwork functioning, will be able to set it for you." She tsked. "You have been away from court for a while, haven't you, Chief Air Minister?"

"Not long enough," Celeste muttered, but she did not

further the conversation. The sooner the bodyguard left her, the sooner she and Loveday might compare notes.

As it was, Wintzen showed every intention of helping Celeste undress as she followed her into her bedchamber.

"You may go," Celeste told the bodyguard, eyes narrowed.

Wintzen crossed her arms over a chest inflating with resistance. "I will not leave you until I know you are safely abed."

"I am perfectly capable of calling for you should the need arise," Celeste insisted.

"Unless someone prevents you from calling," the bodyguard said with a dark look at Loveday.

Loveday must have had enough, for she rounded on the woman. "Who has served the Chief Air Minister the longest? Who watched over her after she fell from the skies and tended her injuries? Who saw her safely to Paris?"

Wintzen took a step back, arms falling. "Very well. When you have finished with your mistress, you may see to my needs as well." She stalked from the room and slammed the door behind her.

"Brilliant," Celeste murmured as Loveday came to join her. "And justified. Thank you."

"They aren't going to make this easy, are they?" Loveday murmured back. She began work on Celeste's ties.

"No," Celeste said with a sigh. "And I hate that you must sleep with that woman. Even the beds in that room look hard. Take some of the pillows from here. If anyone questions me, I will say there were too many on the bed."

"You may find a number of people questioning you," Loveday told her, "and not about the pillows." Quickly, she repeated what she had learned below stairs.

"Then it is as bad as I feared," Celeste said when she

finished. "My mother is not the only one at court to risk her life for the Emperor. We must be on our guard."

"Agreed," Loveday said, finishing her work. She went to the wardrobe along one wall and opened a drawer. "It seems your captains thought of everything. There are nightgowns in here."

"Take one," Celeste insisted. "We will have to see about more clothes tomorrow."

Loveday turned, an armful of embroidered India cotton pressed to her chest. "Do you think we will be here so long, then?"

"Long enough," Celeste allowed. "Tomorrow, I will have someone go and nail a notice to the door of l'Ecole of new leadership. That will alert Josie and Amélie that the plan is succeeding. Then we will go through the office and see what we can use to repair the air ship. If you give me a list of what else is needed, I will see it ordered, but we will need to find a way to send the supplies to l'École. First, however, I intend to see Marcel."

Loveday raised a brow. "*Gardien* Wintzen is not going to like that."

She didn't.

The next morning, she argued all the way through a breakfast of porridge and bacon that Loveday brought up from the kitchens.

Celeste refused to allow the bodyguard to bully either of them further, and so, shortly after breakfast, she and Wintzen descended the stone stairs toward the dungeon beneath the Emperor's palace. A uniformed guard unlocked the door at the top of the stairs, and three more waited in the antechamber at the bottom. One led her deeper, Wintzen right behind.

When he reached the bottom of the next flight down, he stepped aside. "Third door on the right," he told Celeste with a jerk of his scruffy chin down one of four corridors that branched off the flagged center square, where four soldiers playing cards at the table rose to their feet and saluted. "Are you certain you don't want help?"

Celeste eyed him. "This is the man who murdered my mother. I don't expect what I have to say will take long."

He nodded, and she stalked down the stone-walled corridor to the third oak door banded in iron and locked with an iron padlock.

"Allow me," Wintzen said, reaching around her to pry open a little window at about eye level. What, did she think Marcel would be armed?

Torchlight trickled past Celeste through the three-by-six-inch slot into a space perhaps six feet deep and four feet wide. She could not make out the floor. There was no light within, and somewhere, water dripped.

"Marcel?" she called into the darkness.

Her friend's dusky face surged up in front of the slot, and Celeste took a step back in surprise.

Wintzen must have mistaken her reason, for she pounded a fist against the door. "Back! Show some respect for the Emperor's Chief Air Minister."

"La Blanchard? But I was told she died." Marcel's voice was no more than a croak. Had they given him no water, no food? Celeste's stomach twisted.

"Madame Blanchard is dead," she made herself say. "I am

her daughter, Mademoiselle Blanchard, and I have the honor of serving Napoleon in her place."

"Celeste?" His fingers, filthy with grime, gripped the bars of the little window. "You returned? I promise, I did not kill your mother. You know I could not."

"I have been told many things since I returned from Switzerland," Celeste told him, praying he would have enough sense left to play along. "Friends I knew since childhood are abandoned. My life's work is destroyed. But I have found other friends now, and they will see me through."

He was silent a moment as if digesting that. His brown eyes never left her face. "I am glad you have new friends. I had friends once, too."

"A true friend stands by you in adversity," Celeste said. "A true friend will not allow you to suffer but will do everything possible to keep you safe and free you of your bonds. A true friend understands who your enemies really are and seeks to defeat them."

"Do you have such a friend, Mademoiselle Blanchard?" he murmured.

"I do," she said. "He is strong and valiant, and he will not give up the fight. Neither will I."

"Your friend is a fortunate fellow," he said. "I hope he realizes that *La Blanchard* had more enemies than she knew. They may not be satisfied with her death. He ought to advise you to be on your guard."

Tears burned in her eyes. "I should advise you of the same, Monsieur Delaguard. There will be a reckoning for what was done, and soon."

She stepped back, and Wintzen slid shut the window with a snap.

"He will not escape," she told Celeste as if to comfort her. "No one escapes from this dungeon alive."

Which was exactly what Celeste feared.

When Celeste and Wintzen returned, Loveday could see by her friend's pallor and the worry in her eyes that the visit to the gaol had confirmed the worst. While she helped Celeste out of her redingote, Celeste was able to communicate in snatches of whispers exactly what Marcel Delaguard faced.

The poor young man. To see his prospects plummet from those of a career aeronaut to those of a prisoner in one long fall—to be the scapegoat while persons unknown plotted against Celeste's family—no wonder Celeste looked as though she might faint at any moment.

They entered the office as though it were a sanctuary.

"This task is exactly what I need," Celeste admitted, laying out paper and ink for a list, and surveying the racks of materials and shelves of reference books. "Can there be any cure for melancholy more effective than imagining mechanical devices?"

"I think not," Loveday said. "Though I would give a steam boiler for an apron and gloves—to say nothing of something else to wear. We shall be covered in dust and cobwebs by day's end."

"Luckily, there are steam boilers in the laundry, and we may have our clothes washed—or at least brushed. So. Let us put aside our worries and begin."

"We ought to number the racks and shelves, starting at the door and working to the right," Loveday suggested. "Or should we empty everything out into the middle of the room and file it in order of its purpose?"

"The first option," Celeste said. "We must know what we have." She glanced at Wintzen, who, it was clear, had no intention of assisting, but only of standing next to the door with her arms crossed, gazing straight ahead. "My mother was an organized person. This should go fairly quickly. I will make a list of the items needed most urgently, both for repair and for supply."

Translation: *Lark Deux is my first concern. Then the school, and Josie and Amélie. Then getting supplies back to Arthur and Emory.* And somehow, Loveday knew, Marcel's freedom must be a part of everything on that list as well.

As the afternoon wore on, Loveday's hands became more and more filthy, and the list on the desk became longer and more smudged. On hand were curved sail needles and thick, sturdy thread to repair the torn gas bag, and barrels of lifting gas. There was even a cask of bitumen to brush over the seams of the gas bag and make it airtight. But missing was anything resembling rigging rope, and none of the treated canvas of which gas bags were made. There were yards of silk, but not nearly enough. There were any number of tools—turnscrews, hammers, crowbars. But not a single pulley or clamp for the rigging. There were gears and sheets of copper to replace the damaged piping, but nothing to heat them with, and certainly no forge with which to build an engine. All in all, the office was both wonderful and maddening.

Had it been ransacked after Madame Blanchard's death? Or had she simply not replenished the Corps' most often used supplies?

Celeste opened the large double doors of a cupboard in the

middle of a wall of bookcases filled with engineering treatises and explanations of physics. Loveday expected to see jars of nails and screws.

"Quelle surprise," she exclaimed as a tinkling tune began to play. "What is this?"

Brushing cobwebs from her hands, Loveday joined her and stared. "Is that a court dress?"

"On an automaton?"

As though the cupboard were a massive music box, the automaton turned in a circle within, showing the gown from every angle while a tune unfamiliar to Loveday spooled from somewhere she could not see—the pedestal, perhaps? The undergown was made of cream silk, its corded bodice sparkled with brilliants, and a high lace collar was of wonderful engineering. Designed in the colors of the Aeronautical Corps, the deep-cut open gown in cerulean velvet was trimmed with black braid.

"What is that tune?" Loveday's mind felt mazed at the extravagance of both gown and automaton.

"It is the *Chant du Départ*. The Emperor's favorite song." Celeste, too, sounded blank.

"That would appear to be the work of Monsieur Patenaude," came Wintzen's voice from the door. "Likely built right in this room."

"But… a court dress?" Celeste said. "In a workroom?"

"It would be convenient if she were summoned to the Emperor's presence unexpectedly, I suppose," Loveday said in wondering tones.

"Or perhaps it was a demonstration of some kind. When officials visited. Or the Emperor himself."

"I suppose we will never know. But one thing we do know

—it was definitely meant for occasions with short notice. Like the Emperor."

Celeste elbowed Loveday in the ribs for her pertness in making a joke at his expense, and Loveday laughed, dancing out of range. "Come, the sun has gone down over the roof opposite. It is time to clean up and make you presentable for your first dinner in the *Salle des Fonctionnaires*."

But Celeste shook her head. "I cannot do it in my flying costume. Let us wait a day or two—we must, after all, give them plenty of time to hear the gossip about me."

"But—" Loveday and Wintzen both began.

Celeste raised a hand. "It is too soon, and I am too fatigued. We will have three trays brought up and call it a meeting of my personal staff. And if anyone argues with me, I will lock them in this cupboard."

Loveday would have purchased a ticket to watch that.

Especially if it were Wintzen. Or Captain La Croix.

CHAPTER 12

Saturday morning dawned with weather as unsettled as Loveday felt. Clouds heaped up over the avenues of elegant buildings, threatening rain, while whirlwinds chased litter and leaves across the gardens overlooked by their rooms.

Where were Arthur and Emory this morning? Had they been discovered, or were they still safely concealed? Were they able to find enough food? And what of Mama and Papa? They must be half mad with worry now that it had been nearly a week since they had so blithely set off. Blithely and with a greater lack of preparation than anyone could have guessed. Oh, if only she had not allowed Arthur to—

No, she must not blame him for her own foolishness. They had all got themselves into this predicament, so now they must get themselves out. As quickly as possible.

If only there was a way to send a message to Arthur, and another to Hale House! With a sigh, she gazed at the pigeons ranged along the gutters and perched upon the waterspouts of the other buildings in the great quadrangle. One might tie a note to the leg of a bird, if they could be trained sufficiently to find the recipient's direction. But training would take months. Better to build a bird, and invent a way to give it both propulsion and direction.

Clearly one could spend a lifetime inventing the smaller devices upon which more magnificent ones could be built. Was that the philosophy that lay behind the works of the missing Monsieur Patenaude? And why, exactly, was he missing?

"Are you going to while away the entire morning at the window, or fetch breakfast?" Wintzen's voice came from the doorway.

Loveday had already noted the neatly made bed opposite hers and had hoped vainly for a cup of tea. Alas, Wintzen's idea of her duties did not allow for such things. If tea were to be found, Loveday must find it, and that meant a trek to the kitchens.

"She will do neither." Celeste stood in her bedchamber doorway, still in her nightgown. "Aimée, if you will assist me?"

She snatched up her underthings and gown, still a bit smudged about the ties and hems, and went in. As she helped Celeste dress and then was helped in her turn, Wintzen persisted.

"How shall you occupy yourselves, then?"

"I will return to my office and continue my work," Celeste said, as though it were obvious. "I am sending Mademoiselle Jourdamour with a message to my former modiste. I must be clothed as befits my station. As well, I am of a mind to have Madame alter the court gown we found to fit me. Everyone knows such things are never in the front ranks of fashion. I could wear it for another twenty years, and it would still be appropriate."

Loveday had read reports in the newspapers of ladies at court in London who still wore the hoops of the King and Queen's youth. No one seemed to think it unusual.

"I shall be happy to go," Loveday said. For of course Celeste meant no such thing—or at least, not entirely. "I must remember to take along a lunch, and perhaps a sketchbook where I might make notes and sketches of what I see in the city." *I shall take food to Josie and Amélie, and the list of supplies we need.*

Celeste nodded. "An excellent idea."

"I shall stay here, with you," Wintzen said in tones that brooked no argument.

"Of course," Celeste agreed pleasantly.

After a good breakfast of boiled eggs and tiny meat pies, to say nothing of the handled bowls filled with a delicious liquid called *café au lait*, Loveday returned the trays, smiled at the *maîtresse de cuisine*, and requested a hamper for a picnic. To her surprise, a basket was filled without comment, and Loveday added several of the little meat pies and another baguette. While she regretted that they would not go to the poor waiting in the street outside the kitchen door, their purpose would be fulfilled if Josie and Amélie received the nourishment instead.

She collected the list of supplies and the address of the modiste from Celeste, and set off. The wind pushed her down the avenues, making her skirts snap about her. Repeated glances at the sky made her wonder whether on her return journey she might have to turn the empty hamper over her head to keep off the rain. As she turned the corner, she glanced back to see if the wind had discommoded anyone else. Someone was just withdrawing into a deeply recessed doorway. She would do the same, had she not a more urgent errand.

When she arrived at l'Ecole des Aeronautes, she glanced up and down the street. A tingle had come and gone between her shoulder blades, and she shivered. She would be glad to get inside.

Ducking into the narrow alley, she circled around to the workshop door to face the impenetrable stone walls once more. The building looked just as deserted as it had the other night. More so, perhaps, in the daylight, when there should be open doors, students at the windows, and activity in the streets. Not this stony, immobile silence, as though it might be set upon if it moved.

"Amélie!" she called up to the window, hoping they were within hearing. "Josie!"

The window was flung up. "Loveday! We've been so worried. What have you there?"

"Breakfast and more. Have you a rope?"

Down it came, and with its end knotted about the handles of the hamper, breakfast rose swiftly and vanished into the room beyond. The rope ladder came down, and Loveday wrapped her skirts around her shoulders and climbed it as quickly as she could, lest someone in a window opposite should look out and see her drawers and stockings on full parade.

When she landed on the floor, Amélie pulled up the ladder and rolled it neatly. Then she closed and latched the window against the wind and turned to hug Loveday. "Join us while we enjoy the feast you have brought."

"No indeed," she retorted, hugging Josie. "Celeste sent it for you."

She followed the girls downstairs. If she had been tempted to take off her pelisse after a warm walk carrying a fairly heavy basket, she was no longer. It might be the end of August outside, but in here, it was already approaching October. She could only hope that by the time it really was autumn proper, they would all have left Paris far behind and would no longer need to worry about the chill.

In the kitchen, Loveday could see Amélie add up the contents of the basket, divide it by two, and calculate how many days they could make it last.

"Do not fear," she said quietly. "We will send more, for as long as we need to."

The two girls fell upon the food the way the chickens did at home, as though they were hawks. "What news?" Josie said around half a meat pie consumed in one bite. "We have been beside ourselves with worry when you did not come back."

Loveday began her account with the audience with the Emperor and ended with Wintzen's remaining behind with Celeste. In between there were *automoutons*, the *Salle des Fonctionnaires*, all the kitchen gossip, and La Croix and Toussaint.

"I have heard of them," Amélie said. "They were no friends to *La Blanchard*. On one occasion they even made her weep with rage."

"It was terrible," Josie said, sitting back, her appetite satisfied for the first time in… how long? Loveday wondered.

"I doubt they have changed." Amélie reached for the list Loveday had brought. "Our task now is to do as much as we can for Celeste while they are none the wiser." Her gaze ran down the list, and she handed it to Josie. "We have treated canvas. Only about six lengths, though." She held out her arms to indicate the width of each panel.

"That should be enough. And lifting gas?"

Josie dimpled. "Oh yes. Barrels of it. It is the primary reason we agreed so promptly to board up the school. The last thing we want is for the army to requisition it."

"The Chief Air Minister would be happy to do so, immediately." Loveday's smile became a conspiratorial grin, then faded. "The question is, how may we get the supplies to St Malo, where the air ship is concealed?"

"Another fictional secret test flight?" Amélie asked.

"Using a test ship built where?" Josie asked, her chin leaning on her hand. "Everyone knows the school is boarded up. And it is not likely *La Blanchard* would have commissioned a ship built elsewhere."

"Wagons and drays go in and out of Paris all the time," Amélie suggested. "There are no longer guards at the gates—Napoleon is confident he is in no danger here in his capital."

"So we might send a wagon to St Malo," Loveday mused. "Do you have one?"

"Oui," Josie said. "But not a steam wagon—only one drawn by a horse."

Hm. "I wonder if the Chief Air Minister could requisition one. It could then be stolen."

"It could. And the thieves would be hanged or their hands cut off," Amélie pointed out. "The laws are very strict about that."

"Because of the looting when Napoleon first came to power," Josie explained, though Loveday was sure she could not have been more than a child at the time.

Loveday imagined the busy roads going in and out of

Paris. She had seen them herself—no one could tell one load from another, or question his neighbor about what he carried. Bundles and objects tied up with canvas all looked the same, unless you were transporting furniture.

Furniture. Country roads. Fascinating vehicles.

She sat up straight. "How large a parcel would the supplies for *Lark Deux* make?"

Josie's eyebrows rose at such an odd question, but she looked around. "From your list, and what you have told me already exists… plus the barrels of lifting gas…" She gestured toward the enormous hearth, where six men could have stood and conversed comfortably. "It would fill that, at a guess."

Loveday deflated. "For a brief moment, I had visions of our building one of those marvelous two-wheeled conveyances. What did Celeste call it? The one upon which a lady is not permitted to ride if she is to remain a lady?"

"The *chaise roulante?*" Josie asked. When Loveday nodded, the girl sighed with regret. "How I wish we could. But imagine how large the platform would need to be in order to convey so many barrels of lifting gas. We should take up the entire road and be found out instantly."

Loveday rose. "We will think of something. For now, mark off the things on the list upon which you can lay your hands, and I will take it back to Celeste. She may have an idea we have not thought of, while we order the remaining supplies."

"And then?" Amélie asked.

"Then perhaps it will be La Croix and Toussaint who will weep with rage," Loveday said.

~

AFTER SENDING Loveday to the school, Celeste did her best to keep up appearances. She went to her office, but the racks of materials and tools did nothing to cheer her. Oh, what Marcel would have made of this! Yet there he was, poor brave man, moldering in the dungeon.

She wiggled her mouth back and forth as she sat behind the desk, trying to think of a way to rescue him. The dungeon seemed impenetrable. First, she would have to unlock the upper door with keys she did not have, sneak downstairs past two sets of guards, and unlock Marcel's door. She would have to help him up the stairs and through a good portion of the palace, including other staff standing guard. With little food and water, would he have the strength to make it that far? And once out of the palace, she had to transport him to the school to meet Josie and Amélie. All of Loveday's inventions did not seem enough.

"You are troubled," Wintzen said from her place beside the door. She seemed to have no difficulty standing, for she looked more like a statue than a woman, with her stone-grey skirts and rigid posture.

Celeste pasted on a smile. "I have been appointed the Chief Minister of a department critical to the success of this war yet plagued by accidents and missteps. Most would find that situation troubling."

A whirring click broke through the quiet.

Wintzen pushed off the wall. "Do not move."

Celeste swallowed. "It came from there, behind the window draperies."

The bodyguard stomped across the carpet and swept aside the velvet.

One of the *automoutons* was busily polishing the wainscoting between the window and the racks. It seemed to have been polishing for some time, for the paint was beginning to peel.

"Dummes Schaf," Wintzen muttered, but she bent and repositioned it, and it trotted away from the wall on its jointed mechanical legs. *"Mouton stupide."*

Celeste drew in a breath of relief. "You call them sheep, too?"

"Les automoutons, oui," Wintzen agreed, seemingly unaware that she had adopted Loveday's name for them. She watched the little device as it bumped into the desk leg before reaching the racks and positioning itself to begin work on that portion of the room. "They were one of the simpler things Monsieur Patenaude invented for the Emperor. A waste of his talents."

"He was the Grand Inventor?" Celeste asked, remembering what Loveday had told her.

"Oui. I do not know who the Emperor will find to replace him."

"Then you think he is dead?"

Wintzen shrugged. "Dead or captured by the enemy. Either way, his genius is lost to us." She frowned at the device as if willing it from the room. "But how did this *automouton* reach your office here? It did not come in with us, and I doubt your assistant would allow it in."

Not unless Loveday planned to take it apart and study it. Even as Celeste glanced to the *automouton*, it shuddered and its feather tail stopped its whirling.

"It is broken?" she asked.

Wintzen held up a hand and approached it cautiously. "No. The cleaning tail is lodged behind this barrel." Before Celeste could call out to stop her, she wrestled the barrel aside to free the *automouton*. Of course, the door concealed behind the rack obligingly popped open.

"A secret passage," Celeste marveled as if seeing it for the first time.

Wintzen peered down the passage, then closed the door firmly and repositioned the barrel. "They are everywhere, like the Emperor's spies."

"You expect us to be spied upon?" Celeste ventured, as though unaware that Wintzen herself was chief among them.

Wintzen returned to her station next to the main door. "But of course. You are important."

Being important to three people was hardly an achievement, even if one of them was an emperor. "And if I were unimportant, would the spies leave me alone?"

"No," Wintzen said. "The spies only leave you alone if you are dead or expected to be shortly."

Celeste swallowed.

Just then, someone knocked on the door to the office. Wintzen whirled and cracked open the portal. She must have recognized their visitors, for she stepped aside and pulled the door wider.

La Croix and Toussaint stood waiting in their cerulean dress coats, the latter's black boot tapping his impatience on the threshold.

Celeste rose. "Captains. I did not send for you."

La Croix's face turned red from his clean-shaven chin to the roots of his blond hair.

"You requested that we apprise you as to the state of the Corps, Chief Air Minister," Toussaint said as if she were an aged doyenne who required reminding where she'd put her snuffbox. "We have gathered the information and are prepared to share it with you. But if you would prefer to remain in ignorance should the Emperor call for you…"

Of course she would not. Celeste bit back a sigh and nodded to Wintzen to allow them entrance. "Come in, then. Tell me all about the Aeronautical Corps."

She would have loved to slap that self-satisfied smile off Toussaint's lean face, but she kept her hands to herself as he and La Croix sauntered into the office. Wintzen crossed the room to position herself at Celeste's left elbow.

Celeste remained standing. They were gentlemen enough that they could not sit until she did. They would have a long time to wait. She lifted a brow.

"Tell *La Blanchard* our numbers," Toussaint ordered his comrade.

La Croix blinked, then rallied, even as Celeste struggled to accustom herself to being called by her mother's sobriquet.

"We have twenty-four of the balloons your mother designed," he explained, "and fifty men who are trained to fly them."

Celeste frowned. "So few? At one point, the Corps had more than a hundred men and women ready to fly, and each had a balloon."

La Croix grimaced. "Those steam cannons the English developed have taken their toll in the air as well as on the ground."

"And the school was closed," Toussaint reminded her. "We cannot recoup our losses without fresh recruits."

She opened her mouth to offer to reopen the school, then closed it again. While she still wanted to see the school returned to its former glory as well, how could Loveday, Amélie, and Josie repair *Lark Deux* in secret if dozens of new students were clogging the corridors and all too eager to talk to outsiders about what they saw?

"I will assess the school's suitability to be reopened," she told them. "If it seems feasible, I will determine an accelerated schedule."

La Croix grinned, then seemed to remember she was the enemy and shut down his smile.

Toussaint inclined his head. "An excellent suggestion, Minister. We will need to look for teachers as well, with your esteemed mother and father gone and you busy at the helm of the Corps. A shame one of the last students turned traitor. When you visited him, were you able to learn anything about why he wanted to harm your mother?"

Celeste glanced at Wintzen, but the bodyguard was watching Toussaint with narrowed eyes, as if she could see through his lies. Had she gossiped, or had the imperial guardsman who had let them in spread the story? Either way, she could not allow the captains to know she believed utterly in Marcel's innocence.

Celeste put on a sorrowful look. "Alas, Monsieur Delaguard was not forthcoming. But perhaps you could enlighten me. Surely you investigated."

"Why?" La Croix asked. "It was clear who was guilty."

She rather thought so as well. "Then no one examined the balloon? The explosives?"

"There was little left of either, Minister," Toussaint said. "But let us not speak of things that must distress you. Suffice it to say that your dear mother was lost to us, and you have been found. We look forward to a prosperous future together."

"Then you have plans," Celeste said. "Good. What are they?"

La Croix looked to his comrade. Toussaint smiled. "We hope to rebuild the Aeronautical Corps to surpass its former glory under your mother."

"More balloons, more aeronauts, certainly," Celeste allowed. "But what else? An improved envelope, perhaps, such as I tested on the flight to Switzerland? The ability to go higher? Farther?"

"All within our grasp," Toussaint assured her, "now that you are here to provide us with the vision."

"And the design," La Croix added.

Toussaint's cheek twitched as if he had bitten the inside of his mouth.

Celeste's pulse broke into a canter. "And why would you think I would know how to design a better balloon?"

"Because you are *La Blanchard*'s daughter," Toussaint said smoothly. "Surrounded by her tools, I have no doubt something will come to you. By the by, an old friend asked to be remembered to you. The Comte d'Angeline. He expressed interest in renewing your acquaintance."

She nearly shuddered like the *automouton* at the very thought of the man the Emperor had ordered her to marry. Did Toussaint know the story? Was he merely trying to knock her off course, like a squall on the Channel?

"Please give him my regards," Celeste said, "and assure him my time is entirely devoted to seeing the Emperor's dream become a reality."

"Then you will see us invade England?" La Croix asked eagerly.

"You said you wanted the Aeronautical Corps to surpass

its former glory under my mother," she reminded him, mouth dry.

"Just so," Toussaint agreed. "And to that end, we will have more information about the Corps for your review by tomorrow morning."

He bowed, and La Croix followed suit.

Celeste could only watch them stroll from the room. She had given them no reason to suspect her. But they had given her no information she could use to her advantage.

Stalemate.

CHAPTER 13

By some miracle, Celeste appeared to be alone in the office when Loveday returned. Her friend's brows rose as Loveday brought in the food hamper as though it contained lead balls and leaned on the door to make it latch securely.

"Where is our grey shadow?" Loveday whispered.

"Down there." Celeste nodded toward the door of the secret passage, which now stood open a couple of inches, the barrel of lifting gas once again lying properly in its rack, like a bottle of wine.

"Is that wise?" Loveday asked in astonishment. "What if she is making a report to her masters?"

"She would do that in any case," Celeste said as Loveday handed her the list from Josie and Amélie. "She does not need to sneak about in secret passages. She is seeing where it goes, and whether it poses a danger to us. But never mind her, let us speak quickly, before she comes back." She glanced down the list. "I must confess I had hoped that l'Ecole would have many more of the things we need than this list indicates."

"I know." Loveday cleared two rolled-up sets of plans from a hard chair and seated herself, pushing her windblown hair from her eyes. "Josie says that everything Marcel was working on was confiscated when he was arrested, and some of the supplies we need were among them." Loveday leaned forward, hardly able to contain her delight. "But not his velocipede. Why did you not tell me such a wonderful device existed?"

"We have had other things on our minds." Celeste took her in more closely this time—windblown hair and all. "Loveday Penhale, you didn't ride it back to the palace!"

"I did, and then I hid behind a bit of topiary in the gardens and disassembled it." She grinned. "It's in the hamper."

Celeste let out a bark of laughter, then clapped both hands to her mouth. "We must keep it a secret," she hissed, lowering her hands. "Just in case we need a speedy getaway."

"I thought the very same." She picked up the hamper—really, the iron steed with its gears and wheels seemed much heavier in pieces than when she'd wheeled it so easily out of its cupboard at the school—then heaved it onto one of the empty lower racks. She rearranged a few items so that a wicker hamper looked more at home, with a sextant and a pair of compasses on its lid for good measure.

Then she flung herself onto the hard chair once more. "What do you think of our list? Is it a hopeless case?"

"It is a difficult case," Celeste admitted. She tapped the paper where items they needed were bare of the necessary X beside them. "Pulleys, rope for the rigging, clamps. Things we might find in the steam works in Truro are utterly impossible here. We are forced to order them from the Emperor's manufactories."

"But surely the Emperor need not approve every little

thing?" Loveday asked. "Is the palace so large because of its impressive state apartments, or because it is filled with a bloated bureaucracy who live to make progress difficult?"

"The latter, I am afraid. But there is still hope." Celeste folded up the list. "I am meeting with our two favorite captains tomorrow to discuss augmenting the Aeronautical Corps. I believe I may be able to slip our orders in with necessary equipment for that effort, only with a much shorter delivery time."

"But then we must get it to our friends outside the city." Loveday dared not say *St Malo* aloud, even when they were alone. "Josie and Amélie and I talked over some possibilities, but the chances of success are not very good."

"Remember what you learned reading mathematics treatises," Celeste said, lowering her voice. "The simplest solution is often the most elegant."

"The simplest solution is to load everything into a furniture cart on our friend Monsieur Charpentier's return trip home," Loveday said flatly.

Celeste blinked. "What a very good idea."

"But how are we to accomplish it?" Loveday could practically see plans forming and being discarded behind Celeste's dark eyes. She herself had discarded a dozen such as she'd sped back to the palace.

Footsteps were rapidly approaching—a brisk step Loveday recognized instantly. "Shh!"

In a moment Wintzen slipped through the door, seized the barrel of lifting gas from its place, and stood it in front of the rack. "I have discovered where this goes, Minister."

"I had no doubt you would," Celeste replied. "And?"

"It runs behind these rooms and the next two suites of

offices, with doors opening into each one. Similar construction exists all over the palace so that the servants may clean and deliver materials without being observed, or taking up room in corridors traveled by important officials."

Loveday wondered how important the servants might be considered if they were to stop performing their duties and the officials had to clean and carry for themselves.

"So we are in no danger from that quarter?" Celeste asked.

"No. But I would dearly love to requisition a locksmith. Sadly, even if I did, it would take days for the requisition to work its way up to the Lord Chamberlain and be approved."

Loveday choked back a snort as her previous question was answered. "I can make a lock," she said, glancing about her. "Goodness knows there are enough parts and gears here. If you can locate a broken padlock for me, I can fit it up to be useful again."

Wintzen stepped back to the door of the passage, moved the barrel, and disappeared within. Just as Loveday had begun to hope she and Celeste might begin to converse again, she reappeared, a padlock dangling from her hand. "It has no key. It was lying a few yards up the passage."

"It will need no key. But only the three of us may open it." Loveday got to work making a replica of the lock she used to keep on the door of her workshop. Before her younger sisters grew up enough to realize just how unsuitable and dull her activities out there really were, and lost interest in trying to get in.

Oh, if she could only see her sisters again, she would welcome them at any moment of the day!

While Celeste and Wintzen discussed La Croix's and Toussaint's visit, the latter showing a surprising breadth of knowledge about requisitioning supplies for the army that could be applied to outfitting the Aeronautical Corps, Loveday built the lock. And when it was completed, she took one of the *boîtes d'alerte* and began to disassemble it.

"What are you doing?" Wintzen demanded. "That was made by Monsieur Patenaude. Stop that at once."

"He may have made it, and very well, too, but I am making it useful. While I am working, you and Celeste might practice with the lock. It has three gears inside that may be initiated with a hairpin. See if you can open it."

Naturally Wintzen must go first, in case something built by Celeste's own assistant in her own presence should blow up in her face or be used to assassinate her. But to give the woman credit, she figured it out before Loveday was even halfway through her adjustments to the *boîte*. By the time she had given it to Celeste to open, Loveday had nearly finished.

Wintzen nodded. "It will do."

"And it has the advantage of needing a hairpin," Celeste said with some satisfaction as it popped open for her. "I think we may safely agree that La Croix and Toussaint will not be opening it—unless they are in the company of a lady."

"And if that lady should be I," Wintzen said, "I shall pretend no knowledge of it. I prefer rooms to be secure, and locks to work."

Loveday flicked a glance up at Celeste. Was this a sign that Wintzen considered her duty to Celeste above her obligation to the two captains? She had said that she had been seconded to the palace guard, and in tones of some pride, too. Perhaps she was not in the captains' employ after all.

Even so, Loveday was not about to ask. The odds of

receiving a truthful answer were so small they could not be calculated.

"There." She regarded the little *boîte* fondly, with its two discreet wires now extending three or four feet from under it. "The leads go in the passage, the *boîte* on this side of the door. When someone steps on them, the *boîte d'alerte* will do as its name suggests. Only instead of waking us, it will chime to alert us that someone has approached."

Wintzen's brows rose in as close as she could probably come to a look of admiration. Then she said, "You will be disappointed when it is only the servants, come to clean."

Celeste shook her head. "I will not permit anyone but we three in here alone. If I am to design a new balloon for the Emperor, that is considered a state secret. Only invited guests will enter, and that only when you and I—or you and Mademoiselle Jourdamour—are here. Is that clear, Wintzen?"

"Perfectly. I approve." The woman nodded. "I will find another broken lock for mademoiselle to refashion for the servants' door."

They did not need her approval, but Celeste looked relieved to have it, all the same.

"I shall affix the one we have to the main *porte*," Wintzen announced, and collected it from the desk where it lay open.

They heard the scrape of the lock upon the latch outside, and then the sound of a step away. Studying her handiwork? Another few steps, then silence.

Has she gone? Loveday mouthed to Celeste.

Hardly. Celeste rolled her eyes. "She has been with me every moment," she whispered.

But this behavior was so unusual that Loveday could not resist. Silently, she opened the door a crack.

Wintzen stood on the other side of the corridor, her white-blond hair in its neat braided crown illuminated by the light from the window. But it was no servant with a polishing cloth standing there with her. As Loveday's gaze fell upon him, a gentleman in a tailored coat turned away and walked back toward the staircase. As Wintzen watched him go, Loveday closed the door and crossed the room with a swift, silent step.

"A man," she whispered to Celeste. "Not La Croix or Toussaint. Not in uniform. Not a servant."

"A sweetheart?" Celeste whispered back, eyes disbelieving, in a tone she might have used to say *A unicorn?*

Oh dear, she must not laugh. It was serious. Who was that man? Wintzen's posture had told Loveday it was no stranger, yet in the three days they had been here, Loveday had never seen the bodyguard speak to any of the staff. Only La Croix and Toussaint, and even then in the briefest of terms.

Wintzen came back in as though her only concern had been the success of the lock. And when she said not a word except to ask if they were ready for the midday meal, Loveday's instincts tingled as though they had been the leads to the *boîte d'alerte*, and someone had just stepped on them.

MADAME FINETT, Celeste's former modiste, must have taken their request for new gowns seriously, for she arrived at the palace on Sunday just after the required morning church service, which Celeste and Loveday had been able to avoid with the excuse of having nothing suitable to wear. The famed modiste brought a young assistant, Marie, to confer with

Celeste. She brought so many swatches of fabric and fashion plates with her that three of the winders had to be enlisted to carry them up to Celeste's suite, leaving an unwound *automouton* wandering disconsolately.

"But of course you would come to me," the slender seamstress said as Marie moved around Celeste to confirm her measurements. "Who else has the knowledge, the style to dress the Chief Air Minister?" She waved a languid hand, and Marie scuttled back, only to pull out a small leather-bound book and pencil. From her place beside the door, Wintzen very much looked as if she wished she could be elsewhere. So did Loveday, seated nearby.

"Four new court dresses," Madame Finett reeled off to her assistant as she too walked around Celeste, who was standing in the middle of the bedchamber. "I will not remake your mother's gown. I am an *artiste*. Three ballgowns, two dinner gowns, an opera gown, five walking dresses with jackets, an evening cloak, two pelisses, and all the necessary accoutrements. I had one gown of yours your dear mother could not bear to take possession of when we thought you lost. You may have that for now."

"And a flying costume," Celeste reminded her, trying not to think about her mourning mother, so distraught she could not bear to see a new dress meant for her.

Madame Finett wrinkled her long nose. "I have not designed those. A shame Madame Hortense Tisserand is no longer available."

Celeste remembered the well-endowed woman who had helped her mother design the uniforms for the Aeronautical Corps. "Did she retire from her work?"

"Who knows?" Madame Finett spread her elegantly

fingered hands. "One day she was at her shop, the next—*poof!* She is gone." She turned to Marie. "Undergarments and clothing for the boudoir as well."

"*Oui, Madame,*" Marie said, scribbling in the book.

The modiste eyed Celeste. "You had a passion for blue, if I remember."

Celeste almost smiled at the reminder. She'd tried to convince her mother that she would wear only blue, then had Marie secretly remake an older dress so the silk for the new one might be sent to l'École to build the balloon that had carried her to England. A shame she could not use such a ploy now.

But Marie was staring at her with a slightly panicked look on her face, as if fearing her past sins were about to come to light, so Celeste merely nodded. "*Oui,* blue. Any shade will do."

Madame Finett *tsk*ed. "Any shade will *not* do. We must consider your position and your coloring. A rich, deep blue and bright cerulean, I think, augmented with crimson and primrose. Yes, I can see it now." She smiled toothily.

"And you will gown my assistant as well," Celeste said with a nod to Loveday, who, surprisingly, suddenly had the same panicked look as Marie.

Madame Finett glanced at Loveday, fine black brows up. "I have some grey bombazine I cannot use for anything else. I will contrive."

Oh, that seemed unfair. "*Non, non, non,*" Celeste said. "She accompanies me everywhere, including into the Emperor's presence. I cannot have her looking like a dowd. Please, Madame, only you could find a way to make an assistant coordinate with her minister."

Madame's pale gaze drifted off into the middle distance. "Coordinate. Hm. Primrose, yes, to go with her fair coloring. I think it can be done." She snapped her gaze back to Celeste. "Marie will take her measurements, and you will send her for fittings, *oui?*"

"Of course," Celeste promised.

She looked to Wintzen. "I will need the measurements for that one as well. The Emperor will pay."

Wintzen met her look for look. "That will not be necessary. I wear the uniform of the Aeronautical Corps."

"I will send you her measurements," Celeste said, trying not to grin.

Wintzen glowered at her.

They spent a very pleasant time looking over all the designs. She would never see most of these garments; she and Loveday would have left France behind by the time they were all fitted and finished. But it was fun to imagine, and Madame Finett would still be paid.

"That was very kind of you," Loveday said as she helped Celeste dress for dinner in the gown her mother had not been able to face.

"You should have the benefit of new dresses as well," Celeste said. "Or at least such new dresses as may be had at the Emperor's expense before we leave."

"Wintzen has requisitioned an awful grey uniform dress like hers from palace security. It is better than nothing and will do." She stepped back "Are you certain you don't want another tray up here? Dinner at the officials' table sounds rather chaotic."

"I want to see what I can learn," Celeste told her. "Even if Wintzen is to accompany me."

"And I intend to dine each evening with the staff," Loveday said, "and see what else *I* can learn."

The idea of facing the Emperor's minions on her own was far less appealing, but Celeste recognized the wisdom of dividing to conquer. So, a short time later, she descended the stone stairway to the first floor and followed the corridor to the *Salle des Fonctionnaires*. She had thought Wintzen's presence might be glaringly obvious, but, as the lady had said, nearly every official had brought a bodyguard. The long table was necessarily crowded and the volume of noise nearly deafening.

It didn't help that many of the officials had brought *boîtes d'alerte* with them. Some bronze, some porcelain with gilding, the boxes sat beside their places and let off a frantic clattering that nearly shook them off the table. At each alarm, an official would snatch up the piece of paper the box spat out, leap to his or her feet, and dash from the room, leaving their bodyguard to pick up the box and pelt after them.

"You will not leave the room," Wintzen informed her as they found places near the bottom of the table.

The man to her right cast her a frown. "Are you a Chief Clerk?"

"Non," Wintzen told him before Celeste could answer. "This is the Emperor's Chief Air Minister. You will treat her with respect."

The fellow paled. "A thousand apologies, Chief Air Minister. But this part of the table is reserved for clerks. You must go higher."

"The minister," Wintzen informed him in chilling tones, "sits where she likes."

He did not speak to them again.

At least some of the others were more welcoming. The woman on her left, who introduced herself as the Clerk of the Clocks, was more than happy to drone on about the importance of keeping time and the place of clockwork in the Emperor's plan.

"Then you have been at your position for some time," Celeste said when she could get a word in edgewise.

"Three weeks," the woman said proudly. "I was chosen immediately after we lost the previous clerk."

She almost hesitated to ask. "An illness, I take it?"

"No, indeed," she confided. "He could not handle the strain of this important position and left without a word."

"That makes at least four of them," Celeste told Loveday that night in her bedchamber. She had not stayed until the dessert course, but she had insisted that a footman take a plate to Marcel, claiming that he must be made to see what he would shortly be leaving behind. Wintzen had glowered sufficiently that Celeste did not think the footman would disobey her command.

"The Grand Inventor," Loveday mused, "the Minister of Public Works, a modiste to the Aeronautical Corps, and the Clerk of the Clocks."

"An unlikely quartet," Celeste said, pulling on her nightrail. "But their disappearance merely underscores what happens when one displeases Napoleon. We would be wise to look industrious, or we may be next."

CHAPTER 14

The following morning, attired in her new grey working dress, Loveday smoothed the fresh sheet of paper on the workbench that ran along one wall of the office. She now had paper, pencils, a stack of slender, leather-bound notebooks, and a smattering of various wheels and gears from the racks that looked useful. Her own journal, with its sketches of wheeled vehicles and steam-powered airships, was concealed at l'Ecole for safekeeping. So, for the moment, her world held no greater pleasure than the prospect of fresh paper.

As long as she did not think about Arthur and Emory. If her mind traveled west too often, she would not be able to think at all, and there was too much danger all around them for that.

"We must design an air ship that requires every single part we need for *Lark Deux*," she had whispered to Celeste this morning as she tightened the strings of her friend's short stays. "And much as I hate the thought, we might consider a metal gondola, not wood. It would not withstand a cannon-bomb, but it would certainly protect us from rifle balls."

"We must be seen to design something," Celeste had whispered in reply, over her shoulder. "I will have everything delivered to l'Ecole."

The question Loveday must now answer was whether or not to design a ship that actually worked.

It would be fairly straightforward, she thought, gazing at the paper and rolling a pencil between her palms, to design an air ship that possessed a fatal flaw. An engine made of a copper alloy that would explode at a certain heat and altitude. An additive to the lifting gas that would expand the gas bag past its known tolerances and guarantee the seams would fail. The result would be the entirety of the Aeronautical Corps falling out of the sky.

She shuddered at the thought of so much death. Of being responsible for it. No, there must be another way.

Besides, there would undoubtedly be test flights. Many of them. Training flights, too. One simply could not guarantee that all the ships in the fleet would suffer catastrophic failure all at once, on the day the Emperor decreed he would invade England.

No, it must be something more subtle. Something in common use that could be triggered on a single occasion—when the ships lifted for England. Aeronauts could be deposited in the sea and still be rescued, and she would not have their deaths on her conscience, even as an act of war.

She began to sketch a gondola. Not the thing of beauty the boatwright at Mevagissey had created for her and Celeste, but along the lines of their clumsier first model. They would not use coaches, of course, as tidy as that would make carriage houses all over France. But what about a metal shell? That would seem to the Emperor to be madly advanced, since at the moment the baskets of his balloons were all made of wicker, according to Celeste. And the expense might even beggar his treasury—an added benefit.

Her pencil flew along the paper.

Not rigging of the kind Celeste and she had designed, either. Ropes, certainly, but—aha. Ropes passed *under* the gondola in copper channels, that was it. So that it could be held from the bottom, not suspended from the top. Another advancement. Lots of rope on this model, so they could reconstruct their rigging when the supplies were somehow delivered to Arthur and Emory.

The lock on the main door to the corridor clicked open and Celeste came in, closely followed by Wintzen, who had escorted her to inspect the Corps, and thence to the Requisitioning Office to meet the Master of Materiel and issue orders for supplies.

"What is this?" Wintzen joined her at the table.

It was all Loveday could do not to turn the sheet of paper over and conceal her sketches. Instead, she lifted her pencil and answered politely. "It is a preliminary design for an advanced air ship for the Emperor."

Wintzen gazed at it for a moment without comment. Then she said, "How many troops will it carry?"

"I had thought four to six."

Wintzen shook her head. "At that rate, we will manage to get one company of aeronauts in the air, and no more."

"She is right, Mademoiselle Jourdamour," Celeste said

reluctantly. "We must lift our eyes beyond what has been accomplished before, and imagine ships that can carry fifty troops, along with its crew of aeronauts."

"Fifty!" Loveday exclaimed.

Celeste's eyes held a warning. *"Oui, bien sûr.* So I have been advised just now by Captain Toussaint, at the parade ground." Her lashes fell as she considered the sketch on the table. "But of course, any invasion must have an advance guard, and smaller, more nimble scout ships. I assume that is what you are designing here."

"Oui," Loveday said, thinking fast. "If we are to steadily increase our requisitions as well as outfit l'Ecole des Aéronautes to be reopened, we must begin with the new designs at a smaller scale, so that the students may learn as the prototypes are being built. We can then progress to troop transports."

"Exactement," Celeste said with a nod. She put off her redingote and removed a hat similar to that of Wintzen, with its brave cockade in the Corps colors. The men must have presented it to her in the absence of her own. Then she rounded the table to pick up a pencil.

And Wintzen was forgotten in the sheer joy of designing a ship that would likely never be built for an invasion that they would do everything in their power to prevent. Celeste's quick eye absorbed the channels for the ropes under the gondola, and the callout for the pedal system that would work the paddles. Her eyes danced as she shared silent laughter with Loveday, as if she were imagining a team of exhausted aeronauts taking it in shifts to man the pedals, since the design did not include a steam engine. All the French balloons Loveday had seen were built to the old design of an envelope of lifting gas and little manual propulsion. The steam engine, it appeared, was only used for the behemoths.

What, she wondered as she sketched and suggested changes, powered the *sous-marins*? Some kind of closed system? Either that or a contingent of exhausted bathynauts who likely won all their village foot-races on May Day, so powerfully muscled had their legs become powering the wheels that must drive a propulsion system under water.

In and among all the impossible features of this advanced air ship, Loveday and Celeste added item after item that they needed. But how to incorporate the wicker corset, which of course this model did not possess?

After a moment of staring at and through the paper, imagining this contraption, Loveday tapped Celeste on the wrist with the pencil. All around the gunwales of the gondola, which looked suspiciously like the barouche landau driven by Sir Robert Jermyn, with the two halves of its top folded back and its box in front, she sketched in a wicker enclosure on all four sides. In the callout, she wrote in neat capitals, LIFE RAFT.

Celeste pressed her lips together so that she would not laugh, and elbowed her, just once, in the ribs.

CELESTE AND LOVEDAY were debating the malleability of French copper when a knock sounded from the direction of the corridor. Loveday immediately began rolling up the nascent plans, even as Wintzen cracked open the door. Celeste caught sight of a tall footman, who thrust out a box. "For the Chief Air Minister, from the Clerk of the Clocks."

Wintzen nodded. "Set it on the floor."

He was too well-trained to frown, but he complied slowly enough that his confusion was evident.

"Wait," Wintzen ordered. She bent and prodded the box, turning it this way and that. Apparently satisfied, she lifted it in her arms. "You have done your duty. You may go."

He bowed and obeyed.

She carried the box into the room and set it on Celeste's desk. "You have an appointment."

Celeste moved to the desk and gazed down at the box. Made from creamy porcelain, with sprigs of lavender painted on all four sides and gilding decorating the corners, it looked as if it ought to be sitting on a lady's dressing table.

"How do you know?" she asked her bodyguard.

"This is called a *boîte d'alerte* for a simple reason. The person who requests your presence places a message inside. At a suitable time before the appointment, the box alerts the recipient and produces the message."

As if it had been waiting for the explanation to conclude, the box began chiming so hard it clattered against the desk. Celeste took a step back as it ejected a slip of paper from a slot in one side, just like those of the ministers at dinner.

Wintzen seized it and held it up as she read. "The Clerk of the Clocks informs you that you are expected at court in one hour."

"How kind of her—" Celeste began, then sucked in a breath. "One hour!"

"One hour?" Loveday asked as Celeste pressed her fingers to her lips, mind whirling like the tail of an *automouton*. "It is a long walk, but is that not sufficient time?"

"It is not the walk but the expectations," Celeste explained, hurrying to the large cupboard where her mother's court costume still reposed. "This is no afternoon audience in the reception rooms. This is in the throne room. I have only accompanied my mother to court a few times, but I remember the ceremony." She glanced at Wintzen, who had once again taken up her position beside the door. "Is it still so?"

"I have only been at court for a few weeks," she said, "but never have I seen such formality."

"Quickly, then." Celeste opened the cupboard and pulled her mother's court dress from the automaton. "I must change, whether it fits me or not."

Between Wintzen and Loveday, she managed to don the elaborate court dress, with its Van Dyke collar that stood up in starched lace as high as her cheeks. Thank the good Lord she was of a size through the back and shoulders with her mother. The skirts likely would have benefited from a hoop, but she would have to settle with no less than three petticoats, one of them starched, too. The gown was a little tight in the bosom and long at the hem, but she would simply lift the skirts as she walked.

It would do.

It would have to.

"The plumes!" Wintzen hissed as she started for the door with a scant quarter hour remaining. "As Chief Air Minister, you must wear at least three."

Celeste shook her head, panic pricking her. "There were none in the cupboard. Where does one requisition plumes at short notice?"

"Wait." Loveday tugged a box out of one of the racks. "Your mother had peacock feathers. I'm not sure why. Here." She brought back a handful.

"She preferred them to goose feathers for writing," Celeste

explained. "These have not been trimmed yet. *Bon.* Otherwise, I might have punctured myself." She bent her knees, and Loveday affixed three of the feathers in her coiffure. Not nearly elegant enough, but there was no more time.

She should not have been surprised when Wintzen followed her. "Do you not have to dress as well?"

"I am your bodyguard," she said. "I do not need to dress any more than does the furniture in the throne room."

Which was quite dressed enough in its velvets and gilding.

Of course, all the other ministers thronging about His Imperial Majesty rivaled it. Every coat was embroidered with gold and silver, glittering with metal sequins and buttons the size of saucers. The scent of more than a dozen perfumes hung like a cloud under the corniced ceiling. Many of the gentlemen still powdered their hair, and all of the ladies wore plumes of one kind or another. Several glanced at Celeste's head, then bent their own heads to murmur.

Approbation or accusation? She would likely never know. For in the throne room, only the Emperor spoke aloud unless he gave his permission to another.

And there he was, under a massive crimson canopy edged in gold braid a foot tall and held up by statues of golden eagles with ruby eyes that glittered. The top of the canopy was surmounted by a golden crown boasting, of course, an ostrich plume.

Celeste slipped in behind a group of clerks, distinguished by the silver-threaded caplets covering their shoulders. The Clerk of the Clocks nodded to her. The others faced resolutely toward their monarch. Wintzen took up her place a few feet away, gaze sweeping the crowd.

A gentleman in gold brocade was making his bow to the Emperor. "Your most gracious Imperial Majesty, thank you for this appointment. I will not disappoint you."

"I have the utmost confidence in that statement," Napoleon assured him. "My ministers do not disappoint, or they are no longer my ministers."

As the newly appointed minister paled, the Emperor lifted a hand and held it out, palm up, at his shoulder.

Three courtiers stepped forward. One held a bottle of cognac, another a ruby crystal goblet. The third shifted on his feet as if he only wished to escape. The first poured into the goblet. The second handed the goblet to the third. The third lifted it in salute to the Emperor and took a cautious sip.

Everyone in the room went still.

The young man's face broke into a smile, which he quickly swallowed before handing the goblet to Napoleon with a bow. "Your cup, Your Imperial Majesty."

The Emperor took a sip and nodded. *"Bon."*

Everyone relaxed.

From all around the palace, the clocks rang the hour, from tinny pings to resounding gongs.

Napoleon smiled. "Ah, the sound of progress."

His newest minister bowed his way back into the crowd.

Celeste stood through the acknowledgment of three more appointments. She thought her name might be called, but no one so much as glanced in her direction. Slowly, she sidled closer to Wintzen.

"What is the point of this?" she whispered as one of the ministers droned on about liberty, equality, and fraternity. "Do we all need to be here?"

"If you are all here, then it is a perfect time to send spies into your offices," Wintzen murmured back.

Her stomach clenched. Loveday could be in danger. "We must go, now!"

CHAPTER 15

Thank goodness her persona as Aimée Jourdamour was so insignificant. Happy thought indeed—Loveday was not dragged from her work simply to provide an admiring audience for a man who could not get enough attention.

After poor Celeste had hustled from the office in all her finery, Loveday settled in at the workbench with her drawings of the air ship that would never be. Chin in hand, pencil tapping on the table, she considered the changes Celeste had drawn in and extrapolated further. A section of piping here, a storage cabinet there, and what about a double hull? They might do cedar on the inside, iron sheathing on the outside, then run all the piping and rigging ropes between the two layers. After all, if it was never going to fly, one might as well be as extravagant as one pleased.

So absorbed was she that an hour passed before she heard the chiming of a clock. She lifted her head, waiting for the entire palace to ring the hour. Surely Celeste would be back soon? How long did these ridiculous audiences take?

But only a single chime came again.

With a sharp intake of breath, she realized it was not the clocks at all. It was the *boîte d'alerte*, chiming because someone had stood on the leads! In the next moment, the secret door rattled, but of course would not open with the newly designed lock upon it.

Loveday leaped from her stool and dashed across the room, whipping a hairpin out of her Psyche knot as she went. The lock was opened in a matter of seconds, and she flung open the secret door.

The servants' corridor was empty.

"Who is there?" she demanded of the shadowy darkness, like a ninny. What assassin would be so polite as to reply?

Hmph. She made certain the leads were back in place and closed the door with a bang, to let the miscreant know she knew he had been there, then repositioned the *boîte d'alerte* where it had been before. She had no sooner snapped the padlock closed on the hasp than Celeste burst in, closely followed by Wintzen.

"Loveday!" she cried. "Are you all right?"

How had she known? She indicated the rack, now back in place. "Someone was there, but they ran when they found the door locked. I hope it was not a servant."

"A servant would have knocked," Wintzen said. "You are certain you are all right?"

"Yes, but why should you fear I am not?"

"Because we think all that fuss and bother to get me to court was simply to get us out of the room." Celeste unfastened the frogs across her bosom. "Help me out of this gown, would you?"

Loveday removed the feathers, which were in the way, and

handed them to Wintzen. Then she lifted the outer layer from Celeste's shoulders and laid it over a chair. The inner gown with the upstanding lace collar was the fussy part.

"Luckily they did not take my insignificance into account," she said as she labored. "I am happy to report that the *boîte d'alerte* worked perfectly. I was warned someone was standing there even before they tried the latch."

"I am glad you locked the door," Wintzen said, in the first expression of actual humanity Loveday had heard.

"I am, too, rather," Loveday admitted. "I had not a single weapon to hand but a pencil."

"In here?" Wintzen looked amazed. "Why, there is a crowbar, a length of chain, and a fireplace poker, all within reach, to say nothing of those barrels of lifting gas, which could be heaved at an attacker. It is clear that I must also teach you the secondary function of a pencil."

Loveday looked at Celeste, and together they looked at Wintzen.

"You have a very different way of looking at the world," Celeste finally said. "Do you make these observations in every room and street and corridor?"

"I hope you are pleased that I do," Wintzen told her. "Otherwise I should not be a very good bodyguard, should I?"

She had a point.

The intruder would almost certainly return. Perhaps Loveday ought to ask her to give them a brief tour of their own office and teach them how to put the secondary functions of the equipment and supplies to good use.

~

THE NEXT MORNING, much to their astonishment, a member of the Master of Materiel's staff requested admittance to the office, where they were once again working on the new design. Wintzen admitted him, her suspicious glare all but causing him to stammer.

"The supplies you ordered yesterday, Chief Air M-Minister," he said. "I've got them on a w-wagon in the courtyard. Where would you like them delivered?"

The two of them stared at him for a moment before Celeste recovered herself. "The supplies I ordered? You have them ready now? So soon?"

"Yes, Minister. I spent a good part of yesterday evening making certain everything was just as you requested. Is there a problem? Were you not expecting it?"

"I had believed the process to be much more lengthy and complicated," Celeste said mildly. "But I am very glad it is not."

"Well, you're a minister," the young man pointed out, as though this explained everything.

Loveday could only be thankful that *she* had not gone to requisition the supplies. They might still be waiting a month from now.

"My assistant will go with you to make the delivery to l'Ecole des Aéronautes," Celeste went on. "Thank you very much for your work. I will make sure that the Master of Materiel is informed of your dedication to your duty."

The young man blushed. "Thank you, Chief Air Minister."

Loveday shot Celeste a glance that could only be translated as a squeal of delight. While Celeste summoned the footmen to take the supplies on hand in the office outside and load them on the cart, Loveday ran upstairs to fetch her pelisse. She met the young man from the Master of Materiel's staff in the court-yard, just as the footmen were finishing the task. The wagon was pulled by a horse the size of Hugo, though nowhere near as young, and no wonder. Six barrels of lifting gas had been roped to the insides of its walls and the other materials heaped in the middle and roped down under a tarpaulin.

"You do not use the steam-powered vehicles to pull a load of this size?" she inquired after a footman had handed her up to the bench seat and the young man took up the reins to guide the horse through the archway and on to the avenue beyond.

"They were all in use," he confessed. "Old Guillaume here is probably due to be sent to the tanneries, but he is good for this kind of thing. At least he is at home in the streets. These days, horses for the army are not trained as carriage horses. Everyone wants the steam vehicles."

"He won't really go to the tanneries, will he?" Guillaume might be old, but he held his head high, and his strength could be in no doubt even though his tail was going grey.

"I expect so. By the end of the summer, probably."

It was the last day of August. Loveday made up her mind. "I should like to requisition him, then, for service at l'Ecole des Aéronautes. The Chief Air Minister has no means of hauling her balloons to the parade ground when she makes her ascensions. I believe that Guillaume here would be ideal for the purpose."

"But wouldn't a steam vehicle—"

"Among those crowds? Can you imagine it, sir—a horse of this size, with plumes and proper livery? It would be like—"

Oh, who was a famous French woman? "Like Jeanne d'Arc arriving in a chariot."

He smiled at the image. "The Chief Air Minister does look rather like the blessed saint. She is in the stained glass window of our church at home."

And she knew she had him.

"They will be good to him, won't they?" he asked anxiously. "At the school?"

"As good as though he had saved their lives," she assured him, and meant it.

In the Rue des Aéronautes, she guided him around to the area in the rear of the school. When he brought Guillaume to a halt and set the brake of the wagon, she climbed down as nimbly as her skirts would let her. The poor young man was confused at not being permitted to open the gates and drive in to the central courtyard to unload, but she assured him that several of the neighborhood boys who aspired to be students would give her that assistance.

"And when their work is done," she assured him, "Guillaume will have the best of care and a bucket of oats for his good service."

With a sigh of relief, she saw him off on his way to the Tuileries. As she turned back, the rope ladder came tumbling down the wall, and in a moment Josie had joined her.

"Is that—"

"Yes," Loveday said, clutching her arm in excitement. "We must load everything you have ready on this wagon and take it all to St Malo."

"When?"

"Today. Now. We have not an instant to lose."

"But what about the horse? The wagon? I have never

driven such a thing."

"But Guillaume here has been driven by any number of no doubt ham-fisted youths. As long as he has plenty of water and grass to eat, and is rubbed down when you remove his harness, he will be content."

"But we will be called thieves!" Josie was pale. "We cannot steal a horse and wagon from the palace."

"Guillaume and the wagon belong to l'Ecole now," Loveday told her with a smile. "I have just requisitioned them. The poor beast was to be sent to the tanneries—you are giving him a permanent stay of execution."

Josie let out a long breath. Then she turned to call up to the window. "Amélie!" Her sister stuck her head out the window and waved to Loveday. "Take the barricades off the gates. Bring everything out. The hamper that came last night, too. We are leaving."

"When?"

"La, *chèrie*, why are you still standing there? Within half an hour!"

OH, but La Croix and Toussaint were maddening! After Loveday had departed on the wagon, Celeste stood over the desk in the office, staring down at the piles of reports the two captains had obligingly delivered to her.

"Reacquainting me with the Corps indeed," she muttered, picking up a closely written sheet entitled *State of the Stockpile of Suitable Ropes*. There was likely a similar report below it on the state of the stockpile of *un*suitable ropes. They were trying to bury her in minutiae and bring her work to a halt.

Someone rapped on the door. As was her wont, Wintzen cracked the panel so carefully she must have expected an explosive to be simmering on the other side. Instead, she jerked even straighter, threw open the door, then spun to face Celeste, skin pale and eyes fastened on the bank of windows opposite. "His Imperial Majesty, Napoleon the First."

Celeste dropped the report on the desk and curtseyed to the floor as the Emperor strolled into the room, hands clasped behind his back. Thank the good Lord Madame Finett had sent over two more gowns, though how she had finished them so quickly was beyond Celeste. This one was a sky blue, with silver frogging across the breast and along the hem. She at least looked as though she knew what she was about.

As she straightened from her curtsey, the Emperor nodded to her desk. "Already setting things in order. *Bon, bon.* And is this why you left court early yesterday?"

She managed a breath through lungs that had seized up. "I thought your aims better served by diligence."

"As wise as your *chère maman,*" he mused. "I could wish for such devotion from all my ministers. Too many seek to curry favor with pleasant smiles and pretty words."

The comment did not inspire a response that wouldn't make her look like a sycophant, too, so she said nothing.

He paced from one side of the room to the other, studying the racks of materials, the books and maps. Wintzen stood immobile, as if hoping he wouldn't notice her any more than the other tools in the room.

He stopped and speared Celeste with a steely gaze. "And what are your thoughts on our readiness to invade England?"

Dangerous topic, but at least it didn't surprise her. Toussaint and La Croix were determined to see it happen, and the

Emperor had asked her mother the same question often enough. Still, if she sounded optimistic, she might find herself over the Channel in a ship similar to the one in the sketches on the worktable, woefully unprepared to meet the elements and barely able to lift. And if she discouraged his ambitions, she might well find herself of no further interest to his spies.

"The feat is possible," she allowed, and he started to smile. "But we will need more pilots and improved air craft for them to fly if we are to place your troops safely on English soil."

"How quickly can you find these pilots and design these craft?" he asked.

Wintzen coughed, and Celeste saw La Croix and Toussaint crowding in the doorway. Who had alerted them to the Emperor's movements? Well, if they wanted to be involved, she would involve them with a vengeance.

"Why, with our loyal captains behind us, there is nothing we cannot do," Celeste said, with an expansive wave to encompass the men at his back. "Captain La Croix, would you care to answer His Imperial Majesty's question as to when we may commence an invasion of England?"

La Croix paled and fidgeted. "Soon. Very soon."

Never one to be left in the shadows, Toussaint took a step forward and inclined his sable head. "We have been working to see this vision become a reality. Give us a month, Your Majesty, and it will be done."

Celeste stared at him in astonishment while Napoleon nodded. "Excellent news. I did right to choose you as my Chief Air Minister, Mademoiselle Blanchard. You will keep me apprised of progress."

Celeste curtsied again. "Of course, Your Imperial Majesty."

She thought he would leave them then. Indeed, La Croix

and Toussaint were making haste to vacate the doorway so he could pass. But he took another tour of the workshop, head cocked, as if counting every bolt of silk and tub of screws. With a faint click, all the clocks in the room reached the hour and began chiming. From the corridor came the echo of dozens more.

"There is another matter," the Emperor said when they had finished and he had drawn abreast of Celeste again. "The people are insisting that I celebrate my birthday. I was in the field on August fifteenth, but I thought September fifteenth would do. I am told there will be a grand masquerade and fireworks. You will perform. Something amazing, like your dear mother would have done."

Toussaint's mustache twitched, as if he was fighting a smile. He thought to show her up. She had a better idea.

"But of course, Your Majesty," she said. "An ascension to rival all others. I will use l'École to prepare, with your gracious permission."

He snapped a nod. "Of course. You will need the school at any rate to train all these new pilots." He rubbed his hands together. "Perhaps they will be ready by the time of this celebration, prepared to deliver our forces to the shores of the enemy, and victory."

"Perhaps," Celeste said with a smile.

"We will endeavor to bring honor to His Imperial Majesty," Toussaint agreed.

"*Vive la France!*" La Croix put in. Always the safe gambit.

"*Vive la France!*" Celeste and Toussaint chorused. Wintzen said nothing.

His smile pleased, His Imperial Majesty strutted out of the office. Her two traitor captains looked prepared to follow.

"A moment, Captains," Celeste called, and they both stopped to eye her. La Croix's blue gaze wavered, as if he couldn't be sure he could comply with whatever she might request. Toussaint looked more impatient, shifting on his booted feet as if she were keeping him from a more important rendezvous.

"You are very confident we can meet the Emperor's deadline," she told them both while Wintzen came to stand closer to her. "Share with me why."

Toussaint nodded toward the piles of paper on her desk. "We have already shared all the information the Minister could need. When you have finished assessing our progress, we would be happy to answer any questions."

She rather doubted he was happy about anything, unless it meant his advancement. "I will have my questions gathered by Monday. Wait on me at noon."

His brows rose. Was he surprised she would be ready so soon? Perhaps she should be grateful he had yet to take her measure.

He seemed to remember himself, for he bowed. "Of course, Chief Air Minister. We will see you then."

La Croix could not move out of the office fast enough.

Wintzen shook her head. *"Imbéciles."*

Celeste eyed her. "You do not think highly of Captains La Croix and Toussaint?"

"I do not think highly of anyone in the Aeronautical Corps, your own self excluded," she said, heading for the door.

Interesting. How had Wintzen ingratiated herself with La Croix enough to gain this position? Or had it been a hardship post, as punishment?

"Wait," Celeste ordered, and Wintzen stopped to look back

at her. "The Aeronautical Corps has been upheld as the best France has to offer. Why would you denigrate its leadership?"

"Because they do not appreciate what could be achieved," she said. "They think only of their own futures, not the future of France, the future of the world. You talk of craft. Do you realize what we might achieve with an advanced air ship such as your assistant has been drawing?"

Once again, she must go carefully. It would not do for anyone to know that an advanced air ship would be arriving shortly in Paris.

Celeste came around the desk to join her by the door, when it was clear Wintzen was not finished. "With an air ship," her bodyguard said, "continents would shrink to something you could cross in a day. Knowledge could be shared in hours. People could be carried to where they were most needed—whether for education or health," she added.

Celeste cocked her head. "I have heard these theories. Lord and Lady Worthington in England published them in *Philosophical Transactions*, the journal of the Royal Society of Engineers. My mother's assistant, Dupont, read them to me."

"They cannot be the only ones so wise," Wintzen insisted, though the faintest of pinks seemed to be rising in her cheeks.

"Perhaps not," Celeste said. "But I am impressed that you have such strong opinions on the matter. Perhaps you would prefer to be a pilot yourself?"

"*Non,*" she said, though it was not very convincing. "Now, I will leave you to your work. I will station myself just outside the door, to prevent anyone's interrupting you further. Call if you need anything."

She went out and shut the door decisively behind her.

CHAPTER 16

ST MALO

Three days later

The road, its white gravel now golden in the long shadows of the late afternoon sun, dipped into a swale before arrowing straight for the causeway to St Malo. For days now, Arthur and Emory had been taking the watch on this hill turn about. Part of their duty was to make certain no one approached *Lark Deux*'s place of concealment, and if that should happen, to provide a distraction and lead the interlopers away. But mostly they were simply doing their best not to lose hope that some day, some hour, they would recognize the figures descending the gentle slope.

They were learning to recognize people, certainly. The two washer-women who had been so kind as to give Arthur a ride were as regular as clockwork. And there were farmers who took produce in to the market square every day. But none possessed a fall of dark curls or a knot of blond hair as rich as summer wheat.

Arthur tried to find a more comfortable spot at his post

without success. He lay on his stomach behind an outcrop of weathered limestone. It gave him a superior view, especially with the aid of the far-scope, but it could not be said his body appreciated the hard ground or the gravel, for the soil was thin and grass sparse. On the other side of the swale lay the copse of trees, with Emory on watch, concealed in the longer, more luxuriant grass on the hillside.

Following the night they had seen the blue lights and the peculiar craft in the sky, they had done a number of exploratory missions as twilight thickened into full darkness and the moon waxed full. Part of the mission was to steal food. The other part was to locate at least one of the lights and try to determine which of several possibilities was its actual purpose.

They found one at the top of the very hill under which they were concealed, which might mean danger at some point, but for now simply meant a smaller chance they would be spotted as they examined it. Both he and Emory had crouched in the tall grass as the last of the evening insects danced in the air, gazing at what could only be called an *installation*.

He had expected a lantern such as the pirates used, with sides of blue glass. What they found was unlike anything he had ever seen.

In a large, squat holder of brass was a lamp, certainly, but attached to it was a firebox. As they knelt next to it in perplexity, coal clattered into a cavity below, making both of them jump. The blue light brightened as the fire consumed its replenished fuel.

And then they heard the sound they had come to associate with the peculiar balloons that all looked like the original

Lark. Small propellers. But as the puttering sound approached overhead, they heard a chime from the balloon, and a new sound answering it from the very ground. A deeper chime.

Emory, who was gazing upward while Arthur stared down, drew in a sharp breath. "It just corrected its course," he said in disbelief. "When that chime sounded. What does it mean?"

"I cannot tell you," Arthur said, and then realized Emory had probably been talking to himself. "Let us lie in wait for another one."

But from this height, he also noticed something else. "Emory, the lights are in a straight line across the landscape. From this hill, we can see the pattern that only looked random before. It is a guidance system. External, not internal. But how does it work?"

"It seems unusually inefficient for French technology," Emory said, his gaze following the blue glimmers every half mile or so until the haze swallowed them up. "Can the balloons be guided by sound? A vibration like the ones we just felt?" And then he snapped his fingers. "They have to be externally guided. Of course! Arthur, those are not human pilots. They are automatons."

The enormity of it rolled over Arthur in a wave of realization and horror. "Can it be that Boney is going to invade with automatons, not human soldiers?"

Emory shook his head, not in the negative, but in disbelief. "It does not seem possible. Why, it would take thousands of the things, and they must be expensive to build."

"All right, not as infantry. But what about aerial bombs? A small company of flying ships dropping those cannonbombs could cause as much loss of life as any pitched battle on land.

More, for it would be indiscriminate. Imagine the numbers of women and children among the dead."

"I would rather not," Emory whispered. "What can we do?"

Another one went overhead. A chime—an answering chime that Arthur could feel in his bad knee—and the balloon juked to one side, heading for the next blue glow in a field lying close to a hay barn.

"I know one thing—we dare not disable this lamp in case there is a contingent of soldiers whose duty it is to repair them. *Lark Deux* would be spotted immediately."

"Flying automatons," Emory mused, clearly fascinated.

Another one passed overhead, and then two more.

"They come at the same time every evening," Arthur had said. "Is it a patrol? But why in the dark? What are they doing?"

In the days since, Emory had followed the path of the blue lights for miles. Each one, he had reported, was exactly the same as the one on their hill. On one foray, he had been gone two full days, and Arthur had had a hard time of it, thinking he had been captured as a spy. He had returned with a small wheel of cheese and six apples, and a report that he had nearly reached the coast before the increasing numbers of people had caused him to turn back. The automatons were indeed flying to a place called the Baie des Sirènes, the bay where they had seen the *sous-marins* massing.

It was time to consider another trip into St Malo to locate Louen. The War Office must know of this development, now that Emory had confirmed the location. Perhaps Arthur would go tonight.

Even now, as he watched the road and the fields below him, wondering when the farmer was going to take off his hay and discover the air ship in his copse, his mind worried at the subject, nibbling and circling, formulating backup plans should Louen be at sea.

The sound of hooves brought him back to his present duty. In a moment, around the curve of the road came a large wagon pulled by a great brown Percheron. The two women on the seat looked tiny in comparison to the horse and its load—one in a blue pelisse and one in green, both wearing straw bonnets trimmed in matching ribbon. Clearly not farm women. And not Loveday and Celeste, either.

Disappointment nearly made him give up his surveillance.

They drew up just below his post, and the patient horse lowered his head to crop the wayside grasses while the two consulted a square of paper and looked about them, apparently comparing it to the landmarks they observed.

Their voices drifted up to him, their French so rapid he could hardly follow it.

"—but she said that there would be a—"

"—after all this time—"

"You don't suppose they have been captured?"

That came clearly enough, and Arthur rolled to his feet, crouching behind the outcrop.

"—hope, Amélie. If Celeste can, then we can."

Celeste! A wagon full of materials for repair! Could this be the miracle they had been waiting for?

He leaped up and snatched his coat off the ground. No one else was in sight to see him wave it like a flag. *Look up. Look up here!*

"I cannot see a copse of—" The girl in green gasped as she caught sight of Arthur.

"There he is!" She waved, and he plunged down the side of the hill, sideways like a crab to spare his weak leg.

When he came into their line of sight again, he waved them off the road, pointing them around the shoulder of the hill to the copse. And to his utter relief, the big horse turned and set his powerful body to the task.

Arthur could have wept for joy.

Emory had clearly heard the wagon bumping and creaking through the field, for he came at a run through the trees. The young lady at the reins pulled up when she caught a glimpse of *Lark Deux* in her bower of beeches and pines.

"Oh, Amélie, see how beautiful it is!"

"The shape, the perfect curvature! Just as described."

"Ladies," Arthur panted as he loped up. "Allow us to assist you down."

The driver—Josie Aventure, of whom Celeste had told them—laughed and tossed him the reins. "Better you should take our so faithful Guillaume out of his harness and allow him to graze. We are quite capable of getting down ourselves —we have had enough practice."

And she scrambled down without another word.

She offered him her hand to be shaken, as straightforward as any man. "I am Josephine Aventure, and this is my sister Amélie," she said in heavily accented English. "We are very happy to see you alive and well, monsieur. You are the neighbor of Loveday? Arthur Trevelyan?"

"*Oui,*" he said, taking the thin hand in both of his and squeezing it gently. "You cannot be happier than we to see you. Are they well? Loveday and Celeste?"

"They are indeed, and send you ever so many messages,

which I will remember as soon as we have unloaded the wagon."

"Surely it can wait?" Emory approached, and they introduced each other. "We do not have much, but we can offer you and the horse water, and we have day-old bread and carrots."

Another merry laugh. The smaller sister, Amélie, began to work at the knots in the rope holding down the tarpaulin. "They will be a welcome addition to our cold roast of pork and the wheel of cheese. Thank you."

Arthur's knees went weak, not from his old wounds, but from the thought of actual meat. His last full meal had been at the public house with Louen.

Emory helped him unharness the horse and then used a piece of canvas to rub down his sweaty coat. Guillaume was perfectly content to be staked in the rich grass just under the canopy while they turned their attention to unloading the wagon.

Except the Aventure sisters had already begun. "We must unload and stack the supplies in the order in which we will need them for the repairs," Amélie was saying. "If you gentlemen will move the barrels of lifting gas over there, we will begin with the repair of the aft gas bag."

"Then the corset," Josie went on, gazing at the damage, "and finally, the envelope and rigging."

It was like being with Celeste and Loveday again—or rather, the familiarity of the conversation only showed the magnitude of their friends' absence. He and Emory found themselves obeying the orders of two people who knew far better than they what they were doing. And by the time darkness fell, the wagon had been emptied, the equipment organized, and a plan for the next day formulated.

It was a shock to the system to have so much activity after the frustrating, endless waiting and watching of the past several days.

"Two more headstrong, intelligent females with a penchant for mechanics," Emory whispered as they took the buckets hanging from the back of the wagon and went to fetch water for the horse. "What, is this an epidemic?"

"If it is, it is the most welcome that ever struck," Arthur said with a smile. "I have never looked forward to anything so much as hearing all their news of our friends."

"And of learning what said friends have planned," Emory added.

Yes, that, too. Arthur hoped it included a successful ascent and a fast flight back to England… but somehow he had a feeling that it would be much more.

"And after that," he said to Emory as they knelt by the creek that meandered through the north end of the field, "I should very much like to take our guests up the hill. The moon is full tonight. Maybe they can tell us more of these blue lights and balloons with automaton pilots."

"In the absence of Celeste and Loveday," Emory said, "I can think of no one whose opinions I would rather hear."

La Croix and Toussaint arrived a day late, nearly a week after Josie and Amélie had departed, while Loveday was at l'Ecole ensuring all was ready to receive the air ship and its muchawaited passengers. In retaliation, Celeste left the two captains standing for five minutes while she pretended to study a report on rushes gathered in the Seine and their utility for weaving lightweight baskets. She'd already skimmed the report once. The author had concluded after a tortuous hundred pages that such baskets would not be sturdy enough to carry above three passengers. She could have told him that in two paragraphs.

Her time had been better spent following the clues she and Loveday had discovered a few days ago, sprinkled through the reports like breadcrumbs through a forest. It was difficult to believe that her two captains thought she would not read the reports at all, and would thereby miss what was truly going on.

The fact that they had underestimated her would be their downfall.

Finally, she consented to raise her gaze to theirs. La Croix was fidgeting with the braid on one cuff of his cerulean uniform. Toussaint was regarding her, gaze hooded, like a hawk watching for the field mouse to give itself away.

"It appears you have been trying to improve our balloons," she said. "Did you dare to create an advanced design for them?"

La Croix started and confirmed her and Loveday's suspicions. Toussaint inclined his head. "The Chief Air Minister is very wise. We are indeed working on such a wonder, though we have not progressed far without your exalted mother."

Her mother had complained that both her captains were more versatile in flying the air craft than building them, and most versatile of all at pretending to knowledge they did not possess. "You have ruled out reeds, wicker, and tin as the material for an improved basket," she allowed. "What did you settle upon?"

La Croix looked to Toussaint.

"Cedar," the dark-haired captain drawled as if bored by the conversation. "Thinly planed, but sufficient when reinforced with copper piping."

Cedar had been another English approach. She had read the treatise herself at her father's knee and had had the boatwright in Mevagissey build *Lark Deux* using it. Still, she had thought Loveday's use of copper piping to be unique.

"And the envelope?" she asked.

"Silk over a wicker frame. A recent innovation, I believe."

Celeste drew in a breath. A recent innovation indeed, and one that she and Loveday had conceived. It wasn't unknown for inventors leagues apart to reach the same conclusions within a similar timeframe, but still. A knot began to form in her stomach.

"Interesting," she said. "And who made such a discovery? We must enlist their aid."

"I cannot say, Chief Air Minister," Toussaint replied. "Your mother provided the plans. She did not share their origin."

They knew she could not question her mother. Suddenly, the loss rose up and threatened to swallow her whole. Celeste fought off the darkness. If only Loveday were here beside her!

"A shame," she made herself say. "But at least we have the plans. I would like to see them."

Toussaint waved a hand toward the dozens of rolls of paper stacked among the books and upon chairs. "The originals should be here. Perhaps your assistant could locate them, if you explain carefully what you seek."

Loveday had already searched through the rolls. If she had

spotted an air ship that looked like theirs, she would have told Celeste. After a few choice words, no doubt.

"And what is the progress of their manufacture?" she asked.

"We have built several prototypes," La Croix assured her proudly.

And wouldn't the English War Office be pleased if she and Loveday could bring back information about them? "I will inspect them," she said. "Arrange for me to tour the manufactory."

Toussaint inclined his head. "Alas, it is not a fit place for a lady."

Celeste raised her brows. "I am not a lady. I am the Chief Air Minister, your superior, and you will not tell me what is fit for me to see."

Toussaint's lip curled, twisting his mustache out of shape. "But, Chief Air Minister, you should not be risked. Manufactories can be prone to fire, explosions. It is my duty to keep you safe. If you feel I am in error in that, you are, of course, within your rights to demand that the Emperor overrule me."

As if Napoleon allowed anyone to demand anything. Once more, he had put her in a corner with little way out.

She thought quickly. "Then send one of your prototypes to me."

He grimaced. "They are in the testing phase, Chief Air Minister. Some are at the front and others are near Cherbourg. None are currently in Paris."

Of course not. Oh, but he was slippery.

"Very well," she said. "I have requested a briefing from the Minister of War in any case, which is likely to be much more thorough." Had the request even made its way through the layers of secretaries and functionaries to reach the Minister's desk? Whether or not it had, she still took no little satisfaction at the look of blank surprise on his face, before he stretched his lips in a smile. "For now, provide me with weekly reports."

Toussaint inclined his head. "Of course, Minister. Come, La Croix."

Her other captain bowed, and the two left her. It took her ten minutes to overcome her rage at their determination to keep these new ships from her. If only she knew what was happening in St Malo! If only this endless waiting would end!

She must do something. She must get out of here. Visit l'Ecole, and see how Loveday was faring. Find out if she had heard anything at all.

But Wintzen would not leave her alone until bedtime. Worse, Loveday did not return, and Celeste had no idea why. She forced herself to eat dinner with the other officials.

Wintzen scowled as she and Celeste returned to the suite. "Where is your assistant? Am I to do everything around here?"

"She is on a mission for me," Celeste told her, though every muscle seemed to be tightening with worry. "She will return when it has been completed."

She waited only until Wintzen had stomped off to their bedchamber before donning the black velvet evening cape Madame Finett had sent over. Keeping an eye out for guards, she slipped from her bedchamber and followed the servants' stair to the ground floor. She nearly tripped over an *auto-mouton* busily scrubbing at the gilded trim boards along the corridor. Setting it going in a different direction, she patted its fleecy backside and turned for the door.

Wintzen stood in front of it, arms crossed over her broad chest. "Where are you going, Chief Air Minister?"

As far away from you as I can get. Celeste swallowed the words and pasted on a smile. "I could not sleep. I thought a walk around the grounds."

Wintzen lowered her arms. "I will accompany you."

With a sigh, Celeste turned away from the door to the entrance arch and headed for the one to the gardens instead. Her penance was three perambulations around the sculpted shrubbery before Wintzen escorted her back to her apartments. Only then did the woman pull a tightly folded note from her bodice.

"This came for you, Minister."

Celeste rounded on her. "You kept it from me all this time!"

"It is my duty to protect you, even from nonsense such as this."

Celeste struggled to keep her breathing even. "How did it come?"

"A boy brought it to the kitchen door, and they summoned me. The greater question is who sent it."

There could be no doubt. Celeste's hands shook as she read the direction on the intricately folded note. She knew those folds as well as she knew the handwriting.

Josie had written a couplet that could be read by anyone, but understood by only two.

The lark flies with joyous singing
And hears our lady's bells ringing

Celeste refolded the note. "Merely a couplet from an admirer. No need for alarm."

Wintzen crossed her arms over her chest. "What admirer?"

Celeste made a show of shrugging. "How should I know? The position of Chief Air Minister has already attracted attention. I will see you in the morning."

She turned her back and marched into her bedchamber.

Once inside, she pressed a hand to her lips and sank onto the window seat. The skies to the west were filled with stars. The moon was waning, but enough remained to brighten all of Paris below. The watchman's lantern in the garden was a feeble glow in comparison.

What exactly had Josie meant? Was she here in Paris, or had this note traveled a greater distance? *Our lady's bells.* But whose? The great cathedral of Notre Dame had had ten before nine had been melted down in the Revolution. But Josie had not capitalized the name—*our lady.* A humbler church, then? One they thought of as *ours?* Our Lady of Penitence, the much smaller church around the corner from l'Ecole? It had six bells. Was that it?

Six… six…

And suddenly she realized it had been *six days* since Josie and Amélie had departed Paris. Three days to travel to St Malo with the slower horse—three days to make the repairs—but only a matter of hours to return on the third day once the sun had set. Only a matter of moments to pay a boy upon arrival to deliver a message.

Celeste drew a sudden breath that shivered with excitement.

They were here! They must have been able to repair the air ship sufficiently, but something must have been off if Loveday still remained at the school. Had they been spotted? France would have more than her and Loveday's plans, if so.

And how had her mother come by the plans that looked

suspiciously like their original ones—if Toussaint had not been lying? Celeste had tried to send word to Josie and Amélie that she was alive through Madame Racine's connections, but it was clear the messages had never reached them, for they'd been shocked to see her. But Madame Racine would never betray her adopted country by sending information about her and Loveday's discoveries.

But someone had. Whoever had stolen their original plans had been able to reach her mother. *La Blanchard* had had the utmost disdain for spies. Why would she accept that information from one such? And why had she thought Celeste dead, if she had been given plans that clearly showed her own daughter's ideas and handwriting?

Celeste would have the answers to these questions and more, perhaps as soon as tomorrow. They were here! Her whole soul rose in a prayer of thanksgiving.

They were here! And safe!

When she was finally able to sink her head onto a pillow and sleep, she dreamed of bells ringing out in celebration.

The very air tasted sweeter the next morning. Loveday must have slipped inside in the middle of the night and managed a few minutes of sleep on the sofa, for she was up when Celeste came out of her room. Before they could so much as congratulate each other, Wintzen stalked in.

"Derelict," she snapped at Loveday. "You are never here when needed, and you failed to order breakfast."

"Well, I—" Loveday began with a look at Celeste.

Wintzen cut her off with a slash of her hand. "Never mind. I asked for help from the kitchens myself."

As if to prove it, a young man came through the servants' door bearing a large covered tray. He must be new to the Emperor's service, or perhaps he was but rarely given the opportunity to come above stairs, for he gawked at all the gilding and velvet. Wintzen immediately went to inspect the tray, and him.

That didn't stop him from flashing Celeste an impudent grin as he set the silver tray on the table beside her chair.

"I saw you last night," he said.

Did he mean in the gardens? Celeste nodded as she reached for the cream to add to her *café*. "I wished to take the air."

"And that you did!"

"You are too bold," Wintzen complained. She tipped her head toward the door. "Be off with you now."

He schooled his face, bowed to them all, and scurried out. Loveday cast Celeste a look of warning before Wintzen shut the door behind him.

The bodyguard turned to scowl at Celeste. "How did you leave the palace without me?"

Celeste frowned. "You know that I did not."

"I know that you did," Wintzen contradicted her bluntly. "Half of Paris saw you last night, up in the air. The palace is buzzing like a hive of bees. Who else but *La Blanchard* would fly an air ship into Paris? Will you unveil it for the Emperor's birthday celebrations?"

Realization hit, and the café went down hard. Celeste coughed and set down the cup even as Loveday turned white as the china upon the tray.

"What did they see?" Celeste demanded.

"A wondrous craft, by all accounts," Wintzen admitted, excavating her coddled egg with efficient skill. "Sleek, like a corvette in the air. Where did you have it built?"

That she could never admit. "I am my mother's daughter. We have our ways."

Wintzen seemed to accept that. "The Emperor will be pleased. Where is the ship now?"

Why was she asking so many questions? Celeste had ruled out her being in the pay of La Croix or Toussaint. Was she spying for someone else?

She glanced at Loveday, whose color was slowly returning. Her friend must have made a decision, for she lifted her chin. "Where the air ship is being completed is less important than that it be completed on schedule. The Chief Air Minister has asked me to supervise the process. I suggest you stay out of our way."

Wintzen's face darkened, making her look even more like a Valkyrie. "I am ordered to protect the Chief Air Minister, better than her mother was protected."

Celeste could not help but wince at the reminder. "That is enough, Wintzen. My assistant is correct. She has the remit from me, and I may accompany her from time to time to ensure she has all she needs to succeed."

"Not alone," Wintzen insisted.

Celeste puffed out a sigh of frustration. "Her escort will be sufficient."

Loveday nodded agreement.

"She cannot protect you," Wintzen sneered. "She is a lady who knows nothing about fighting. Her hands are too soft."

The lady in question knew a great deal more than Wintzen likely did about wrestling heavy objects into submission. Celeste rose from the table. "If she needs to know how to fight, then teach her."

IT HAD BEEN A LONG, if joyous, night. Loveday had only had a few moments to help guide the air ship down into the school's huge courtyard and greet her friends before she had to return to the palace or risk exposure. Arthur, bearded and scruffy and resembling nothing so much as a pirate himself from the days of living rough, had not been pleased to watch her go. In truth, she had been less than pleased to leave him behind, again. She had hoped to escape to the school as soon as possible this morning.

Unfortunately, to her surprise, lessons began in the office as soon as breakfast was concluded. Loveday could hardly contain her frustration with Wintzen and her perpetual presence, not when her entire body tingled with impatience to run through the streets of Paris to l'Ecole des Aéronautes. To determine the air ship's condition. How had they gone about repairing her, there under the trees? And what had they done with Guillaume the horse? Oh, she would give anything to flee the palace with Celeste!

But that was not going to happen immediately. Celeste had hit on probably the only thing that would have induced Wintzen to allow the two of them out alone, and now Loveday had to do her best to not be a complete failure at it.

What a good thing her body was not that of the average young English miss, whose only exercise might be to walk to church, or even to ride about the estate in the company of a groom.

She and Wintzen cleared a space on the side of the office closest to the secret door. "I would suggest rolling up the carpet," Wintzen said grimly, "but the Emperor has already paid us one visit, and I do not see myself explaining to him what we are doing should he decide on a second."

Loveday wondered how long it would take for the news of the miraculous air ship to reach the imperial ears. The danger of a second visit could be very real.

While Celeste looked on, Wintzen positioned Loveday

opposite herself and explained what she would do. "You defend yourself and then I will tell you how to improve."

Loveday would rather have learned about the improvement first, but before she could do much more than raise an arm to prepare herself, her head rang with a slap.

"Wintzen!" she exclaimed. "My opponent is not likely to be another woman."

Slap—on her chest. Slap—on one leg.

"Defend yourself!" Wintzen said, closing in again.

This time Loveday did manage to block her and took advantage of an opening to get in a punch to the stomach.

Wintzen gasped, but not because of the blow. "You must not do that."

"Do what? What was wrong?"

"The punch. That is the province of the military only."

Loveday's arms fell to her sides. "I don't understand."

"The closed fist is considered a deadly weapon. For that punch alone, you risk being brought before a magistrate for assault."

"But what if the Minister is attacked by a man?" This was so foreign to everything Loveday knew that she could hardly take it in. "Would not the punch be needed to stop him?"

Wintzen shook her head. "In defending her, you must wrestle, kick, or slap. The risk is too great to employ the closed fist."

Loveday shook her head in amazement. What would the French think of the boxing champions that drew such crowds in Truro on quarter days? "I cannot promise to remember that in the heat of the moment. But very well. Tell me how I may improve."

Whatever they might think of Wintzen, she kept her word.

By the time the trays arrived with luncheon, Loveday had been painfully well educated on the art of fighting without the punch. But she learned nevertheless. The second time she slipped under Wintzen's guard, she grasped her in a hold and flipped her off her feet. Wintzen actually laughed as she lay upon the carpet on her back.

It was the first time they had seen her do more than produce a wintry smile.

"It took me a year to learn that move," she said as she accepted Loveday's hand and was pulled to her feet. "You are surprisingly strong for a gently reared young lady, mademoiselle."

"Our household employments in Switzerland are—" She risked a glance at Celeste. "Different."

"The question is," Celeste said, indicating they should join her at the desk for luncheon, "is she accomplished enough to undertake the dangerous task of seeing me safely to my modiste for a fitting this afternoon?"

Wintzen considered this, apparently unaware of any sarcasm. "If you travel in a carriage," she said at last. "Mademoiselle Jourdamour ought to be able to provide enough protection to cross the pavement and reach the door. And," she added, gazing sternly at Loveday, "I expect you to enter before her, and determine the safety of each room before the Minister enters it."

"Of course," Loveday said.

She would have promised to swing from the chandelier in each room if Wintzen had ordered it, if they could only get out of here and over to l'Ecole sooner.

But at length even the longest wait must end. Wintzen ordered the carriage and stood at attention in the courtyard as they entered it, then watched the vehicle lurch into motion and cross to the archway before she turned to go inside.

"As much as she makes me mazed as a pisky," Loveday admitted, "I am glad to have learned a thing or two from her. I hope our lessons continue."

"Mazed or no, you will be sore tomorrow," Celeste said. "Perhaps you might pass the lessons on to me, if we ever get two minutes together in privacy."

"One may accomplish quite a lot in two minutes," Loveday allowed. Then she bounced on the leather seat. "Oh, Celeste, I cannot wait to see our friends again!"

CELESTE MIGHT HAVE AGREED to be driven in one of the Emperor's carriages, but she dismissed the coachman and groom as soon as they reached the street one over from the Rue des Aéronautes.

"I have my own way back to the palace," she assured the coachman when he questioned her instruction. She and Loveday stayed on the corner long enough to be certain he had gone.

"Shank's mare is a hard mode of travel," her friend said as they started for the school. "I should know. I have been doing far more of it than I should like."

Celeste made a commiserating moue. "We will return by velocipede. If you brought mine to the palace, then Marcel's should still be here. If it remains in working order, you can ride postillion."

The thought of her friend in the dungeon dimmed Celeste's spirits for a moment, but she couldn't help her smile as they approached the building. No one could doubt the school was once more in operation. Gone were the barricades nailed over the entrance. Smoke puffed from one of the chimneys, and the ring of hammer on metal echoed even through the stout doors.

Memories assailed her as she walked into the workshop. There, next to the bins that had once held silk for the students' balloons, she had sewn her first envelope under her mother's watchful eye. At the oak worktable in the center of the space, she had debated the merits of hydrogen, hot air, and lifting gas with her father, as he sat in his wheeled chair, blankets covering the legs that would never hold him upright again. His designs, unrealized in his lifetime, were carefully stored in the room at the back, the room her mother had given her for her *laboratoire*, where Celeste and Marcel had planned the balloon that had taken her to England.

Past the romantic shapes of the wicker baskets her mother had used for her celebrated ascensions—a swan, a scallop shell, a fish—she heard voices echoing from the central courtyard. She followed Loveday out into the light.

There, crouched on the flagstones like an eagle come to rest, lay their air ship in a nest of low scaffolding. Amélie and Josie had already put Arthur and Emory to work expanding her.

"Non, non," Josie was scolding from her tall stool beside the trestles where the envelope had been laid out. "Have you never sewn a seam before, *Capitaine* Trevelyan? The stitches, they must be smaller and closer together."

Celeste thought he grumbled something as he sat beside her friend, silk cascading across his lap. He jabbed the needle into the silk, then yanked out his other hand and sucked his thumb.

"But how well you hold that hammer, Monsieur Thorndyke," Amélie said, bending closer to where Emory was pounding out a dent in a sheet of copper on a shelf built out from the observation tower. He had his coat off and sleeves rolled up, and Celeste found the flex of muscle fascinating to watch. Apparently so did Amélie, for she did not so much as look up as Celeste and Loveday entered the courtyard.

Celeste shook off the moment of jealousy and followed Loveday closer. Arthur glanced up then, and the pleasure on his newly shaven face stopped her in her tracks in shock. *Mais non,* his gaze was on Loveday. Her friend appeared transfixed in place, on the far side of a river of silk, but her smile was radiant. "I have never been so happy to see anyone again as I am to see the four of you."

His pleasure dimmed just a trifle before he rallied. "And we you. Last night there was no time, but we have so much to tell you." He stopped when he saw her frowning on the undulating folds of silk.

"You removed the forward canvas gas bag," she said. "Were we leaking that badly?"

Amélie nodded. "You could smell it. But I did not recognize the provenance. *Bain de Evian,* perhaps?"

"*Non,*" Celeste told her, joining them. "Wheal Garan. A mine in Cornwall."

Arthur set aside his needle and thread and rose abruptly, tumbling the material to the floor. "The location makes no difference. England has a sufficient supply of lifting gas to allow us to be a concern to France. That is all we need to share."

EMORY RECOGNIZED the conviction ringing in Arthur's voice. They had had ample time to talk while protecting the air ship. Indeed, he could not remember talking as much with any gentleman of his acquaintance, when not venturing out at night to leave silver in exchange for food taken from barns and cellars or lying in the grass counting unmanned ships. He knew exactly what Arthur thought about this war and how to end it.

But they were deep in enemy territory, and alienating their only allies, after all they had done for them, did not seem wise.

Besides, how could Emory argue with Celeste's logic? Just the sight of her, gowned in a fetching blue dress that reminded him of the flowers his sister Henri tended, made his mouth turn up in a smile.

"You are asking my friends to risk their lives for you," Celeste informed Arthur as Miss Aventure hurried forward with a frown to pull up the material Arthur had spilled. "The least you can do is be helpful in exchange."

"Delighted to be of service," he said, though his tone was clipped. "Just not with England's secrets."

Miss Amélie left Emory's side to venture over and pat the hull of the gondola. "And this, she is not a secret?"

"Not anymore," Celeste said. "My bodyguard, Wintzen, tells me half of Paris saw you come in last night. She thought I had slipped her leash to pilot it myself."

The others exchanged worried glances, but Emory was more concerned with this Wintzen person. "You have a body-guard?" he asked, moving closer. "Are you in danger?"

Celeste shook her head. "I may be, but Wintzen is more likely to be the one endangering me than protecting me. She was clearly placed to watch my every movement."

The courtyard felt colder, though he could think of no reason for the temperature to plummet along with his spirits.

Miss Amélie glanced toward the door. "Did she accompany you?"

"She allowed us to leave," Loveday reported. "But she might still have followed us."

Emory closed the distance between him and the others, until he was standing next to Celeste, thankful more than ever that he had had an opportunity to bathe and shave.

"Which is why I will not stay long," she said with an apologetic smile to him. "Napoleon is planning a grand fête on the fifteenth to celebrate his birthday, including a masquerade ball. As his Chief Air Minister, I am to make an ascension. If anyone asks any of us about the air ship, we will say it is part of my plan for that event."

Having witnessed how badly an ascension could go, he could not like the risk to her. However, Loveday was quick to point out the benefit.

"The ascension also gives us the opportunity to gather supplies," she explained. "We will see them delivered to the school for the expansion of the gas bags and the envelope. Then *Lark Deux* will bear seven without difficulty."

The others seemed to take comfort in that, for even Arthur smiled his approval.

Emory was watching Celeste. "The Misses Aventure told us that your mother died on her last ascension. My condolences."

"Thank you," she said, and he could see the light fading

from her eyes. "I cannot believe she is gone. She was a hero to many in France."

He wanted to gather her to him, murmur assurances against those curls. But he had no right—and likely never would.

"She was a hero to everyone," Miss Aventure agreed. "Still, it is a shame we must leave before the masquerade. I've always wanted to attend one at the palace. Can you imagine dancing through the night with a handsome count?" She fluttered her lashes in Emory's direction.

Celeste shifted, blocking his view of her friend.

"He might not be a count," her practical sister said. "How would you know with the mask?"

Celeste went still, then blinked. Her smile brightened the courtyard, banishing the chill he'd felt. She seized Miss Amélie's hands and swung her in a circle, skirts belling. "Amélie, you are a genius!"

"Yes," her friend acknowledged as they came to a stop. "Why do you remark on it now?"

"The masquerade," Celeste said, beckoning the others closer. "Don't you see? Everyone will be masked. It will be the perfect time to enter the palace and rescue Marcel. As soon as we have him, we will return to the school and leave France behind, keeping this marvelous air ship out of Napoleon's clutches."

CHAPTER 18

To Arthur's way of thinking, it was better to have a dangerous plan than none at all. And better still to have Loveday's agreement. She chimed in with her own assent as soon as he nodded his approval of Celeste's idea to rescue the imprisoned aeronaut. He, of course, had no business attempting any kind of rescue of a French man he did not know. But the coolness of Loveday's greeting today—she'd shown more emotion when he'd reported that the horse Guillaume had been accepted with joy by Louen and his wife for their farm—and his own disgust at his inability to contribute to the repair of *Lark Deux* combined to make him feel a little reckless. He had determined to make himself useful in the way he knew best—the gathering of intelligence.

"Are you certain?" Emory murmured when he told him what he intended. "Should I accompany you? You cannot mean to take on the Emperor's capital alone."

"It is the only way I can do so," Arthur said. "You aeronauts and engineers have your work cut out for you here. I will leave you to it, and find a way to add to our knowledge of what is going on."

Emory appeared unwilling to ask him how exactly he planned to do so, which suited Arthur. If his friend were questioned, it was better he knew nothing of Arthur's activities.

"Let Loveday and Celeste know, will you?"

Emory promised to do so. "They won't like it."

Arthur knew that. He didn't like it, either, but needs must where the devil drove.

So, over the next day or two, and in consultation with Josie, who possessed a disturbing knowledge of the less savory neighborhoods of Paris, he cast a wide net—in the public houses of the Pigalle, on the docks and warehouses of the districts downstream, even the boatmen poling people across the Seine behind Notre Dame for a few centimes. And gradually a whisper here, a friend of a friend there, a conversation overheard somewhere else began to sketch in the outline of a map in his mind.

A map that led him late on Friday to the very outskirts of Paris, where he could see the fields in the distance as he climbed down from the back of a farmer's empty hay wagon. But close at hand, on a tributary of the river where warehouses had been constructed to store food and vegetables intended for the tables of Paris, was his destination.

He did his best to slouch and keep his eyes down. To behave not like the heir to Gwynn Place, but a man who might once have been prosperous, but was now down on his luck. Goodness knew he looked it, his clothes showing the wear and tear of living in the rough. Past the warehouses and docks, downstream a little, lay his goal.

It didn't look much like a manufactory—it looked more like a greenhouse, if a greenhouse possessed panes of isinglass tinted blue. Which confirmed that his information, paid for with a mug of ale and an hour of increasingly impatient listening to the man's yarns, had been correct.

He had purposely timed his visit to arrive just after sunset, when there might be fewer people about, but there would still be enough light to see. It also meant, as he tried the doors on the river side and a window or two, that the place was locked up tight. He slid along the side of the building, beneath the row of tinted windows, then stretched up to see what he might see. But the panes were too rippled, and the color seemed to be used not only for creating blue lights in fields, but for ensuring the curious were none the wiser.

Still, he knew from living on an estate with a number of tenant farms that there was always one place where evidence went once it was no longer useful. And sure enough, a little farther along, there was a pit. He settled in the shelter of a clump of tall mulleins to look into the refuse. What information could he glean here?

Perhaps Loveday or Emory could have made sense of the scrap metal, the broken wheels, and a set of gears within a larger metal wheel that might have been some attempt at a mechanical transport. It looked as though a small explosion had sprung the gears and melted some of them. Bits of paper blew about like dried petals in the wind off the river, catching in the sticky leaves of the mulleins. He captured a few of them, squinting in the fading light. Here were what seemed to be pages torn from a journal like the ones Loveday and Celeste used. Like the one that even now was still concealed behind the mantel in his chamber at home. His French, while fairly fluent, had improved in leaps and bounds since they had been here. Still, in the poor light he could not decipher the jumbled partial diagrams. He stuffed the scraps in his pocket. Perhaps Loveday could make sense of them.

Scattered over the ground were more metal parts, only smaller than the heavier ones that had come to rest in the bottom of the pit—pieces as small as the palm of his hand, or the size of coins, made of brass, tin, and copper. Glancing about, he gathered up a few, and as he did, he saw something in the soft dirt. He dislodged it and brought up an array of tubes and coils about the size of a loaf of bread. It appeared to have been struck with a pipe, if the row of dents was any indication.

Where had he seen something like this?

And then he had it. In Barnabas Pendragon's cabin, aboard the smuggler's brigantine, moments before the squall had hit. Moments before he'd been thrown into the sea and the ship had gone down with its captain and most of its crew. Barnabas had referred to the device as Old Job's Pisky—the latest model built by Zephaniah Job, the smugglers' banker and a talented inventor. The Pisky—like the sprite that made people mazed in the head, or crazy—had been designed to maze the navigation of the *sous-marins*. Arthur had dearly wanted to write to the War Office after his rescue to inform them of it, but in honor he could not. He was sworn to secrecy.

Had the French seized one instead, and taken countermeasures?

The evening star twinkled out in the deep blue sky over the distant hills, rimmed with a final glow of light. It reminded him of other celestial bodies, manmade and much closer to hand. What if—

He drew a long breath.

What if the French had indeed captured one of Job's devices, and worked out its functioning? Of course its purpose was not to maze their own *sous-marins*, but what if it was to do the opposite? What if it was to guide the unmanned balloons? Is that what was really being built in this manufactory?

"Hey!" The shout froze him in place. "You there! What are you doing?"

Arthur tucked the damaged array under his coat and dashed along the side of the building to the river, where his choices were the nearest dock or a tall fence.

"Hey! Stop!"

He was trapped. Footsteps were coming from both sides now. The river chuckled below, moving fast on its journey toward the Seine, a few miles away through the meadows.

Arthur took a deep breath, clutched his battered prize to himself, and leaped.

WINTZEN SEEMED ODDLY content to have Celeste and Loveday visit l'Ecole on Thursday and Friday, but the bodyguard was not amused when they returned Friday afternoon on velocipedes. Loveday had reassembled the one that had been in the hamper. Now Wintzen eyed the iron frames as if they were snakes with fangs extended. "You rode here on such a thing?" she demanded.

Celeste leaned her iron steed against a rack holding colorful bolts of silk. "We borrowed them from l'École. They are swift and sure, and they require no feeding. Or winding," she added, thinking about the clocks and *automoutons*.

"And anyone you passed on the roads might have taken a swing at you." Wintzen shook her head. "Will you have no care for your safety?"

As if to ensure as much, she doubled her efforts, as though her goal was never to give Celeste an opportunity to breathe again. If Celeste moved from the desk to the worktable, Wintzen followed. She insisted that they remain in the palace on Saturday, and she inspected Loveday's work as if expecting to find plans to blow up the place. She refused to give Celeste and Loveday a moment together Saturday evening, going so far as to wait while Loveday helped Celeste change for bed and then escorting Loveday to the room they shared.

On Sunday, after a highly elaborate worship service with the Emperor and his court, Celeste kept her bodyguard busy long enough for Loveday to escape to the school. As if to get even, Wintzen stood so close to Celeste's left shoulder at the desk that she had trouble composing her note to Madame Finett about masquerade costumes for seven people. Wintzen even grabbed and read each order Celeste placed for silk, cedar, and copper.

"I do not see how these orders could be a danger to me," Celeste complained as her bodyguard took the next letter out of her hand before the ink was dry. "I see no need for you to read them."

Wintzen let the letter fall on the stack growing upon the corner of the desk. "I am memorizing the names of the vendors, to be certain I know who may be coming to the office. Is all this for the air ship that flew into Paris?"

She should have known her bodyguard would not have

forgotten that. As Wintzen walked over to the plans on Loveday's worktable, Celeste rose to join her.

"You should keep this design from prying eyes," Wintzen said, gaze roaming over the drawings.

This was no *Lark Deux,* but the ironclad vessel that could not fly. Still, Wintzen was right. Celeste reached for the edge of the paper, then paused. She had come to respect Loveday's orderly mind. Even at home, she was likely to store her designs in the same place, the same way, each time. With Wintzen breathing down her neck, she would not have left her designs so scattered.

"Did you touch this?" she asked her bodyguard.

Wintzen crossed her arms over her chest as if to hide her fingers. "No. Why?"

"It's been moved." She readjusted the paper, and a pencil rolled off the worktable to clack against the floor. "And look here, you can see the indent of other markings, like a shadow."

"Someone has copied it," Wintzen growled. "Careless spies."

Celeste stiffened. "But how? We've been here all day. The main door is locked when we are out, and I never heard the alarm sound on the secret door."

In answer, Wintzen stalked to that door. Only then did Celeste realize the *boîte d'alerte* was missing entirely from its place inside the workshop.

Wintzen wrenched open the door. With light streaming down the tunnel from the office, it was easy to see that the passage was empty.

The bodyguard bent, and when she turned, she held pieces of porcelain in her hands. A long lead dangled down.

"Smashed," she said, extending the pieces toward Celeste. "It never stood a chance."

The box was indeed a mangled mess, as if it had been struck repeatedly with a hammer. The lock Loveday had built had clearly been breached, the door opened, and the evidence left in the servants' corridor. A shiver tiptoed up the back of her neck.

"Roll the barrel of lifting gas back in place for now," she told Wintzen. "We'll find another way to secure the door when Aimée returns. Until then, I am keeping these plans at my side."

"And I will remain watchful," Wintzen promised.

They would all have to remain watchful. Someone else knew of Loveday's false design. The moment a real engineer looked at it, he would know they had been deceived.

And would come to find out why.

CHAPTER 19

When Loveday arrived at l'Ecole on Sunday on the velocipede, having escaped the Tuileries, she felt like an air ship that had been loosed from its mooring ropes and found a measure of freedom in the sky. She would never complain about Mama and Papa's insistence on propriety again. Compared to the prison that the palace had become, she and Ros and Gwen were almost as independent as men. They could go where they wished in each other's company. She had her little cane whiskey in which to make calls. And no one ever told her that she had to walk half a mile to fetch breakfast—and practically at dawn to boot.

She leaned the velocipede against the wall inside the door and found Amélie and Josie in the courtyard, rigging a silly little basket shaped like a scallop shell to its brightly colored envelope. The balloon for Celeste's ascension on Wednesday. It looked like a lady's lapdog next to the sleek dignity of *Lark Deux*. How was it even possible to pilot such a thing with only paddles and a single rudder?

With a smile, Josie knotted a rope and said, "Your friend *le capitaine* and Monsieur Thorndyke are in the workroom, Loveday. I believe they have some questions that only you can answer."

She thanked them and hurried through to the workroom, puzzled. The people with the answers to engineering or aeronautical questions were already here.

"Loveday." Arthur's tense features relaxed into a smile as she stepped through the doorway. "We were beginning to worry."

"It is maddening, not to be able to call one's life one's own," she said, untying the wide grosgrain ribbons of her straw bonnet. "Wintzen has adhered to us as tightly as a teazel, and there was no shaking her off until now."

"Has something happened to make her increase her watchfulness?" Emory asked.

"Some plot is always afoot, it seems. But the strangest thing has nothing to do with Wintzen. It is the disappearance of these court officials. Has Celeste told you?"

The gentlemen nodded. "I suspect that Wintzen's caution increases with every whisper of speculation in the corridors lest Celeste be next."

"I confess that her greater vigilance gives me relief, if nothing else," Emory said.

"It is not you under her thumb," Loveday reminded him. "But let us speak of more congenial things. Josie says you have questions for me?"

Arthur nodded and indicated a sorry heap of scrap metal and trash on the worktable. "What do you make of this?"

Arthur would never make light of her mind, nor sport with her, so he must be perfectly serious. Still, she approached the table with no small amount of skepticism.

Until she looked closely at the pieces of paper, which looked as though they had been torn from a journal much like Celeste's original one, which had been found washed up on the beach below Gwynn Place. Here, too, the paper had had a soaking. It seemed to be a callout for a spring mechanism. And this was a bit of a paragraph that seemed to describe a brass casing. A third was a list of parts, the paper torn down the middle to leave the words incomplete.

"How very odd," she murmured, turning them over. "The hand is very neat. Old-fashioned. And look—this word?" Arthur leaned in to read it, and she caught the scent of cedar and clean cotton. Belatedly, she realized someone must have found him a new shirt to replace the one in which he had spent the last week.

"*Guidage*," Arthur read aloud. "*De guidage*. Of guidance?"

"It is not a common word in this context," she said. "More often, such as on the rolls of plans created by Madame Blanchard, one sees the other word. *Diriger*. To steer."

"Guidance," Emory said. "As in a system of guidance, such as the beacons with the pulse of sound we discovered at St Malo?"

"I wonder." Loveday gazed at the scraps, which someone had thrown away. "Was someone unhappy with his work? Were these torn up in frustration? Or destroyed by another who did not want them found? Where were they?"

"In the rubbish pit behind a manufactory where the Seine flows into Paris. They are hardly readable—I was discovered and had to swim a good distance using only one arm."

She looked up from the table in sudden alarm. "One arm? Were you injured?"

Arthur laughed. "No indeed. I was ferrying that oddity there and did not want it to go to the bottom of the river."

Oddity was right. She turned her attention to what seemed to be a damaged array. Tubes, gears, and bent clockwork, to say nothing of a line of dents that made it look as though it had been clubbed with a crowbar.

"What about this made you risk your life to bring it here?" she finally asked.

"I have seen something like it before," he said. "Have you ever heard of Old Job's Pisky?"

Loveday flashed a smile. "If I have, will you promise not to tell Papa?"

"My lips are sealed," he said, and in spite of herself, her gaze dropped to his mouth.

Goodness. How very forward.

She blinked her attention back to the damaged mechanism. "I only heard Thomas Trevithick talk about it once. He is an honest man, but even he is not above the acquisition of a fine French brandy. Apparently Zephaniah Job once asked for his assistance with a device that could confuse the—"

She stopped as a sudden thought struck, and the three of them stared at one another.

"Confuse the guidance mechanisms of the *sous-marins*," Emory finished. "I've heard of the device as well. Arthur and I believe that there is a system of beacon lamps running between Paris and the coast to guide unmanned balloons, using a similar mechanism."

Loveday's mind leaped past disabled *sous-marins* and straight to the matter at hand. "A version of Old Job's Pisky? To confuse the mechanisms of… what?"

"Not to confuse them," Arthur said. "The opposite. And I

think they succeeded. Emory and I saw them in operation, over St Malo. The lamp in the ground sent some kind of sound or pulse, and the balloons corrected their course, heading for the next one."

"Preparations for an invasion seem to have begun, even without the companies of aeronauts Napoleon wants," Emory said. "We think these unmanned balloons and the *sous-marins* are massing on the coast, and they will cross with one of the beacons aboard each *sous-marin*, to guide the balloon across the water."

Loveday could hardly take it in. Unmanned craft? Was it possible? "Who could build such a thing?" Her mind was only half in the room, the other half being somewhere in the skies over the Channel. She picked up several bent gears and examined them. Then her attention sharpened and she came back to earth. "I have seen work like this before."

She collected the wheels and gears, their construction delicate but strong, the cogs precise in shape. The stamp in the center, of a circlet of beads and a pair of compasses.

"The *automoutons* at the palace—the little cleaning sheep. And the *boîtes d'alerte*—the boxes that alert people to their appointments," she translated for Emory. "They all have this kind of construction inside. Made by—" She looked up. "Made by Monsieur Patenaude, the Emperor's Grand Inventor. Who is at present missing."

"Perhaps not," Arthur said, gazing at the parts. "Perhaps he has been ordered to work at the Emperor's manufactory, on something so secret that no one may know where he is."

IT TOOK SOME DOING, but Celeste managed to convince Wintzen to fetch the dinner trays that night after Loveday had returned from the school. She wanted to talk to Loveday about what she and Wintzen had discovered, and the light in her friend's eyes told Celeste that Loveday had her own news to share. The moment her bodyguard was out the door, Celeste leaned her back against the portal and looked to Loveday.

"*Vite!* She will return soon. I must tell you about the plans."

"And I must tell you about what Arthur discovered," Loveday countered.

A few moments later, when all was revealed in concise, breathless sentences, they stopped and stared at each other.

"Someone else knows about our new plans," Loveday said. "And may already be creating their own prototype to match."

"Not so quickly, I think," Celeste said, her mind leaping ahead. "There are only so many suppliers, and the requests of the Chief Air Minister must be honored first. At least, I hope my position still holds that much weight. And I have hidden the plans for the false ship in your wardrobe for now. Even false, there are enough advancements on those plans that Napoleon will want them."

"I'll take them with me to the school for safekeeping," Loveday promised. "Before I leave tomorrow, I'll also see about a better alarm for the secret door."

Celeste nodded. "*Merci.* When I think someone might be standing a few feet away, watching my every move..." She shuddered.

Loveday laid a hand on her shoulder. "Not much longer. With any luck, we'll be away on Wednesday night."

She could only pray.

Wintzen returned then, frowning at them both as if she suspected they had been plotting treason in her absence. But that frown was nothing to the way she scowled at La Croix the next morning when he came with the first of the weekly reports Celeste had requested.

"So you are ordering supplies and considering options," Celeste summarized when he'd ground to a halt like a badly sprung clock, his gaze continually darting between her and Wintzen. "Remarkably little progress if you intend to launch by the Emperor's birthday celebration."

In two days.

He raised his chin. "We are moving along as planned. And what of the school? Is all in readiness for our new pilots?"

She had walked into that snare easily enough. "It will be soon," Celeste promised.

He emboldened himself to take a step closer to her desk. "Perhaps I should see it for myself. So I know how many recruits to seek."

"No need," she said, rising. "I can tell you that we have a dozen beds for male students and another dozen for female. Just see that you find pilots. Dismissed."

He bowed and left. The slump of his shoulders gave her comfort that she had revealed nothing of use to him. A shame she could also say the same for him. How cordially they were concealing everything important from one another!

"I will visit the school this morning," she told Wintzen as the door closed behind her captain. "I hired some of my mother's former students to help prepare it for attendance again, and, given Captain La Croix's concerns, I would like to see how they fare."

Wintzen prowled closer. "Your assistant has already gone to the school. She can give you a report when she returns."

All at once, her patience fled. "You are impeding my work."

"I am keeping you safe," Wintzen countered.

"Do you dare imply that your work is more important to our glorious Emperor than mine?" Celeste demanded.

Napoleon's name, like her mother's, rarely failed to bring instant obedience. But Wintzen merely narrowed her eyes. "Yes."

"Then you are mistaken," Celeste said, turning for the door. "The Emperor cares nothing for my life, so long as I bring him closer to his plans. To do that, I must visit the school." She went to the other velocipede waiting beside the rack.

Wintzen positioned herself in front of the main door. "I will accompany you, then. We can take a carriage."

Oh, but she was maddening! The bodyguard would never be content to remain outside, and, given her unknown allegiances, she could not be allowed to see the air ship. But perhaps there was another way around her edicts.

Celeste leaned the velocipede back against the rack. "Very well. We can call upon Madame Finett and have you fitted for your masquerade costume."

That at least gave Wintzen pause, for she took a step away from Celeste. "I need no costume."

"I must attend the masquerade," Celeste informed her as she advanced. "If you are intent on protecting me, you will have to attend as well."

"I will attend," Wintzen allowed. "But I will not dress up."

"It might help you blend in," Celeste suggested, "and give you an advantage over my adversaries."

Her bodyguard appeared to accept that, for she made no more protests as Celeste sent for a carriage. Until it was ready, she might as well keep busy. Accordingly, she delivered the names of the retinue that would accompany her to the masquerade to the Chief Court Minister personally. His own battalion of assistants and clerks protested. It helped that Wintzen stood beside her, glowering at them all. They were reluctantly shown into his gilded office, where a bronze bust of the Emperor watched all proceedings.

A wizened man with fingers likely cramped from dealing with so much paper, the Minister peered up at Celeste through thick-lensed spectacles from behind his cluttered desk.

"So many?" he complained. "Most list only a husband or wife and perhaps a grown child."

"Would my mother do less?" Celeste demanded, chin up. The bust of Napoleon rotated on its clockwork gears in her direction as if giving his approval.

The Chief Court Minister sighed, picked up a seal, and stamped her list. "I will have the invitations delivered to your office, Chief Air Minister."

There were moments when being *La Blanchard* had its benefits.

Her mother's name continued to have its effect at the modiste's as well. Madame Finett was understandably busy with costumes for anyone at court who could pay her outrageous fees. The seven other costumes Celeste had written of were out of the question, but she would find a spare moment to create something *magnifique* for Celeste.

"As we did when your *chère maman* was alive, yes?" she said with a sad sniff.

"Yes," Celeste agreed. "And of course, the court will be agog at your wondrous creations."

She smiled like a cat set among the pigeons. "There is that."

"And I think you must help me with the others," Celeste said, smiling winsomely.

There, the modiste balked. "*Non, non*, Chief Air Minister. You cannot expect so much of me on such a schedule. I have already overworked my staff with your wardrobe!"

"They need not be your best work," Celeste commiserated. "They are for my staff, after all. And we will need masks as well."

Madame Finett resorted to smelling salts.

"Perhaps," her assistant Marie put in with a hesitant smile as her mistress attempted to recover her wits, "we could use some of the older costumes that have been returned—altered to fit, of course."

Madame Finett rolled her eyes skyward as if hoping to see *La Blanchard* ready to swoop down and save her. "I suppose we must do what we can for the Emperor."

"*Bon,*" Celeste said. "You have my measurements and those of my assistant. Please measure my bodyguard now. If you will allow me the use of your seamstress's tape, I will endeavor to gather the rest."

Madame Finett did not appear pleased with the idea, but Marie volunteered to instruct Celeste in the art. Celeste could only breathe a sigh of relief. Amélie and Josie would likely fare well at the modiste's, but they were far too busy working on the air ship to be spared. And how would Arthur and Emory manage? The captain was fluent in French, but that aristocratic manner was difficult to hide. Emory wouldn't have been able to understand more than a few words. And Marcel was in no position to be fitted.

"Length from the neck to the waist," Marie instructed, handing Celeste a line of string on which knots had been made. "From the hip to the ankle and from the shoulder to the wrist. Then around the waist and around the chest. That should give me enough to go on."

Celeste thanked her, and she and Wintzen rode the remaining distance to the school. Now came the most difficult part of her plan today.

Wintzen knew an air ship had been brought to Paris. How was Celeste to prevent her bodyguard from seeing those who had flown in it?

$\mathcal{C}$eleste rushed into the courtyard at l'Ecole. "Hurry! Wintzen is just outside. We must hide the captain and Monsieur Thorndyke!"

It had been the flimsiest of excuses. Celeste had pointed out that anyone might sneak in through one of the windows on the ground floor, and her bodyguard had set off on a circuit of the building to be sure none of the windows had been tampered with. But at her cry, all Celeste's friends jumped into action. In a moment, Loveday and Arthur were hidden behind the air ship, and Emory, Celeste, and Josie were rolling shut the doors from the workshop to the central courtyard.

"Go!" Celeste urged him when only a few feet remained of the opening. He must have decided his clothes could use an airing, for he wore the baggy trousers and loose smock shirt Marcel had often donned while working. In fact, those looked very like her friend's wardrobe.

He must have borrowed some of Marcel's stubbornness as well. "No," Emory said. "Not until I know you are safe."

Her heart squeezed. "Then stay away from Wintzen. She will know you for an *Anglais*."

He nodded and shoved the door closed with a final thud.

When Wintzen entered a few moments later, there was nothing to see except Amélie and Josie industriously sweeping the floor while Emory stacked bolts of newly delivered silk into bins.

That didn't stop the bodyguard from prowling around the space, peering into every corner, and poking at every rack. Celeste left her quizzing Amélie about the safety of ascensions to take Josie aside.

"I know you are busy checking the silk for any small holes," she murmured as she drew out the knotted string and offered it to her, "but can you make another measuring tape just like this?"

Josie took it with a frown. "A seamstress's measure? *Certainement*. I have one very like this."

"We need one exactly like this," Celeste told her. "You and the others must be measured for your masquerade costumes. I thought I would measure some, and Loveday can measure the others."

Josie cast a look toward the big doors as if she could see Loveday on the other side. "Mademoiselle Penhale is very wise when it comes to gears and calculations. I am not sure how well she fares with fabric. I will make the measure and use it on her, Amélie, and *Capitaine* Trevelyan. I can estimate Marcel. My sister can measure me. You measure Monsieur Thorndyke."

An *automouton* set up capering inside Celeste at her friend's knowing smile. She shook off the feeling. While Josie duplicated the measure, Celeste went to retrieve a journal and pencil from her own laboratory at the back of the space. They had been so busy the last few days, she hadn't had a moment to visit before now.

Everything was as she had left it when she'd abandoned it for England months ago. Perhaps Josie and Amélie hadn't had the heart to clean out the room. The last journal she had used right before the trip was still lying on the scarred worktable. She opened it and thumbed back to the last entry.

But the words were not in her handwriting.

She is gone, our beautiful daughter, and it is all my fault. Oh, Jean, what a miserable mother I have turned out to be. She wanted only to follow you, and now she has.

Celeste pressed her hand to her mouth to hold back a sob. Poor *Maman*, thinking she was alone. Celeste should never have left. She should have stayed—tried to find another way.

But there had been no other way.

She knew that. The Emperor had made it clear that her family would be punished if her mother did not give him his cherished invasion. Celeste had only been trying to help. She hadn't known she'd be leaving everything and everyone behind, forever.

She drew in a deep breath as she turned to a fresh page. She still had a chance to do something that would have made her parents proud. She must focus on the task at hand.

When she came out of the laboratory, Josie offered her a length of measuring cord with a wink. Shaking her head, Celeste went to where Emory was now polishing a bit of brass with a rag, trying hard not to look as if he were watching Wintzen's every move.

"Come help me with this basket, Third Year," she commanded in French, beckoning with one hand so he would understand. He followed her around the stack of baskets until they were out of sight of her bodyguard.

"I need to measure you for your costume," she explained in English.

"I see." He looked disappointed for some reason. "Measure away. Though I must warn you that my father's tailor has complained of the numbers often enough. It seems I have unusually long legs."

Drawn to her attention, they did seem long. Though the rough trousers hid their form, she knew them to be nicely shaped, too, from the time he had dressed for the Midsummer Ball. Celeste forced her gaze back to his. "Turn around, if you please."

She placed her journal and pencil on the gunwale of one of the thicker baskets, then set the measure at the base of his collar and let it hang.

"What are these?" he murmured as she worked, as if noticing their surroundings for the first time.

She glanced at the whimsical shapes as she came around him to measure his arms. "My mother used these for her ascensions." She nodded to the one that had been crafted to look like half of an eggshell. "She hated that one. The Emperor asked her to wear feathers, so she would look like a chick."

Emory frowned. "I understood your mother was highly regarded."

"She still is," she said, being careful to measure his legs on the outside. "But as she fell from favor, she was forced to agree to whatever whim possessed Napoleon. I have not been put in such a position. Yet."

As she straightened from peering at his ankles, she found the room unaccountably warm. Surely they were saving the coal for the steam engine, not a fire.

"I cannot like your being so close to him," he murmured. "He's a madman."

"He's the Emperor," she informed him. "He's allowed to do whatever pleases him."

"What arrogance."

His face had settled into harsh lines. Strange that she and Loveday had once thought Emory arrogant. Now she knew it was not self-centered ambition, but the hope of making a difference that drove him. Thanks to their work, his father's mine was producing again, not only tin but lifting gas for the Prince.

Lifting gas that could carry England's air ships into France and end this war, once and for all.

"Let us not talk of the Emperor," she said, offering him her best smile. She craned her neck to see into the workroom, where Wintzen was now interrogating Josie, as if she thought the measuring cord might somehow be used as a garrote. She might have a few more moments with Emory.

"You have seen firsthand, now, what it takes to fly and repair an air ship," she said, pulling back. "I have not had time to talk to you of it. What do you think?"

His smile lifted, and she could have floated right up with it. "I could grow accustomed to being in the skies." His smile faded. "But I fear my future lies underground."

"In Wheal Thorne," she surmised. "But all is well there, *non?*"

"Quite well, for now. My father, however, likes to remind me that his days of running the mine are numbered. He expects me to take over."

Celeste wrinkled her nose. "What a waste of an engineer. Have one of your sisters take over. Henrietta seems born to the task."

His brows rose so high they nearly climbed into his sandy hair. "A woman, running a tin mine?"

Celeste put her hands on her hips. "Surely you have realized by now that a woman can be many things."

He chuckled. "With you standing there looking as if you're ready to take up arms, I'd be a fool to disagree."

"And you will never be a fool," she said, dropping her hands. "Just give it some thought. I believe you will find your sisters receptive to the idea of having control of their future. Now, I must finish."

"Allow me," he said, and he took the measure to wrap it around his waist. Celeste noted the number he reported. When she looked up, she found him struggling to pull the measure up under his arms.

"I do not think I can accomplish this alone," he confessed.

Swallowing, Celeste went to adjust the cord.

She had never been so close to him, even when they had danced at the Midsummer Ball. Her head was pressed nearly against his chest as she reached around him to level the cord. She could sense the rise and fall as he breathed, feel the warmth radiating out of him. Glancing up, she found his lips oh so close to hers. If he bent just a little…

As if he realized it as well, something lit in his eyes. Celeste stilled, waiting, hoping.

"*Fini,*" Josie announced, joining them. "Do you have

Monsieur Thorndyke's numbers? I will measure Loveday and *Capitaine* Trevelyan and deliver the numbers to Madame Finett. That is who you are using, *oui?*"

Celeste found her breath and stepped back with a nod. Her fingers shook, but she managed to write in her journal and hand the book to Josie. Emory coiled the measure and offered it to her friend as well. It was all very aboveboard and proper.

As Josie bustled off, Emory moved closer once more and lowered his head to whisper in her ear. "I hope you will save me one of your waltzes at the masquerade. You just held me in your arms. I should like to return the favor."

Before she could answer, Wintzen stalked up to them. "Is this student bothering you, Chief Air Minister?" she growled.

Celeste stepped back, even as Emory stiffened. "No. I was instructing him on his choice of basket. Something larger, then, Third Year."

Emory must have understood the command in her voice, if nothing else, for he managed a bow and turned to go. Wintzen stepped aside to allow him to pass, but she watched him all the way across the workshop.

"I do not trust that one," she said. "He is too old to be a student."

"We must take our recruits where we find them," Celeste said.

Wintzen shook her head as if she was not convinced. "We should return to the palace. Your assistant will return soon."

Not soon enough for her, but much as she would have liked to help her friends at the school, the best she could do at the moment was to take her bodyguard away. So, she would go.

Even if her heart bid her to stay.

D o you think she will carry us all to England?" Arthur's voice was low, though now that Celeste and Wintzen had gone, there was no danger in their speaking. The walls of the courtyard were thick, and Josie, Emory, and Amélie were in the workroom, laying out the silk on the trestles for the little vessel that would carry Celeste in her ascension.

"I think so." Loveday laid a hand on *Lark Deux*'s sleek side. "The gas bags are sound—do you smell lavender?"

"Not unless you are wearing scent," he said with a smile.

"Not I. I should frighten Celeste too badly if I did. Both of us associate the scent with lifting gas now. *Leaking* lifting gas."

"I smell nothing." He gazed upward, where the corset had been repaired. "The envelope will be stretched over it tomorrow?"

"Yes, and then it will be ready for the day following." A whirl of butterflies took up residence in her stomach. "Can it be possible that in two days' time we could be home?"

"Please God it may be so. And then?"

She turned to him. "What do you mean? Then you and Emory submit your reports to the Prince, and wait for him to agree that we should win his prize."

With a smile, he said, "I am learning how single-minded you are."

"It is a failing," she confessed. "Mama wishes I could be single-minded about ladylike accomplishments, like painting in watercolors, or playing the pianoforte."

"But then you would not be you, and we should not be here, attempting to foil the Emperor's plot against England."

"We would not be here if I had not fallen in with your reckless challenges," she retorted. "We might be foiling plots from the safety of Cornwall."

"And that, I am afraid, is one of my failings. It is an advantage in the heat of battle, but at home, or aboard experimental air ships, I must temper it with sense. But you have not answered me."

She had not forgotten. She simply didn't know how to reply. "I cannot see into the future, Arthur, even with a far-scope," she said. "If we do not win the prize, then I suppose life goes on as before. If we do, then perhaps Celeste and I will have the means to build *Lark Trois*."

"Will you need to, if the plans are sent to the War Office and the Prince orders a fleet constructed?"

"But what if air ships are not only for the use of the War Office? What if they can be used in place of the Royal Mail, or even in place of coaches so that ordinary people may travel?"

"Perhaps such a vision lies far in the future," he suggested. "I was thinking merely of next week. Or Michaelmas."

She had to laugh at herself. "There I go again. Single-minded."

"Thinking of next week—or Michaelmas—keeps my spirits up," he said.

Above them, twilight was gathering in the skies. She ought to leave soon, before the lamps came on, while she could still see to pilot the velocipede.

"Thinking of calling upon you, or of dancing with you properly at the Harvest Ball, keeps my spirits up as well." His voice had become softer. "Do you think of that also?"

"I do," she allowed. "Though thinking of home sometimes makes me weep. It is better, don't you think, to think through our escape instead?"

He was silent, as though she had somehow disappointed him. Then he said, "On the battlefield, I spent many a sleepless night planning how to keep my men safe. I suppose you are right. It is nearly dark, Loveday. I think you ought to be going. There are unsavory characters about on the streets."

"I have my velocipede," she assured him. "Its speed will outstrip that of any footpad."

He touched her cheek. "I know. But for my sake, be careful. I will look forward to seeing you in the morning."

As she boarded the velocipede and sped away down the Rue des Aéronautes, she could swear she still felt that warm touch upon her skin. What a featherhead she was, with all her talk of the War Office and the future. Talking around his question as though dancing a quadrille, instead of answering it.

Oh, why had she not simply said, *Yes, Arthur, I would be delighted to have you call, and I would dance every dance with you at the Harvest Ball and shock all the sticklers in the neighborhood without a thought.*

It was no wonder that poor Mama despaired of her. She

was perfectly capable of speaking up when it came to mechanics. Arthur had proved himself an able and congenial companion-at-arms. He was handsome and the heir to Gwynn Place. She trusted him. Why could she not simply say what she felt?

Gritting her teeth at herself, she came out of her exasperated thoughts to realize she must slow down, for a carriage pulled by two horses seemed to be disabled in the middle of the Rue des Pénitents. Two men were standing at the rear looking at the wheel, but it did not look from here to be badly damaged. She must maneuver around them.

The sound of an engine came from behind her. Goodness, how had that steam wagon come so close—she would be run into the back of the carriage—

A narrow lane opened just to her left and she put a foot down and spun the velocipede just enough to dive into it. To her enormous irritation, it ended not at the next street, but in the blank wall of a house. Well, the wagon must be past by now. She spun her mount again and headed up to the Rue des Pénitents.

Four men stepped into the mouth of the alley, blocking her exit.

"Out of the way!" she shouted and leaned into her trajectory so they would know she meant business.

They did not move. She was too close—

One of them grabbed her—

The velocipede went spinning past them and died on the pavement.

"Let go of me!" She kicked and slapped and even bit but got only a mouthful of wool for her pains. Her stomach was loose with fear, her mind blank of everything but escape—and the certain knowledge that somehow Toussaint was behind this, and she would be tortured to reveal what she knew of Celeste.

"Is this the one?" her captor panted.

"*Oui,*" said the man who had picked up the velocipede. "*L'Anglaise.* Shut her up before someone hears."

L'Anglaise?

Her captor swung her into the carriage, the other tossed in the velocipede after her as though it weighed nothing and climbed in as well. Her captor clouted her across the temple, and as the horses were galvanized into motion, her mind seemed to spiral away.

Her last thought as she struggled against the dark was the terrifying realization that they had called her *L'Anglaise.* Not *La Suisse*—the Swiss woman.

They knew. And in a flash, she knew why. She must have written something in English on the false plans.

She would not be questioned. Or even tortured. She would be executed as a spy.

CELESTE SET TO work as soon as she reached the office in the palace. She had more letters to write, and not even Wintzen could make her go to dinner in the *Salle des Fonctionnaires* until they were completed. A smile threatened as she pulled a piece of pressed paper toward her. At Hale House, Mrs Penhale had been so careful of each sheet of paper. Here, Celeste could have covered the walls had she so desired. She sharpened her quill and began to write.

Wintzen craned her neck. "What do you order now? Are you not going to dinner?"

"Nothing that need concern you," Celeste said. "And no, not until I finish."

"Everything you do concerns me," Wintzen countered. She held out her hand. "Give it to me."

Celeste had an almost irresistible desire to clutch the letter to her chest and stick out her tongue at the woman. Instead, she put on her haughtiest look. "You are my bodyguard, not my emperor. Go find me a footman so I can see that these are delivered."

Wintzen glared at her.

Celeste glared back.

Wintzen flounced out the door and slammed it behind her so hard the maps on the bookcases trembled.

But that didn't stop her from reading the top address as Celeste handed the footman a stack of letters.

"The battery at Le Tréport?" she asked. "Why are you writing to the shore defenses?"

Celeste waved the footman out the door before answering. "They must be alerted before the Emperor's air ship armada can pass safely. We wouldn't want to fire on our own craft, would we?"

Wintzen frowned. "Are we truly so ready to fly, then?"

"We will be," Celeste said, thinking of the air ship waiting at the school. "And I am taking no chances that an air ship goes down before it reaches England."

"Very wise," her bodyguard said, face clearing. "But is it France's air ships or the one you're building in the school that concerns you?"

Celeste stared at her bodyguard. Wintzen's arms were

crossed under her bosom, as usual, but her head was cocked as if she were deciding which method to use to throttle her.

"Why would you ask such a question?" Celeste asked, stalling for time. Clearly something had given her away. What had she said? What had she done? How could she counter it?

Wintzen held up one finger, then went to open the secret door and peer down the dim passage. Whatever she saw must have satisfied her, for she shut that door with a nod.

"Empty," she said. "For now." She turned to face Celeste, motioning her closer.

Against her better judgement, Celeste joined her beside the racks, where they were both out of sight of the windows.

"Dupont sent me," she whispered.

Celeste reared back. "Dupont!"

"Shh!" Wintzen cautioned, finger once more at her lips. "Forgive me for not telling you sooner, but I wasn't sure I could trust you. Your Emperor ordered Dupont to the front, as if she were no better than a piece of coal to be fed to his behemoths. She escaped by dead of night and brought her knowledge of flying to us."

Celeste was utterly bereft of speech.

Of course her former governess and companion had known about flying. Like Celeste, she had followed Sophie and Jean-Pierre Blanchard all over Europe as they demonstrated their abilities. She had not only been Celeste's confidante, but her mother's as well, after her father's death.

"You are a member of the Karlsruhe Confederacy," Celeste whispered in realization. "The army of the Prussian and Bavarian states fighting on the eastern front."

Wintzen nodded. "Dupont suspected your *liebe Mutter* had

been killed to prevent her from telling Napoleon what she knew."

"And what did she know?" Celeste all but begged.

Wintzen shrugged. "She only told Dupont she was concerned for the safety of France. Perhaps if she had known you were alive…"

A great many things might have been different. Celeste sighed. "Is Dupont aware they have blamed Marcel for my mother's death?"

"*Ja*. I send reports every week. I was originally ordered to watch the Emperor, but being assigned to you was an unexpected benefit."

"Not much of a benefit," Celeste said. "You've seen how La Croix and Toussaint have me caged."

"Caged… if you were trying to rebuild the Aeronautical Corps," Wintzen said. "But you are not."

The statement was as much command as fact.

"I am not," Celeste agreed. "But I wish I knew what La Croix and Toussaint were doing."

The bodyguard held up her hand again, then tipped her head toward the racks. Was that a noise from the secret passage?

Wintzen grabbed the door and threw it open. An *automouton* trotted into the room and set to work on the wainscoting.

"*Dummes Schaf,*" she muttered, shutting the door behind it. She turned to Celeste. "I can tell you a little of what your captains plan. They have sent air ships to the front. The vile things pin us down. They spy on our every move. Worse, they drop little explosives that cause much damage and death."

Celeste shivered. "Even my mother's."

"We must stop them," Wintzen said with far more faith than Celeste felt at the moment. "They are inhuman, these pilots. They just keep flying, as if nothing else matters."

"Nothing else *does* matter, in the sky," Celeste said. "My father taught me that. The rush, the exhilaration, it can be a drug." She glanced to the piles of reports on one corner of her desk. "And yet Toussaint tells me they have few pilots and can find no others. Who are these men and women who are plaguing you?"

"I wish I knew," Wintzen said. "But more, I wish we had a way to stop them."

She and Loveday were trying to do just that. Another ally was always welcome.

"There may be a way," Celeste said. "If you had your own, more superior air ships."

"You could do this?" Wintzen asked, eyes widening.

Celeste waved toward Loveday's now empty worktable. "You've seen the false plans. Perhaps fortunately, so have others. But if you help us, it will take only a few changes to make them real. Any engineer will be able to use them."

Once more Wintzen cocked her head, but Celeste could no longer see the gesture as a threat. "What would you have me do?"

Even though she knew they were alone, Celeste lowered her voice. "I came here with three *Anglais* in a new air ship. We were fired upon and have been repairing the ship at l'Ecole. Now we plan to rescue Marcel and escape France. That's why so many are coming with me to the masquerade. Amélie and Josie, who you met at the school, will stay with my balloon until I make my ascension so that no one can tamper with it. Monsieur Thorndyke, the Third Year you did not trust, will accompany me to the ball to protect me."

She bristled. "*I* protect you."

"When we planned this, I did not know you were working with Dupont," Celeste reminded her. "I feared you were in La Croix's pocket. Now I have a better role for you. When all eyes are on me and my ascent, you will accompany Loveday and a gentleman who is helping us to retrieve Marcel. Amélie, Josie, and Monsieur Thorndyke will join you once you are outside. They will return to the school, where I will bring the balloon down in the courtyard. We fly out just before dawn, when everyone is sleeping off the celebration, and you can take the plans to the Confederacy."

Laid out like that, it sounded so simple. Yet a dozen things could go wrong at every turn. As if just as tormented by the thought, the *automouton* let out a squeak of protesting gears.

Wintzen looked ready to do it violence.

"It's stuck again," Celeste explained, bending to free the little automaton from the crack in the doorway.

A doorway that had been soundly closed only a few moments ago.

She yanked open the door just as the light at the end snuffed out.

She whirled. "Someone was here, listening to us."

"I will discover whom," Wintzen promised. "Do not leave this room until I return for you. And if I don't return before the dinner bell sounds, run for the school and don't look back."

CHAPTER 22

Celeste barely had time to pace the length of the racks and back, avoiding the industrious *automouton* in the process, before the secret door swung open, and La Croix stumbled into the room. She stiffened, until Wintzen emerged behind him, hand clamped on the back of his neck like a vise.

"This rat was scampering down the passage," she announced, giving him a shake. "What would you like me to do with it? Drowning? Poison? I can arrange for either."

Celeste tried not to gape. Surely her bodyguard was only trying to frighten the captain. If the whitening of his face was any indication, the gambit was working.

But Celeste had another idea. "By no means," she told her bodyguard. "We must make our guest welcome. Have a seat, *mon capitaine.*"

He had enough of his wits about him that he could yank himself out of Wintzen's grip and make a show of sauntering to the desk and seating himself in Celeste's chair.

The insolence!

"I will tell you nothing," he said, glowering.

Celeste made a moue as she pulled up another chair in front of him. "Because you know nothing. I determined that the moment I met you."

His face flamed. "I know enough to keep you from triumphing."

"Do you?" She leaned back as if she couldn't care less. "Because you were spying on me."

"But of course. Everyone spies on everyone in the Emperor's court."

Wintzen gave her a look as if to say, *I told you so.*

"So I have heard," Celeste allowed. "But I think you discovered more than you bargained for, *non?*"

He glanced at Wintzen as if concerned what she might do if he told the truth, then leaned toward Celeste across the desk and lowered his voice. "You hope to leave France. I will help you, if you help me."

Whatever she had been expecting, it was not that. "What?"

"I will help you," he repeated as if her time in the skies had damaged her hearing. "Toussaint must be stopped. He's mad."

Once more she exchanged glances with Wintzen. Her bodyguard cuffed the captain on the shoulder. "Explain," she demanded.

He winced. "Always he has been ambitious. He wanted your mother's position, but the Emperor favored her. When he received the plans for the air ship, he saw the opportunity to prevail."

"Then my mother did give them to him?" Celeste asked, still trying to fathom how her mother had laid her hands on the plans she and Loveday had developed in the tack room at Hale House.

"That is the story Toussaint told when pressed, to the

point that *La Blanchard* questioned him about it. In truth, they came from one of the Emperor's spies in *Cornouaille*."

Celeste put a hand to her stomach, which had just done an acrobatic roll. "The Emperor has a spy in Cornwall?"

La Croix snorted. "The Emperor has spies everywhere."

Apparently so, if he could be bothered with Hale House and a small estate in the Cornish countryside. But no, it would not have been Loveday's home that drew the spy. Arthur Trevelyan and his work for the War Office, perhaps? Or the advances of the steam works in Truro? What she and Loveday had designed would have been an unexpected benefit.

She and Loveday must employ all their powers to find the spy when they returned. Between one moment and the next, it had become an international imperative.

"And so Toussaint sought to profit from these plans," Celeste said, bringing them back to the case in point.

"Worse," he said, eyes haunted. "Toussaint believes he can build an air ship armada, with pilots loyal to him alone. Then he can not only win the war, but overthrow Napoleon and rule the world."

She stared at him.

"Where are these air ships?" Wintzen demanded, hand once more going to the back of his neck. "How many do you have?"

"I don't know!" He struggled in vain to avoid her. "I thought you might have guessed. I was hoping for something, anything, to counter his schemes. You cannot want France under his thumb."

"I cannot want France under anyone's thumb," Celeste informed him. "But I will not allow France to dominate the rest of the world, either. Think, Captain La Croix. Toussaint must have said something that would give us a clue as to where the machines are being constructed." Then a memory flashed in her mind. "Cherbourg. He said a few were being manufactured in Cherbourg. Is that true? Only a few?"

"*Non,*" La Croix said. "Nearly all come from there. But the most important part—the brain, if you will—is being made separately, for safety. Somewhere close to Paris," he insisted. "And he has the Grand Inventor there to help."

Just as when she climbed above the skyline in her balloon, the vista opened before her, and Celeste knew what they must do.

"Wintzen, we are going to the school, and we are taking Captain La Croix with us. I know someone who will know how we can destroy these air ships—or their brains—before any more of them launch. My mother's explosives were dangerous enough to cost her her life. Let's see what other damage we can do with them."

"ARE you certain she is all right?"

"She looks terribly pale. That will be a bruise by morning."

"Who is she?"

Loveday could hear. That was a good sign. But her eyelids felt so heavy it was impossible to move them.

"I think she is coming around." A man's voice.

"Mademoiselle?" An older woman. Loveday smelled the scent of face powder. Good. That was two of her senses working properly.

She felt as though she were swimming up from the sea

floor at home. Past the rocks, past the carpets of mussels, to the wavering light at the surface.

"La, the poor one. What do they want from her, I wonder?" An older man. "So young—what possible use can she be to them?"

"Do not ask that," the woman said. "Look, she is awake."

Loveday's eyes fluttered open even as she checked that her fingers and toes still worked. "Who are you?" she whispered.

Three anxious, middle-aged faces hovered over her.

"I am Hortense Tisserand," the woman said. "Until recently, seamstress to the Aeronautical Corps. With me are Monsieur Patenaude, the Emperor's Grand Inventor, and Monsieur Cadran, formerly the Clerk of the Clocks at the palace."

"But you are all missing," Loveday said, then wished she hadn't.

"Who has said this?" Monsieur Cadran asked as Madame Tisserand helped her sit up. She had been laid on a pallet in a room that contained nothing else but a table and three chairs, a bowl and ewer, and a chamber pot.

"Everyone is talking of it," Loveday said. "In whispers. Many are afraid they will be next. Is the Minister of Public Works here, too?"

"*Non,*" Monsieur Cadran said, his gaze falling. "Not after he created *Le Guidance.* Once they had what they wanted from him, his drawings were destroyed, and he was executed."

Le Guidance. The lamps with the pulse of sound. Loveday moistened dry lips. "Are you confined in here?"

"*Oui,*" Monsieur Patenaude said. "The Emperor requires our skills. And our silence. My poor sister probably thinks me dead."

"And my wife," Monsieur Cadran said sadly. He was a slender man with a kind face and old-fashioned curls that must be natural, for they were filthy yet still held their shape.

"I have no husband now, but my sisters and my assistants are likely beside themselves," Madame Tisserand said. "But mademoiselle, who are you?"

"I am Aimée Jourdamour," she said. "I came through the lines with Celeste Blanchard when her prototype balloon went down in Switzerland."

Madame Tisserand gazed at her. "If you are *une Suisse*, then I am an automaton," she said bluntly. "We are all prisoners here. We have no secrets one from the other. Now, I will ask again. Who are you?"

Perhaps it was time to do away with the pretense and begin living as herself.

"My name is Loveday Penhale," she said at last. "I flew here from Cornwall, in England, with Celeste Blanchard in the air ship we designed together. You see, Celeste succeeded in achieving *La Blanchard*'s ambition. She flew from Paris to England four months ago."

Monsieur Cadran drew in a breath, his eyes huge.

"She lived with my family and together we built our ship. The air ship that Napoleon dearly wants in order to begin his invasion of my country."

"So you are a spy, then," Monsieur Patenaude said. "What a pity."

"Certainly not," Loveday told them with some heat. "Our landing here was an accident. We came too close and were shot down near St Malo. We were never supposed to be here at all, and now Celeste has become Chief Air Minister and is supposed to make an ascension in two days' time, and I very much fear that Toussaint and La Croix will murder her the way they murdered *La Blanchard.*"

At this end of this recitation Loveday had to stop to take a breath.

"Sophie Blanchard was one of my dearest friends," Madame Tisserand said quietly. "They told us it was an accident. That the balloon had caught fire."

Loveday shook her head. "I do not know how they did it, but it was no accident. Celeste's return has put a crimp in their plans… whatever those are."

"Which I suppose brings us to why we are here, my dear," Monsieur Patenaude said.

"Why should three of Napoleon's most highly regarded officers be in a locked room?" Loveday asked, looking about her. "Where are we?"

"In a tiny village called Medrun, on the outskirts of Paris, where Napoleon is manufacturing parts for his *automatons volants.* His automaton pilots, for the new air ships."

"The new air ships." The ones Arthur and Emory had seen flying to the coast. "The ones being built in Cherbourg?"

"You are very well informed concerning state secrets," Monsieur Cadran said, his eyes narrowing slightly.

"I am assistant to the Chief Air Minister. Toussaint let it slip one day. But tell me—are these the ones using that system you mentioned—*Le Guidance?* Did the late Minister work out the functioning of the device that confuses the navigation of the *sous-marins?*"

Monsieur Patenaude's eyes nearly fell from his head. "Now I see why you have been imprisoned with us. Even for the Chief Air Minister's assistant, you are far better informed than it is safe to be. Does she know as much as you?"

"More, probably, by now," Loveday said bluntly. "But is it so?"

"All you have said, yes," Monsieur Patenaude told her. "The automatons pilot the ships according to a path laid on the ground—*Le Guidance*. Some call it the *feux de piste*."

Trail of fire. That made sense. In a way. If she had been designing such a project, she would have made the pilots self-guiding—

"But there is more to it," said the Clerk of the Clocks. "The *sous-marins* are being fitted with *Le Guidance* so that the automaton pilots may be steered across the Channel."

"So we surmised," Loveday said softly. "And are they to drop bombs on the unsuspecting population?"

"*Oui*," he said, chilling her with his bluntness. "The *sous-marins* will also ferry troops, and other balloons with live pilots will carry soldiers. In the confusion the enemy will be unable to defend itself."

"The enemy," Loveday said. "My family. My neighbors. For of course Cornwall will be a target, lying so close."

"No indeed," Madame Tisserand said. "They will begin with Portsmouth, then move north and east until they reach London. Once the south has fallen and been occupied, the rest of the country will follow."

Loveday felt sick. "And you are assisting with this effort, madame? Sewing silk for envelopes for the automaton piloted ships?"

"I assist because if I do not, I will become more intimate than I like with Madame Guillotine," she said with dignity. "Were it up to me, I should serve the Corps happily in its efforts to provide help to the injured, or to explore new parts of the world in these air ships. I am not a supporter of

Napoleon as I was in the beginning. Before I saw what he has become."

"He is mad to conquer, and he has infected others with his madness," Monsieur Patenaude said. "But we are helpless in the matter. We must create our devices that go in the heads of the automatons, that respond to the *feux de piste*. The most technical and difficult of the many parts of the whole."

"Your wonderful devices are being corrupted," Madame Tisserand said, laying a gentle hand on his arm. "Degraded. As are the men and women who follow Napoleon without question."

"Degraded and helpless," repeated Monsieur Cadran, his shoulders slumping.

"You are not," Loveday told them. Cautiously, she got to her feet and found that her head no longer swam. Her limbs did not tremble. "What you are is locked in."

She marched to the door, pulling a hairpin from what was left of her chignon. In less than a minute, the lock clicked open in response to her persuasions, and she opened the door just a crack.

One or two lamps burned in the warehouse, enough to reveal that it was divided by a series of workbenches where clearly the prisoners were assembling the automaton brains and sewing envelopes and gas bags. Celeste would swoon if she could see the number of bolts of silk, stacked high enough to tilt. There was only one door, and it was set into a larger pair where a wagon or steam vehicle could come in and be loaded. Beside it were crates, dozens of them, stacked up higher than her head. Clearly a wagon was expected to collect the finished brains in the very near future.

Near the benches were a table and chairs. Four soldiers in

the blue uniforms of the army laughed and joked amid the remains of their meal. Two of them had been in the coach with her, and one of them had left her with this bruise on her temple. A pack of cards waited, and set upon a barrel of lifting gas was a bottle whose graceful shape likely contained brandy.

"We cannot get out," Monsieur Cadran said as she closed the door quietly and rejoined them, pulling up her hair and repinning it as best she could. "They never leave. The shift is changed every four hours, so they are always fresh and alert."

"They will not be so alert once they finish that bottle of brandy," Loveday pointed out.

Madame Tisserand snorted. "Four soldiers of the army?"

"What about the lifting gas?" Loveday said.

"What about it?" Monsieur Patenaude said. "Do you suggest we come up behind them and hit them on the head with it? It would take two of us to lift one barrel and we would never get across the floor without being shot."

Clearly her companions were not aeronauts.

"Have you never breached a barrel of lifting gas?" she asked.

Three heads shook in the negative.

"Do you know its characteristics?"

"What are you getting at, mademoiselle?" Monsieur Cadran was clearly not used to being the least knowledgeable person in the room.

"Simply this." Loveday joined them on the pallet, kneeling so she might lean in and speak softly. "Lifting gas renders a person unconscious. If they breathe in too much over too long a period—say, an hour—death can result. We simply breach two barrels of it and wait."

"What about us?" Madame Tisserand said in horror. "You do not mean to kill us all, do you?"

"Certainly not," Loveday said. "We remain in here with the door closed. When the soldiers are rendered unconscious, we cover our noses and mouths, and drag them some distance away."

"Why?" Monsieur Patenaude wanted to know. "Why not leave them and flee? We can steal one of the boats at the docks."

"Because that leaves all the automaton brains in all those crates still available to Napoleon," she said. "We can take your drawings and schematics, but we must set fire to the warehouse and destroy everything else."

"All our lovely devices," said Monsieur Patenaude. He sounded almost sad.

Loveday could hardly blame him.

CHAPTER 23

rthur hadn't been sure what to make of the woman who was Celeste's bodyguard when she and Celeste had barreled into the school that evening, but *Gardien* Wintzen proved to be surprisingly resourceful, and the uniform of the palace guard impressively persuasive. Within moments of their leaving l'Ecole, where Captain La Croix remained in the custody of Celeste and the Aventure sisters, the bodyguard, Arthur, and Emory were tucked up in a *fiacre*, the little carriage hired for two hours in the middle of the night. In their pockets were enough of *La Blanchard*'s explosives to blow up the warehouse sleeping by the river.

"I hope you are right, Monsieur," Wintzen said to him, "and Mademoiselle Jourdamour is where you suspect her to be."

So did Arthur. As the *fiacre* bowled along the lamplit avenues, which eventually became streets, which soon became the familiar gravel roads on the outskirts of town, white in the scant light of the waning moon, his certainty flagged more and more. What if he were in error? What if she were even now in the dungeons of the Tuileries, injured or worse? What if—

"There." Emory pointed. "Are those the buildings you spoke of?"

He must leave off his dreadful imaginings and deal with the matter at hand. "Yes. The one a little way downriver. The supplies for the automatons come by boat, to the docks, so that they are barely noticed."

After Wintzen paid the driver of the *fiacre* and he departed, Arthur waited until the sound of the horse's hooves faded into the night. Then he led his companions along the route he had taken before, until they reached the river side and could hear the water lapping at the pilings of the docks.

"We must first—" Wintzen began, when Arthur clamped a hand upon her shoulder for silence.

"We have company," he whispered. They ducked into the paltry shelter of the willows growing on the bank.

The door to the warehouse creaked open, and someone held up a lamp. Two figures struggled out, carrying what appeared to be a soldier. He was bareheaded, and his arms hung down lifelessly.

And then the figure holding the lamp raised it. The face was swathed in fabric—a petticoat?—but he would recognize that golden hair anywhere. Arthur sucked in a breath and smelled the scent of lavender. A wave of relief the size of the combers on the beach at home swamped him.

"Loveday!"

The lantern lowered a trifle. "Who is there?" came muffled through the fabric.

"Arthur, Emory, and *Gardien* Wintzen," he said. Why was

she not being more cautious? "What has happened? Are you all right?"

"Perfectly," she said. "We are escaping. Come and help get these soldiers to safety before we set the warehouse afire."

Emory chuckled. "We might have known. It appears she is none the worse for her ordeal. Come. Let us do as we are bid."

While Wintzen exclaimed over the presence of the missing dignitaries of the court, he and Emory and the two older gentlemen wrestled the unconscious soldiers into one of the flat-bottomed punts so common on these waterways. He had stolen one himself the other night when he'd come ashore, and floated nearly all the way to Notre Dame before abandoning it and making his way to l'Ecole with the damaged Pisky. They untied it and sent it on its way downriver with its sleeping burden, then joined Loveday and her two female companions on the bank in front of the warehouse.

"Madame Tisserand and I have collected all the sets of plans we could find," Loveday said, raising her lantern so that Arthur could see the rolls of paper in the woman's arms. He could also see the dark bruise on her temple.

"Loveday, you are hurt," he exclaimed. "Who did that to you?" His hands tingled with the urge to strike the miscreant who dared to touch her.

"You just sent him downriver," she said. "But never mind that, we have not much time before the next watch arrives." In a few brief sentences, she told them what her three companions had shared with her, so clearly that he could see where all their speculations fit. "You are saying that dozens of these automaton brains are at this moment inside?" he repeated incredulously.

"Stacked in crates, ready to be loaded on wagons," she said, nodding. "We must set this place afire without further loss of time."

"I think we can go one better than that," Emory said.

"We brought a number of *La Blanchard*'s explosives," Wintzen told them. "They have quite short fuses, however. Placing them will be very dangerous."

Arthur's gaze met that of Loveday, glimmering in the lamplight. "I have some experience with explosives," he said to Wintzen, though his eyes did not leave Loveday's. "I can plant them."

Distress filled Loveday's face, and a measure of pleading. "You must not go inside," she told him. "The building is full of lifting gas."

"Then here is what we will do," he said, thinking as quickly as though he were on the battlefield again. Which, he supposed, he was. "We must all get in the boats and get as far downriver as we can in the minute or so before the explosives ignite. We will meet at the landing at the bottom of the garden of Notre Dame."

"My companions and I cannot go into the city," Monsieur Patenaude said, shaking his head. "We will be blamed for tonight and executed once it is discovered our bodies are not in the wreckage." He looked at Madame Tisserand and Monsieur Cadran. "I have a cousin in the Marais who will take us in tonight and keep his mouth shut in the morning. Then we will quietly disappear."

Madame Tisserand nodded. "I can go to an old friend in Provence."

"And I to my son's house in Grenoble," Monsier Cadran said. He offered his hand to Loveday. "Promise me you and your friends will be safe. *La Blanchard* in particular."

"I promise," she said, and there was not a person on the bank who did not believe her. *"Bonne chance."*

Monsieur Patenaude's gaze had not left Wintzen's face. "I have an old school friend in Brussels," he said. "He winds the clocks in all the churches. I believe my Flemish is still up to the journey, and… perhaps we may meet again under happier circumstances."

Unaccountably, visible even in the uncertain lamplight, the redoubtable Wintzen blushed scarlet. "Perhaps we may," she croaked.

In the distance, Arthur caught sight of a lamp, and his quick ears the tread of boots marching in perfect step on gravel. "We have no time to lose. The guard will change shortly. Quickly—to the boats."

Emory hustled the three officials into a punt—Monsieur Cadran seized the pole and pushed off. Then he and Wintzen climbed into another. Loveday handed Arthur her lantern and scrambled into the third to wait for him.

From the lantern's flame, Arthur lit the fuses of four of the explosives and yanked open the door of the warehouse. He lofted them inside as hard as he could, slammed shut the door and scrambled down the bank. Loveday already had the pole in hand, and his knee gave out just as he stepped into the punt. He collapsed in a heap while she steadied the little craft and poled it out into the current.

In moments they were a hundred yards downstream. He got his feet under him, cursing, and lifted his head. "I can take over if you—"

With a *crump!* like a cannonball striking a behemoth, the warehouse exploded, sending up a writhing tower of flame into the night.

And three little punts hurried away on the current, unnoticed by anyone as they disappeared around a curve of the river into darkness.

IN ANY OTHER CIRCUMSTANCES, Celeste would have spent part of the evening marveling at the differences her friends had made on the air ship. The hole in the gas bag had been patched with sheets of treated canvas, both bags filled with lifting gas, and the main ropes replaced with thicker strands to accommodate the greater weight. Amélie reported that stores of coal and water had been replenished as well, and she had included some provisions for the journey. All that remained was to finish stretching the envelope over the corset.

"So much silk to be such an appalling color," Josie said, watching the ripple of the material across the trestles. "With the additions of what we had here, it is more than we had ever imagined."

Celeste tugged the envelope back into place for the third time in as many minutes.

Amélie frowned from where she sat beside a trussed-up La Croix. "Did you find a wrinkle?"

"*Non,*" Josie surmised with a smile. "She is worried about Mademoiselle Penhale and Monsieur Thorndyke."

Celeste smoothed her hand over the material. "I am worried about them all. What if this one is lying?" She tipped her chin toward the captain.

"I have told you all I know," La Croix said in an injured tone. "You should have let me go with them."

"You should have told me sooner," Celeste countered. "Then perhaps I might have learned to trust you by now."

He grimaced and shifted on the chair as much as his bound arms would allow. "And I did not know whether to trust you. Your mother said you had died trying to cross the Channel, but you claimed to have gone down in Switzerland. And now I find you have thrown in with the *Anglais* and the Karlsruhe Confederacy. And you fear to trust *me?*" He rolled his eyes.

From somewhere in the distance came a hollow boom followed by several bangs. The sound pushed her to her feet.

"They have destroyed the manufactory," Amélie said as if commenting on the weather.

"They will be fine," Josie assured Celeste, reaching out a hand in support. "They are very clever."

"Sometimes," Celeste said, thinking of her father, "clever is not enough."

"When is that?" Amélie asked with a puzzled frown.

Josie rose from her seat beside the trestles. "They will return soon. What will you do with him?"

La Croix glanced between them, then began shifting again, as if he saw something on their faces that boded no good for him. "I am your ally. I will obey your least command."

"Bon," Celeste said. "Then here is one. Make sure Toussaint has no more copies of the design for the newest air ship." While it was a false and wildly expensive design, it still contained enough advancements to be valuable to the Emperor.

His head bobbed in a nod. "At once, as soon as you free me."

"We will wait for Wintzen," Celeste said, watching him. "She will accompany you."

He did not so much as wilt. Was that a good thing, or was he so confident he could overcome the highly trained woman?

The ensuing hour saw the completion of the stretching of the envelope, and the stretching of Celeste's nerves to the breaking point.

And then, as the churches rang three of the clock, the back door rattled. She and her friends spun. Celeste's heart jumped as she spied Emory, along with Loveday, Arthur, and Wintzen. All limbs were intact; no one limped. Indeed, except for the wrinkles and stains on Loveday's gown, they might have been out strolling down the Champs-Élysées together.

And then she spotted the bruise on Loveday's temple. She rushed forward to meet them. "You are safe! What happened? Are you hurt?"

Loveday accepted Celeste's hug. "I am not hurt. I had the matter in hand, but help was appreciated." She pulled back to explain what had happened at the manufactory. Celeste heard enough to know they had found the Grand Inventor and the others who had gone missing and rescued them before destroying the devices. She moved to Emory's side. She could see he was unharmed. There was no need to confirm it. Yet she reached out to take his hand and hold it tightly.

He did not pull away.

"Then they are gone, the automaton controls for the air ships?" La Croix put in when Loveday had finished.

She frowned. "What is he doing here?"

"Helping us," Celeste said. "As much as he is able. He is going to make sure Toussaint has no more copies of your latest plans, Loveday. Wintzen, I would like you to accompany him."

"With pleasure," Wintzen said, narrowing her eyes at the fellow.

"I'll just go along as well," Arthur put in.

La Croix bristled.

"I think," Loveday said, "we've had enough spying for one day."

Arthur looked as if he would argue, but he met Loveday's gaze and nodded.

"Can you trust him?" Emory asked Celeste.

"We must," she said. Letting go of his hand was harder than it should have been, but she managed it to go plant herself in front of La Croix.

"Listen to me," Celeste commanded, and his gaze snapped up to hers. "You know our plans. You could betray us to the Emperor, but he would likely ask you questions that would implicate you in my mother's death, at the very least."

He paled. "I am innocent."

"And more than one innocent has gone to Madame Guillotine," Celeste reminded him. "You will say nothing about our plans, to anyone, especially Captain Toussaint. In exchange, I will arrange to exit my position in such a way that no one but you can fill it."

His mouth hung open a moment. Then, "You would do this? What about Toussaint?"

"Leave him to me," Celeste promised. "I know just how to give him the attention he craves."

CHAPTER 24

"I do not think I can bear the waiting." Loveday fidgeted about their apartments in her chemise the next day, practically wearing a path in the soft carpet between the door and the windows. From the window of Celeste's room, she could just see the topmost curve of the balloon for her friend's ascension, striped in brilliant colors.

"For the costumes to be delivered?" Celeste, in her chemise as well, turned and grasped her hand. "Please, my friend, you are making me even more nervous than I am—and I did not think that was possible."

The preparations were all complete, her toylike balloon moored in the gardens between the Tuileries and l'Arc de Triomphe du Carousel, where hundreds of people had gathered already in anticipation, though it was barely sunset.

"No, not the costumes—for this to be over." Loveday reached for calm, but even as she did, the latch to the main door turned, and they both hid themselves behind the door with a frisson of alarm.

It was no assassin. Only Wintzen.

Celeste crossed the room in two strides. "What news?"

Loveday no longer saw the other woman as a Valkyrie—a hawklike gaoler—the enemy. Now she saw her as a woman similar to herself—a stranger in a foreign land, here only to fight for what she believed in. And perhaps to fall in love, just a little, if that exchange on the banks of the river had been any indication. Clearly she and Monsieur Patenaude had noticed each other before.

Wintzen closed the door and locked it. "I have confirmed that no more copies of your plans exist in the palace or the barracks, and particularly in Captain Toussaint's possession," she said rapidly. "But oh, the rage and the fury, my friends!"

"What do you mean?" Celeste clasped her hands as though to still their nervous trembling. "Has the Emperor found us out?"

"No indeed. His Imperial Majesty has been closeted with his couturier all the afternoon and may not be disturbed." She rolled her eyes. "Toussaint was informed about the destruction of the manufactory and the automaton brains. My informant said he was incandescent with rage."

"Oh, I should have liked to see that," Loveday remarked. "What a pity he did not fall into an apoplexy."

"And spoil my surprise?" Celeste flashed a grin over her shoulder, then turned back to Wintzen. "Does he have any information about it at all?"

Wintzen shook her head. "He believes the conflagration to have been caused by an accident with the lifting gas. The four soldiers on duty at the time know nothing, remembering only that their prisoners were locked up tight and they were drinking brandy."

"So we are all dead, then?" Loveday said. That would likely be useful.

"Until the men question how they came to be found in the river. The army will investigate after the Emperor's birthday celebration, but when they do not find any bones—"

"We will be long gone by then," Celeste said. "What else?"

"Only that he plans to call back one of the prototypes from Cherbourg and use it to recreate both brain and ship for his armada." She made a moue of apology. "He says that if a mere girl can design an air ship, then another one of 'these tinkering types' should not be difficult to find."

Loveday was saved from a disdainful retort by a knock on the door and had once more to hide. But this time it really was the costumes—three enormous boxes filled with silk and velvet delights delivered by a footman. Loveday dove into hers and held up the dress it contained.

"A shepherdess," she said with a shake of her head. "Do they expect me to wind the *automoutons?* Ah, well. At least Marie has added pockets."

The poke bonnet with its waving feathers concealed her hair, and the shepherd's crook might do to trip a pursuer in a pinch. But the best part was the mask. If she were to stay dead, then she must conceal her features—and the bruise, which was turning a fine color—behind the velvet half-mask. Celeste even took a pot of rose lip salve and added rouge to it, to color her lips in a violent red pout so that no one might recognize even her mouth.

When they were dressed in all their finery, Celeste looked from one to the other. "Are we ready?"

"I have been ready for what seems like hours," Wintzen grumbled, adjusting the shoulders of her costume.

"But you have an important part to play," Celeste reminded her. "You and Loveday will be saving the life of an innocent man while I distract the entire palace with my ascension."

"You do not need to remind me," Loveday said. "Is the barrel of lifting gas concealed?"

"It is," Wintzen said. "I told them it was brandy, to celebrate the Emperor's birthday, and they were not to breach it until the moment they heard the cannons fire for the ascension."

"*Bon.*" Celeste straightened her back, and the sequins on her costume glittered in a river of fire. "Let us go to the ball."

Loveday would never forget the glittering elegance of the stream of people climbing the vast marble stairs to the *Grande Salle de Bal*. Figures from Greek and Roman history, creatures from myth and legend and literature—there were even a dozen Princesses of Wales, each more rotund and spoiled than the next.

In the ballroom, the orchestra struck up "Flight of the Angels" as Celeste's name was announced, and at the bottom of the steps a host of partners rushed forward to offer their hands, their hearts, their very fortunes if only the so beautiful Chief Air Minister and her lovely attendants would favor them with a turn upon the floor.

Giggling, flirting in a manner that would make her sisters stare had they been there, Loveday could hardly choose among a merman in seafoam green satin, a knight in silver lamé armor, or a man in court dress who insisted he was a Bourbon prince. With a tinkling laugh, she chose the merman, and swam off through the crowd to dance her very first waltz.

~

Celeste watched as the courtier led Loveday off to dance. How wonderful to see her friend appreciated, if only for her charms. The gown of the shepherdess too easily masked that agile mind. But he would learn once she spoke.

She glanced around at her own choices. One was a long-limbed fellow in brown stockinette to which any number of silk leaves had been strategically affixed to make him appear a tree. His rough brown mask hid his face, but that shock of blond hair looked familiar. La Croix, perhaps? He would be doing all he could not to be obvious while attempting to keep an eye on her.

Another was dressed in a long black domino with a round glittering white mask of a smiling moon that gazed down on her benevolently. "How original," he said. "Our Chief Air Minister dresses as one of her staff."

That drawling voice could only come from Toussaint. Celeste ran a hand down the cerulean silk of her fitted jacket, setting the sequins to flashing in the light from the chandeliers. "Few of my staff are fortunate enough to be dressed by Madame Finett. Besides, you forget, sir. I must perform shortly. What did you want me to wear in the air, a hoop skirt and feathers?"

Someone nearby tittered. It might have been the tree.

Another man shoved into their circle, a small gilded mask barely concealing his tiny eyes. The circlet of gold leaves upon his broad head and white gown girded about a stout waist proclaimed him a Roman senator. A shame he had already spilled something on his girth, or perhaps the deep red was meant to be blood.

"Did I hear the dulcet voice of Mademoiselle Blanchard?"

Her voice was in no way dulcet, but she recognized *his*,

and fought the tremor that went through her. *"Non,"* she said. "You mistake me, sir."

"My lord," Toussaint purred with a bow. "There is no mistaking that noble head, that regal mien."

The Comte d'Angeline smoothed back his old-fashioned wig, sending a shower of white powder down onto the marble floor. "Alas, too true. I am always at a disadvantage at such events." He turned once more to Celeste. "But you—how magnificent you look. I have been waiting to hear when we might honor the agreement I reached with your *chère maman.*"

"Agreement?" Celeste said with an airy wave that belied her frantic pulse. "The only agreement I must honor is my commitment to serve our illustrious Emperor."

"Vive la France!" the tree proclaimed.

Definitely La Croix.

"But the Emperor requested this match," the comte reminded her, lips pursing as if he desired to take a bite out of her.

"Before he knew I could give him what he most wants," Celeste said. "The invasion of England. You would not want to interfere with that, surely?"

Did Toussaint tense? The moon seemed higher all of a sudden. Did he think she knew?

The comte cleared his throat. *"Non, non.* Certainly I would not wish to interfere with the Emperor's plans. We will speak more when the war has ended and he is victorious."

Since she intended to make sure the Emperor was never victorious, she merely smiled.

"And when the war is ended," Toussaint put in, "a great many things will change."

Brazen, but it only showed how confident he was in his

ability to overthrow entire governments once he had found others to help him build his nasty toys. Well, he would soon learn his mistake.

Celeste turned to her bodyguard, who was dressed in the white tunic and golden belt of a Greek goddess. "Diana and the moon seem well attuned. Perhaps you two would care to dance."

Toussaint began to demur, but Wintzen stepped up and seized his arm. "I accept." She all but dragged him out on the floor.

The comte puffed out his chest. "You will partner me, Celeste."

"*Non.*" A tall hunter in a green wool jacket and brown hose pushed to her side and took Celeste's arm in a possessive grip.

"Alas," Celeste said over her shoulder. "This dance is spoken for. Perhaps another time." She followed the hunter out onto the floor. "You are learning French," she murmured in English to Emory as he took his place across from her.

"*Non,*" he said again, and Celeste almost giggled.

The orchestra struck up the music. A waltz! Emory's head turned, the feather in his hat waving, as couples began swirling around them.

Celeste stepped closer. "You once offered to teach me to dance. Allow me to teach you instead. Put your hand here." She took his hand and placed it at her waist. "And take my other hand, so. *Parfait!* Now, we move to the count of three. *Voilà.*"

With a bit of pushing and pulling, she showed him the movements. As in many things, he learned quickly. After the first few stanzas, he was moving effortlessly around the room. Oh, but she could wish for the swirl of silk about her legs instead of the sleek leather *pantalons* Madame Finett had contrived. She glanced up from watching his feet to find him gazing down at her through the mask with such tenderness she almost missed her step.

The music faded, until the only beat was the beat of her heart, the only sensation the touch of his hand at her waist. And she had thought flying exhilarating!

Then the song ended, and couples parted. She stood gazing up at him, hand still clasped in his. She was supposed to go somewhere, do something, but nothing seemed more important than this.

All around the palace, the clocks began striking the hour in a din of brass, silver, and gold bells.

The ascension. Their flight to freedom.

"We must go," Celeste told him. "Quickly."

He released her and followed her from the ballroom.

Thousands had by now gathered in the courtyard between the palace and l'Arc de Triomphe du Carousel. More clung to the wrought-iron fence that edged the parade grounds. Their murmuring voices rose into a chaotic chorus as she appeared on the crimson carpet that led from the main entrance of the palace to her balloon. The silk envelope swayed in a rising breeze, like a bubble floating against the massive stone archway. The four soldiers representing the branches of Napoleon's forces at the top of the marble Corinthian columns gazed down at her—infantry, cavalry, navy, and aeronaut. She thought the aeronaut might be smiling.

Emory tugged at her hand, and she stopped to face him.

"Let me come with you."

Over the cheers of the crowd, she could barely hear him,

but her heart leapt all the same. She shook her head. "I cannot. The balloon is only balanced for one."

The torches around the parade ground gilded his smile. "At least you have a sound engineering reason for refusing me."

"And only an engineering reason," she assured him. "When we return to England, we will ascend, just you and I. You will see Cornwall from an entirely different vantage point."

"And you can venture down into the mine, with me," he said. "I guarantee you will never look at lifting gas the same way again."

"It is a promise," Celeste said, giving his hand a squeeze.

In answer, he pulled her closer and kissed her.

The crowd roared its approval, the sound pressing against her and nearly knocking her off her feet. Or maybe it was the kiss.

"Celeste! *Tiens!*"

Though Amélie had appeared beside them, her voice seemed to come from a thousand leagues away. Celeste pulled back. Emory wore the most fatuous smile, as if he had discovered a new source of lifting gas. She could believe it. She felt as if she were floating already.

"I will see you at the school," she told him, then turned to stride for the balloon.

CHAPTER 25

The cannons on the edge of the parade ground boomed to announce Celeste's journey down the red carpet, and Loveday's partner, dressed in an aeronaut's uniform, danced her to the door under the balcony where the servants came and went.

"That, I believe, is our song," Arthur said.

"Where is Wintzen?" she whispered. "We have not a moment to lose."

"She will come," he assured her. "Once she puts La Croix in fear of his life for the second time in two days. I am coming to like that woman."

She had to smile. "I am, too, rather."

He touched the corner of her mouth. "There. I have been wanting to do that for days. No," he corrected himself. "I have been wanting to do *this* for days."

He leaned in and kissed the tiny dimple at the corner of her mouth.

All thought of Wintzen, of the crowd around them,

vanished like a mist in the sun. "Captain," Loveday said breathlessly.

She forgot what was to come after that as he leaned in again and kissed the dimple on the other side.

And when she took a breath to say something intelligent, his lips found hers fully, and she spiraled away into the utter newness of such intimacy. Oh, how soft his mouth was, for such a battle-hardened man. Why had no one ever told her that a man's kiss could feel like this?

Someone cleared their throat and said the name of Celeste's assistant.

In the next instant, a cool breeze fanned her face and she opened her eyes to see Arthur standing stiffly next to her while Wintzen raised an eyebrow.

"You have found a way to occupy yourselves while you waited, I see," she said.

Loveday thought her face might catch fire and ignite her mask, so fiercely did she blush.

"Are we ready?"

"Yes," Arthur said. "That was a kiss for luck."

"I hope it was a powerful one, then."

Loveday bit back the crazy urge to assure her that it was indeed, and instead followed Wintzen through the door and into a servants' corridor.

Ten minutes of turns and stairs made Loveday endlessly thankful that they had someone so familiar with the palace on their side. They emerged at the top of a stone staircase that reeked of lavender. She pulled a handkerchief from her pocket and saw that Arthur already had his pressed to his nose. In the anteroom, the soldiers lay like marionettes with their strings dropped. A brandy glass lay smashed on the flagstones.

Wintzen removed a set of keys from one of them and flew down the passage like the Valkyrie she truly was. In moments Marcel's door was open and he was blinking in the unexpected light. A dreadful smell wafted out, as though the poor man had not even a pot for his convenience, only straw.

His dusky skin had a grey undertone, and his eyes had filled with sudden fear.

"Celeste has sent us," Wintzen told him. "Come. We are setting you free."

Arthur wedged his shoulder under the young man's arm, Wintzen on his other side. Together, they half-carried him up the stairs. As they went, Loveday unlocked all the other cells, filled not with thieves and murderers, Wintzen had told them, but with anyone who had ever opened his mouth in criticism of Napoleon. On his birthday, was it not fitting that they should all be released?

And then she ran up the stairs and out into the cool night, where Arthur was waiting.

"Vive la France!"

The crowd chanted its favorite phrase over and over as Celeste made her final checks, Amélie and Josie confirming.

"Ropes in place and taut," she all but shouted to Amélie. "Basket and envelope secured."

"Ballast bags filled and stowed," Amélie shouted back.

"Explosives and lantern ready," Josie added. "And water, in case."

No one wanted to shout in case of what. Venturing into

the skies was dangerous enough. Carrying the explosives only compounded the risks.

"We are ready." Celeste nodded to her friends, then turned to face the palace. On the second floor, a balcony had been constructed, covered against the elements, holding gilded chairs upholstered in crimson velvet. Already, His Imperial Majesty was coming into view, and the crowd shouted their love even as they changed their chant.

"Vive l'empereur. Vive Napoleon!"

He raised a hand in mock humility.

Others came in behind him. The Empress Marie Louise, the generals who were not out leading troops, a few favored officials, his personal bodyguards. The tree that was La Croix and the moon that was Toussaint.

Celeste curtsied in his direction, and the Emperor inclined his head.

Then she turned to the crowd and raised both hands. Slowly, the cacophony quieted. Faces turned toward her, eager, awed. They remembered her mother's ascensions and expected the same or better. A shame to disappoint them, but, with any luck, the more exciting show would be happening on the Emperor's viewing platform shortly.

"To honor our most glorious Emperor," she shouted, "I ascend into the heavens."

Once more, the roar pushed her, this time toward the balloon. She turned and took hold of the ropes to swing herself into the shell-shaped basket. So small, compared to the basket she'd flown in to England. Which itself had been merely a hamper compared to the air ship she and Loveday had constructed.

An air ship she could only pray would take them safely away from this madness tonight.

She checked the explosives and lantern one more time, confirmed that her package was in place, then nodded to her friends. Amélie and Josie loosed the ropes together, and the vessel rose into the sky to the cheers of the crowd.

Always before, she had been one of the crowd, head tilted back to watch her mother rise. Now she was the one gazing down at the faces, searching for Amélie, Josie.

Emory.

He lifted a hand as if to beg a ride. Soon, she promised herself.

She bent and retrieved the *boîte d'alerte* she'd borrowed from the palace. She wound it twice, then slipped it into the spiderweb she'd constructed for it. Carefully, she tossed it over the side as she passed the viewing platform.

The Emperor caught it, even as his guards converged on him. He waved them off, then removed the material that had allowed it to float down. The sound of its chimes was obscured by the noise, but she could see the slip of paper pop up and the Emperor studying it. The last thing she spied before the roof of the platform cut off her view was the Emperor whirling toward Toussaint, finger pointed to send his guard into action.

It seemed he took a dim view of a would-be minister who thought to usurp his throne.

Celeste smiled, wind brushing her cheeks, as the basket progressed up the arch. The bronze Horses of St Mark at the top looked ready to leap off their plinth and into the basket with her. She counted off the seconds until she topped the stone. Time for her next trick.

Bending, she lifted an explosive ball in one hand and the lantern with the other. A stray breeze set the basket to swaying, but she kept her feet. How had her tiny mother managed this? She'd hated loud noises and crowds. Yet she'd gone up again and again.

"For you, *Maman*, and for Papa," Celeste murmured, pressing the opening of the lantern to the wick of the explosive.

The twine caught, sizzling and sparkling. She waited a moment until it neared the paper shell, then threw the ball as far as she could away from the balloon.

With a bang, the ball burst, sending silver sparks down at the onlookers. She could hear the cheers.

Cautiously, she moved the few steps the basket would allow in the other direction and tossed out another ball. Golden sparks showered down.

She set the lantern back in its holster, where its heat could not affect basket or envelope, and set about working the ropes. A little more to the east, but not too far south, or she might come down in the Seine. Thank the good Lord for a wind from the west tonight. Even in this more primitive balloon, she should have no trouble reaching the school.

Having corrected her course, she sent down a few more explosives to keep up the pretense. Her mother would have done better. Her father would have done best of all. He knew how to make every eye follow him. Tonight, she rather hoped to be a disappointment, so that no eye would bother any longer to follow her—or see where she landed.

She glanced out again, looking for the spire of the Tour St Jacques to give her a better fix on her position. Though the moon was fading to a crescent, something crossed it, growing larger. *Non!* She could not have been so late that Loveday would launch without her.

Fear and frustration mingled inside her. What had happened that the air ship should be in the sky now? Why wasn't it headed to the north?

Why was it bearing down on her?

She could hear the chug of the engine, see the flash of moonlight on the envelope. But that wasn't their air ship. This one was smaller, more like what she and Loveday had originally developed.

And there was a single pilot at the controls. As the craft veered closer, she could see the silhouette—tall, stiff. Once more moonlight flashed, this time on a bald brass dome, and she realized this was one of Toussaint's unmanned craft.

They just keep flying, as if nothing else matters.

Wintzen's words came back to her as the soulless automaton's vessel swung straight at her, its sharp prow aimed at her fragile balloon.

"Halt! Who goes there?"

A guard at the gate stepped forward, taking in the disheveled trio. What a sight they must look—a goddess, a shepherdess, an aeronaut, and a ragged jester in a jingling cap.

Loveday whooped with laughter, and Wintzen turned to stare as though she had gone mad. Loveday staggered like a sailor on shore leave and pointed at the guard.

"You are in cuss—cos—costume too!" And she went into

another gale of laughter. "I want to guard the gates—mus' keep out all the sheep!"

Wintzen laughed a hearty laugh, and the three of them staggered practically into the guard, who stepped out of the way in disgust.

He fanned the air in front of his nose. "You reek of lavender gin. What happened to this one? He stinks of worse than that."

"Too much drink and too many horses in the stable," Arthur snorted with laughter. "Oops. Can't return the costume now."

"You are a disgrace to the Emperor," the guard said with disdain. "Get out of here."

The four of them staggered off, whooping now with real laughter and an almost hysterical relief. They crossed the broad avenue and dove into the shadows of the tall buildings that would give them cover.

Loveday tipped back her head to search the night sky. "Where is she? Has she ascended yet?"

A cheer came from the direction of l'Arc de Triomphe du Carousel, and a spangled shower of sparks fell from the sky like a waterfall.

"There!" Wintzen pointed. "Come, she will overtake us if we do not hurry."

As fast as they could, she and Arthur carried Marcel, his arms looped over their shoulders. Loveday could see that Arthur would not last long at this rate. He was limping already. At a deserted square, she called a halt, panting.

"There she is," Marcel croaked. "But what is that?"

For another shape had appeared, closing in on the position of the silly little scallop shell and its single precious passenger.

Arthur drew in a harsh breath. "That is an unmanned ship. It looks just like the ones we saw massing near St Malo. It is on a direct course." His voice became urgent, and he hauled poor Marcel to his feet. "Come on—we must get to the school and raise *Lark Deux* at once!"

If Celeste rose, the air ship had enough distance that it could counter. She needed to descend, quickly. She reached up and grasped the opening of the great gas bag, pushing on the copper valve on the cap that closed the end. Sucking in a breath and holding it, she opened the valve and let the lifting gas out into the night. When she could hold her breath no longer, she shut the valve and turned to gulp in fresh air.

The air ship chugged past above her, amidst the drifting scent of lavender.

So, this was one of Monsieur Patenaude's grand creations. Small wonder Toussaint wanted to keep them out of the Emperor's sight—and her own. She tugged at the ropes to turn toward the school again, all the while keeping an eye on the air ship.

Slowly, it turned. It was going to come at her again.

She glanced down to check her altitude. She was just over the rooftops of the highest buildings. The denizens of the city had come out onto the squares, roads, and balconies to watch the show.

Oh, that Mademoiselle Blanchard. So like her mother. See how she performs.

See how she dies.

Non. She would not follow *Maman* and Papa down that dark road. There had to be something she could do. The automaton was a machine. What could it know of the vagaries of the wind, the effects of temperature and altitude? She was the daughter of Sophie and Jean-Pierre Blanchard. She had been born to fly.

She grasped the gunwale and studied the terrain. As the night cooled, the city would give off an updraft, but it was too late to catch that thermal. Besides, the sooner she landed, the sooner she could escape the automaton. It would never be able to maneuver among the warren-like streets of Paris.

But neither could her balloon.

Something flashed below, there and gone, in a pattern much like the one smugglers used, or so Marcel had told her. But no one was signaling a smuggler here. They were signaling an automaton, as Emory and Arthur had discovered.

Her head jerked up in time to see the air ship bearing down on her again. Too late to sink. Her only choice was to rise. She leaped to the ballast bags and began heaving them over the edge. She could only pray anyone watching below could find shelter before the bags hit.

The balloon gave a jerk and shot skyward. She had a glimpse of a metal face, staring down toward the ground, before the air ship passed below her.

The light and a pulse signaled the things, Emory had said. Small wonder the *automoutons* were forever heading toward a window or a lamp. And she'd wondered whether they wanted to escape as much as she did!

But she was still rising. Across the silver ribbon of the Seine, the spire of Notre Dame was far below her. She had to be at least five hundred feet up now. If the air ship sent her down, there was no chance of survival.

A light flashed below, and the air ship began to turn again. Who was controlling the devilish thing? Someone in Toussaint's pay, certainly. He would have been so pleased to show himself superior to her.

She could not help her smile as she remembered the look on the Emperor's face as he'd turned toward the captain. Toussaint could well be in the dungeon now. Very likely La Croix would be granted his deepest desire and be named Chief Air Minister by morning.

Still, technical questions crowded her mind. What was the automaton's range of movement? It could turn the craft and rise and descend. Wintzen had said the ones at the eastern front could drop explosives. How close did the signaler or signal have to be to control the device?

The *sous-marins* might lead them over the waves, but if they succeeded in crossing the Channel, what would happen once the automatons reached Britain's shores and released their bombs? Were there spies beyond Cornwall waiting to take control of the skies and of England?

The very thought chilled her. So did her options. She could vent more gas, up to a point, and then she would not be able to stop her descent. She could drop more ballast, including the lantern and the last of the explosives, but if she rose too high, she would either freeze from the cold or pass out from the thin air.

The air ship was coming for her, the automaton oblivious to the death it wielded, obedient only to its guidance system. She had to find a way to defeat it.

She just needed to think.

JOSIE AND AMÉLIE released the last two ropes and flung themselves through the gate in *Lark Deux*'s gunwale. Marcel lay on the bench in the stern, and they joined him as the air ship rose like an eagle spreading its wings. The courtyard—the school—the neighborhood fell away beneath them, and Loveday eyed her gauges.

"Nearly to full steam," she said. "Bring her about and lay a course to the last location we saw Celeste."

"Aye, Captain." Arthur tossed a grin over his shoulder, and he and Emory got to work with the vanes.

As gracefully as any mighty bird with an enormous wingspan, *Lark Deux* came about. "Ah, how very lovely she is," Amélie sighed. "Loveday, permit me to work the firebox?"

"With pleasure," she said. "Josie, are you and Marcel all right?"

"From prison to the skies," Marcel said weakly. "I have never been so well in all my life."

"No more talking," Josie ordered. "Drink this water, and then try some bread and cheese."

"There," Emory said, pointing. "She is just to the west of the river, and that obscenity is still in pursuit."

"We must fly directly over it," Loveday said, "and hope that Celeste does not choose that moment to throw her ballast."

"She cannot see us coming," Emory said. "Her envelope

obscures everything above her. We must watch for our opportunity."

Loveday agreed. "Pressure at full steam," she said. "Let us go take care of this pest and save our friend."

"And if that thing truly is Toussaint's prototype," Arthur said, "I will take great satisfaction in depriving him of it."

Within minutes they had overtaken the pair, and as Celeste's ship swung desperately to the south to evade it, Emory and Arthur brought *Lark Deux* over the automaton, stooping upon it like a hawk.

"Now, Amélie!" Loveday called.

Amélie took an explosive bomb the size of a melon and lit its wick. When the flame reached the paper twist, she tossed it over the side. The automaton ship had an internal corset, but no one seemed to have read the callout in their original plans that specified a certain tension to the fabric. The bomb sank between the ribs of the corset and hung in the envelope like a baby in a hammock.

"Get us away!"

But Emory and Arthur had already put *Lark Deux*'s shoulder to the wind, following Celeste's fleeing course.

The bomb exploded, its shower of sparks meant to entertain instead igniting all those yards of silk. The envelope and its wicker corset went up like a Roman candle, folded into a twist, and the gondola plummeted to the ground with a crash they could hear from the sky.

CELESTE LEANED over the gunwale to watch as the unmanned air ship plunged to the cobblestones, smashing forever the prototype Toussaint had hoped to use. Relief brought air rushing into her lungs.

But there was still the little matter of descending. Her attempts to evade the air ship had driven her closer to the Place de la Bastille. The prison had been demolished during the Revolution, but the Emperor had insisted on commemorating the event by parking one of the earliest behemoths, shaped much like an elephant, in the center. The thing was easily twenty feet tall. Coming down on it would do her balloon no good.

To the south was the Canal St Martin, at least where it exited the tunnels carrying all sorts of interesting things that had been washed down the drains. She shuddered, remembering how the water had claimed her first balloon on the way to England. That wouldn't do, either.

Yet she was coming down. Already the rooftops were closer. The basket bumped a spire, setting it to spinning. She clutched the lines to keep from falling out.

The sound of a steam engine puffing made the hair on her neck rise. Did Toussaint have more than one air ship in Paris? Where was it? She bent to peer under the balloon, looking north, south.

There!

Their own precious *Lark Deux* swung past her, Loveday at the helm, and Amélie, Arthur, and Emory on the gunwales.

Emory threw out a rope. Celeste leaned as far as she could, but the twine slipped through her fingers. The ship passed, turned, came about. This time, it was Arthur who threw. Celeste managed to snatch at the rough strands and hold on tight.

"Tie it to the rigging holding the envelope to the basket,"

Arthur shouted, hands cupped around his mouth. "We can tow you until we can find a spot to set down."

"No good," Celeste shouted back. "Not enough power. I will pull you down, too."

Already, the air ship was slowing as it struggled to bring the balloon along. The massive bag of gas over her little scallop shell was not designed to be towed. It resisted every tug.

The rope in her hands tugged too, and she realized Emory and Arthur were attempting to pull her craft closer. Behind them, she sighted Amélie, Josie, and even poor Marcel standing ready to help as well. She hurriedly tied the rope to the line, as Arthur had instructed. The team on the air ship pulled, and the balloon inched closer, until the two envelopes bumped and set everyone to rocking.

More than ten feet remained between gondola and basket.

Emory and Arthur had a quick conversation. Celeste could not hear the words, but Emory appeared to be shaking his head, and Arthur appeared to be turning red. Loveday shouted something, and they both looked to her, before they turned once more to Celeste.

"There's nothing for it," Emory called.

"Tie the rope around you and jump," Arthur shouted. "We can pull you up."

He could not know what he asked. She'd watched her father plummet to the earth. She had not been there when her mother had gone down, but she could imagine the scene all too well. To leap from the safety of the balloon, knowing only pain and death awaited?

Trusting her friends to save her life?

With shaking fingers, she untied the rope and wrapped it

twice around her waist before securing it with one of her father's best knots. Then she climbed up on the gunwale, feet dangling in midair.

Lord, have mercy on my soul.

She jumped.

CHAPTER 27

Emory felt as if his heart would plummet toward the ground with Celeste. His hands tightened on the rope even as he braced his feet. She must have reached the bottom of the swing, for the air ship lurched to one side with the additional weight. Her balloon sank past as if intent on following her.

"Heave!" Arthur shouted, and they all pulled. Emory was aware of the Misses Aventure at his back. Though he was weak from his ordeal, Mr Delaguard was pulling as well.

"Hold," Arthur said. "Reposition." Hand over hand, he shuffled closer to the gunwale again, and Emory followed suit.

"Heave!"

It took four more sets, but then Arthur nodded to Emory, who surged to the gunwale and reached out to help Celeste climb aboard. She collapsed, weeping, in his arms. Arthur collapsed on the deck.

Emory held her close, eyes closed and thoughts rising in a prayer of thanks. She clung to him, trembling, this woman so fierce even the emperor marveled at her.

He marveled as well.

"Celeste, *tu as réussi*," Miss Amélie Aventure said. *"Tu es formidable."*

Formidable. Yes. The very word for her. And beautiful and amazing and a pearl of great price a man might give anything to hold.

"Anglaise, Amélie," she said, her breath shuddering. "So all our friends will understand."

"I understood," Emory told her. "And I can only agree."

Celeste blushed.

LOVEDAY WASTED NOT AN INSTANT. "Celeste, when you are able, we need a course for Le Tréport. For now, I will clear the city with all speed."

Emory got to his feet, his hands upon Celeste's waist to steady her. "The prototype is down, but the miscreants guiding it are not. They will raise the alarm."

Even though her hands still shook from her leap from the balloon, Celeste took her place at the instruments, and faster than Arthur would have dreamed possible, they had left Paris and all its dangers behind.

"Do you think Wintzen will make it away safely?" Celeste asked, one eye to the sextant.

"I think it a very good possibility that she will find Monsieur Patenaude through his clock-winding friend in Brussels," Loveday replied, taking her eyes off her gauges and her hands from the wheel long enough to watch the darkened countryside slide away below.

Celeste said, "I wish her every good fortune, though a

week ago I should never have believed I could say such a thing."

"How we disliked her!" Loveday said with a laugh.

"We are approaching Le Tréport," Celeste told them. "Be alert, in case they did not receive my letter—which would be a pity, since it was nearly the only legitimate command I sent in my entire tenure as Chief Air Minister."

They sailed over the mighty batteries and the fortress as harmlessly as if they had been a gull—or an unmanned balloon.

"Well done, Celeste," Marcel said as the rippling expanse of the English Channel opened up before them.

"Set course north and west," Arthur said with a laugh that even to himself sounded like three parts relief.

Loveday shook her finger at him. "What have I told you about giving orders aboard our ship?" she said with what he hoped was mock sternness. "Celeste, ignore him and set a course north and easterly. We are going to Kent."

"Kent!" Emory swung about from the vane controls. "What on earth for?"

"Because Marcel's brother runs his smuggling vessel in and out of the marshes. Marcel told us as we escaped the palace that Etienne would offer him, Josie, and Amélie shelter aboard his ship. We must see to their safety once we are in England, for their lives will be at risk there as much as ever ours were in Paris."

Emory glanced at Arthur, who nodded. "Right, then. North and easterly it is."

With the course set and the vanes locked in position for the next hour or so, Emory joined Celeste in the stern as she talked softly with her friends. Arthur could not fault her for wanting the waning hours of their journey together to be spent in conversation with people she clearly loved. Making plans. Expressing hope that they would be together again.

His gaze returned to Loveday as she walked the few steps forward that would bring her next to him and keep the vessel in trim. He gazed out over the starboard gunwale, where France lay far behind in the darkness.

"You cannot be missing it already," she said, smiling.

"I do not miss it at all," he said in the kind of tone that normally would end a conversation. But his gaze met hers. "I was just thinking. Of what we accomplished, and what Napoleon will do now that he knows the enemy he has been clasping to his bosom."

Loveday made a face, as though wiping the image these words produced from her mind's eye. "We will do all in our power to make certain he does not find Celeste. Though I confess I am worried about the spy that La Croix told Celeste was still concealed in Cornwall. That person clearly stole our first set of plans and had no difficulty getting them into France for Toussaint, war or no war. They may have other talents as well."

Arthur nodded. "My first priority is to locate that person and render him or her powerless."

His tone was grim, and Loveday seemed to shiver in the cool stream of air.

"We will assist in any way we can—after we have won the Prince's prize," she said.

"You are very confident." Then he grinned. "As you should be. Nothing I have ever seen can best *Lark Deux*. She is a wonder and full of endless potential. Just like you." He felt as he had when he had dared to kiss her at the Emperor's ball—

weightless and daring all at once, as though he had jumped from a cliff.

She pressed her hands to her cheeks. Had they suddenly become heated at his words? Had she welcomed them, the way she had welcomed his kiss?

"What do you suppose the odds are that the Prince is still in the south of England?" he asked, to give them both a moment to recover.

"I think that if I were to wager like my sister Gwen, I would wager on his being in Portsmouth. There is no denying that the war is coming to a head. If his information is anything like ours, he would be prudent to inspect his steam ships and see that they are ready to launch. Do not you agree?"

What a woman she was! He had wondered the same himself, but not with this kind of inescapable logic.

"I think I would be foolish not to agree," he said.

"Good," she said. And then, in the light of the running lamp, her eyes met his, full of mischief and something else. "For I would hate to think I had kissed a fool."

And then she dimpled at him and returned to the helm.

"We knew you could not have been guilty," Josie was assuring Marcel as the four of them sat on the deck of the air ship while it steamed toward England. All still wore their masquerade costumes, minus the masks, and Celeste could not imagine a more motley crew.

"Of course he was not guilty," Amélie said with a frown.

"He worked beside us as we helped *La Blanchard* prepare for her ascent."

"We would have known anyway," Josie scolded her, "because he is our friend."

Marcel reached out as if to touch her hand, then drew back. His nails were chipped and filthy, his hair sticking out from under the clown's jingling cap matted with mud and blood. Celeste didn't want to think about what might be crawling through the black curls.

"I know you are my friends," he said, voice rough. "You would not have risked everything for me otherwise. Thank you."

As Josie blushed and Amélie beamed, he turned to Celeste. "The real villain is Captain Toussaint. Even before your mother's ascent, he had taken to having her followed everywhere."

"A national treasure," Celeste remembered with a shudder.

Marcel nodded. "One day, when they were at the school, I overheard him speaking with a new recruit about advancing through obedience, even when that obedience seemed contrary to France's best interests. I found the fellow shortening the fuses on *La Blanchard*'s explosives after she had inspected them. I tried to stop him, but he turned me over to Toussaint even before your mother began her ascent. No one would believe me afterward."

Perhaps this new recruit had been the one controlling the unmanned air ship at her own ascension. "You have no reason to be concerned any longer about Captain Toussaint," Celeste told Marcel. "His star has fallen. The Emperor is aware of all his plans. Anyone associated with him will likely be clapped in gaol as well."

"The package you threw out," Josie said, eyes widening. "You told the Emperor about the air ships."

"*Mais oui*. I did not want to give Napoleon reason for success, but Toussaint had ambitions far beyond the Aeronautical Corps. France is better off with him out of the way."

"*Merci beaucoup,*" Marcel murmured.

"And the automatons?" Amélie asked. "You know I value devices, but they should not be given such power over us."

"The Emperor shares your love of devices," Celeste said. "But I doubt he will approve of the concept of automatons flying his air ships, especially after La Croix explains how one came to crash. He will make a far more cautious Chief Air Minister, with no more of these mad plots."

"Likely Toussaint thought it necessary," Marcel said. "After your mother's death, few volunteered to join the Corps. Everyone but Captain La Croix and Captain Toussaint recognized the dangers of transporting explosives so close to lifting gas."

"And so close to where the English have their steam cannons," Amélie agreed. She glanced up at the corseted envelope of silk above them. "But this? Oh, the Emperor would love to see this."

"Which is why he can never do so," Celeste told them all. "Even a glimpse in the skies might have been too much. I am so thankful we were able to rescue the Grand Inventor, but Napoleon is already seeking another to take his place. France rules the deep with her *sous-marins*, but England must be the ruler in the skies if we are to end this war."

Marcel leaned back to look up at the ribbed envelope above them as well. "Listen to you, talking of ending wars.

With a few craft like this, you may be able to do it. *La Blanchard* would be proud."

Celeste knew it as well. If only her mother and father had lived to see this marvel.

They talked of many things, then, Emory, Arthur, and Loveday chiming in where they could. They even found moments to sleep and eat a little of the provisions Amélie and Josie had put in a basket under the seat in the stern. Darkness gave way to the first glimmers of dawn before they once more neared the British coast.

"So, this is Kent," Celeste said as the air ship began to descend among a tangle of creeks and marshes.

"It is," Marcel said from where he stood beside her on the gunwale, one arm looped through the closest line. With his other hand, he pointed toward an elegant vessel hiding among the reeds. "And there is *Marguerite*, just as she usually is this time of the month, near the dark of the moon."

Their presence had been noted, for figures scurried about the deck of the smugglers' sloop, loosing lines, preparing to sail.

"I'll bring us as low as I can," Loveday told them. "But with nowhere to set down, I fear you'll have to jump, as Celeste did."

"This is farewell, then," Celeste said, throat tightening.

Marcel sketched a bow. *"Au revoir* only. We will see you again. Amélie, Josephine, *allez!"*

They grasped ropes and looked for the opportunity.

"Now!" Arthur called.

Celeste took a step forward, and her friends leaped. She grabbed the gunwale and watched as they let go of the ropes and dropped lightly into the water. Already the smugglers had lowered a longboat to fetch them. She could only pray that Marcel was right, and she would see them again one day.

Emory came to stand beside her. "I'm glad you decided to stay with us."

She nodded, blinking back tears. "Cornwall has become home." She looked over her shoulder at Loveday at the helm, and a sense of rightness swooped down to sit on her shoulders like a warm cloak. "And so we will go home as well."

"Not immediately," Loveday said. She cranked on the wheel to bring the air ship about. "I have a second destination in mind. Hang on."

CHAPTER 28

The sun was well on its way to its meridian by the time *Lark Deux* had traced the south coast and the Isle of Wight could be seen on the horizon, floating in mist.

"We must have a care," Arthur warned. "There are shore defenses on either side of the harbor, and on the Isle of Wight as well. We do not want to be mistaken for the Emperor's advance guard and shot down."

"We will not be," Loveday assured him.

He stared at her, almost as though he had been affronted. He, after all, was the army captain, with far more experience with shore defenses. And what was she? Merely an inventor. An aeronaut. "How are you so certain?"

"Because while the French defenses are designed to repel invaders by land, sea, and sky," Celeste told him, "the English defenses are not."

Illumination of the mind changed the set of his shoulders. "Ah. Of course. Our guns can fire inland and out to sea, but the steam cannon are not designed to fire upward."

"Exactly," Loveday said. "Though that is merely a matter of

time, don't you think?" She cocked an eyebrow at Emory. "If I were an engineer, my next project might be a steam engine on a mechanism that makes it possible for a cannon's barrel to swivel upward."

"I was just thinking that," Emory said, raising his own eyebrow in return.

She laughed, then turned to her duty. "I see the shipyard, and the steam works. We will make a circle—I do not wish to tease our good cannoneers nor cause them any upset this morning. Vanes vertical, gentlemen, if you please. We will set her down on that greensward and make inquiries as to the whereabouts of the Prince."

Working together, now they could be called a proper crew. Each one knew their task, and not ten minutes had passed since the first sighting of the shipyards when *Lark Deux* settled on the grass of the proving ground. It lay just adjacent to the mighty steam works that was the beating heart of His Majesty's shipyards.

Arthur and Emory leaped down the three feet or so and, finding nothing to moor the air ship to but a cannon, looped the ropes around it. When Loveday and Celeste descended, they found themselves surrounded by soldiers, a circle of rifles aimed straight at them.

"Identify yourselves!" shouted the Beefeater directly in front of Loveday. He took in her ruffly shepherdess costume, and Celeste in her leather *pantalons*, and frowned.

Arthur and Emory had frozen in place, their hands raised to indicate they were unarmed.

"Captain Arthur Trevelyan, Thirty-Second Regiment of Foot," Arthur said with a salute, for all he was dressed like a French aeronaut. "We are just arrived from France with urgent information about Napoleon's air forces. In addition, these young aeronauts wish to present our air ship to His Royal Highness for the Prince's prize."

The Beefeater scowled at them all. "I see an— What did you call it? Air ship. But no one coming from France is to be trusted." Three of his companions in the red and gold uniforms of the King's personal guard formed a phalanx around them. "You'll give your information to me, and if I deem it worthy, I may inform His Royal Highness. Or I may simply impound your vessel and arrest the lot of you as spies."

"Please do not do that, Captain," came a warm tenor voice from behind them.

Instantly, every man on the field bowed, and Loveday and Celeste sank to the ground in a curtsey.

"An air ship!" The Tinkering Prince's face was slack with awe, and he pushed his spectacles higher on his nose. "I saw you come in and set down. I could hardly descend the stairs fast enough. Oh, this is a wonder indeed!" He must have noticed that they were still bowed low. "Oh, ladies, please forgive me. You may rise."

And nothing would do but that Loveday and Celeste must invite him aboard and show him the most minute details of the ship, right down to the cupboard under the stern bench containing the food basket. He would have commanded a royal flight, too, had not the captain of the royal guard protested.

"For you see, Your Royal Highness, *Lark Deux* was originally constructed for four crew members," Celeste told him shyly. "We have recently improved her with an additional gas bag, so that she may take seven comfortably, but I fear nine would tax her beyond her present abilities."

"We would be happy to take the captain of the guard and yourself alone, sir," Emory said.

"I must," the Prince of Wales said in tones that would not be denied. "Just a little way. And may I act as crew, too?"

Loveday exchanged an incredulous glance with Celeste. She had thought perhaps a report might be taken in to the Prince to say that *Lark Deux* was complete as an entry for the competition. She had never dreamed her future sovereign would actually want to fly!

"Twenty minutes, sir," the captain of the guard said. "If it pleases you."

"Oh, you are coming, too, Captain," His Royal Highness said with all the delight of a schoolboy with a new pony.

The captain lost his color, but he would never disobey a direct command.

Arthur and Emory helped the Prince and his guard to board, and then Loveday stoked the firebox. "We shall need supplies of coal and water to return home to Cornwall, sir," she said gaily. "I hope you can accommodate us."

"For this experience you may loot the royal treasury and take the crown jewels, as far as I am concerned," he said breathlessly.

"Up ship!" Loveday called. The remaining Beefeaters loosed the ropes, and they fell up into the sky.

The captain of the guard fainted.

The Prince of Wales whooped with glee and then insisted on learning how to work the vanes. He was a quick study. Loveday supervised as he then took the helm, and once they had made a circuit of Portsmouth Harbor and the captain of the guard had regained his senses—"I will not look over, sir, begging your pardon," he croaked—the crew resumed their positions and took her back down into the grassy proving ground.

The soldiers cheered as *Lark Deux* was once again moored to the cannon, and the Prince was piped off the vessel as though he had just christened the newest steam ship in the ways at the shipyard.

"I hope you will accept her as our entry for your prize, sir," Loveday said breathlessly as Arthur handed her down.

"Accept her! My dear Miss Penhale—Mademoiselle Aventure—I hereby designate each of you the Prince's Pilot, and award you the prize without further ceremony."

Loveday gasped and clutched at Celeste, barely able to stop herself from screaming with joy.

"Truly, nothing can compete with this. I promise you, honors will be forthcoming." The Prince gazed up at *Lark Deux*'s hull, shaking his head as though he could not even yet believe he had mounted up into the air like her namesake. "And we must have more of these marvelous craft."

"If we may, sir," Arthur said, "we have vital information about Napoleon's plans for his airborne fleet."

"Yes indeed, all in good time, Captain." The Tinkering Prince clapped a hand on his shoulder. "We will discuss it all over dinner at the Admiralty. I must say, flying certainly does wonders for the appetite!"

And then they lost his attention once more as he circled the gondola, floating as it was two or three feet off the ground. *Lark Deux* tugged at her mooring ropes as though she, like he, was impatient to be once more in the sky.

Loveday's hand found that of Celeste. "We won the Prince's prize!" she said, not quite able to believe it.

"*Lark Deux*'s mere existence ought to have won it, but the

flight proved beyond a doubt her value to England," Celeste said. "I have a feeling that your *chère maman* will reconcile herself to your papa's purchase of the mines in very short order."

The following day

And so, they were homebound at last. Not in the air ship. Prinny had refused to surrender his prize. Instead, he had ordered them conveyed back to Cornwall in the royal carriage, with the wife of one of his engineers as chaperone.

"Even Napoleon would be impressed," Celeste said, her hand brushing the nap of the velvet upholstery. "Though I suspect he would have preferred a clockwork carriage."

"Steam," Loveday promised from beside her. "Emory, you must improve on the one Richard Trevithick built."

They must have all been weary, for they slept much of the way the first two days out from Portsmouth. The royal carriage was given precedence at each posting inn, and everyone from the mail coach passengers to the stable boys gazed at them in awe.

"You are a nine days' wonder," Mrs Meriweather, their chaperone, assured them.

Arthur alone did not appear pleased. Indeed, the closer they drew to home, the more somber he looked.

"What's wrong?" Celeste murmured to Emory as Arthur requested a moment of time with Loveday when they stopped in Exeter to change the horses. The neat white and black front of the White Hart Inn hid a bustling hostelry among the other shops near Market Street.

Emory watched their two friends stroll down the lane

toward the market, Mrs Meriweather ambling behind. "I imagine Arthur is considering the same matter I have been." His gaze returned to Celeste. "We were forced to spend the night together, unchaperoned, when we first arrived in France. A parent would expect a declaration."

She felt as if he had dropped a ballast bag on her head. "A declaration?"

He nodded, face solemn. "Of marriage."

Twice before she had suspected he might be preparing to propose. She had been glad then to have been mistaken. Now she could only wish for a true proposal, one born of affection, even love, not a forced gesture to comply with some stickler's rule.

"Then it is a very good thing my parents are unavailable," she said with far more levity than she was feeling. "There is no one to require you to do anything you do not wish to do."

He was silent, watching her, and the heat climbed in her face.

"There is also the matter of that kiss," he reminded her.

She looked away. "I am sure that was only born of the moment."

"So long as we understand each other," he said in that same calm voice.

"Yes, *bon*, good." Why couldn't she find the same calm? She was chattering! She clamped her teeth together and offered him her best smile as the coachman beckoned them to retake their seats for the journey home.

CELESTE WAS certain the excitement of returning home, to say nothing of Emory's almost proposal, would keep her awake the rest of the way. But she must have fallen asleep, because she woke to the echoing sounds of shouts. For a moment, she thought she was in the balloon, the crowds clamoring below, and panic threatened to swamp her. Then she realized her head was on Loveday's shoulder.

"They think we're carrying the Prince Regent," Emory remarked from the other side of the carriage.

They were passing through Truro, the houses and quays so familiar. Boys ran alongside the coach, and people came out of homes and businesses to wave or curtsey. Following Emory's direction, the coachman stopped at his family's home on the outskirts of the town.

Someone must have alerted his sisters, for they spilled out of the house to stand and stare as the footman climbed down and opened the door to hand Emory out as though he were the prince himself. His father came to stand beside them.

"Emory!" Georgiana, his youngest sister, rushed forward to throw herself into his arms. "We had almost given up hope!"

"You're home, you're safe," his next oldest sister, Thomasina, warbled, joining her.

Mr Thorndyke hitched up his breeches. "Penhale told us he knew you were safe. I knew no Frenchie could keep you down." He narrowed his gaze on Celeste in the window as if any trouble to his son was all her fault. She kept her smile firmly in place.

The eldest sister, Henrietta, moved more slowly to Emory's side, chambray skirts brushing the path from the door. "Have you brought His Highness?" Her usually calm voice sounded the least bit breathless.

"No, alas," Emory said, untangling himself from his younger sisters' embraces. "I promise to tell you all. Only give me a moment."

He turned to the carriage, his gaze meeting that of Celeste. "Thank you, Celeste, for a most educational adventure."

All three sisters gasped, but Celeste could only smile at the way he'd used her first name in public, in front of his family, as if she meant as much to him as he meant to her.

"Thank *you*, Emory," she answered in kind. "I owe you my life."

His smile was softer than the silk of the envelope and promised as much strength. "Now that you and Miss Penhale have won the Prince's prize for your air ship, I fear you may be too busy to entertain me."

His father stared at her, and she could almost see the light of respect dawning.

"Never," Celeste vowed.

Emory's smile widened. "In that case, may I call on you tomorrow?"

"Of course," she said. "*Bonne nuit, cher* Emory."

"Bone wheat," he said, and she had to hide her smile. Someday, she would teach him French.

"What a charming family," Mrs Meriweather said as the coach started away. "I look forward to meeting yours, Captain Trevelyan."

"Hale House next, I think," Arthur told her. "Miss Penhale's father will expect a full report from me. Mr Thorndyke and I were to come with them on this so-called adventure to make certain all went well. All did not."

"Well enough," Loveday put in. "After all, we won the prize, and we have the Prince's promise of future support. Imagine his underwriting the entire venture!"

"Until the next innovation captivates him," he predicted.

"And what did he mean by *honors*, I wonder?" Loveday subsided, apparently in happy contemplation of what that might mean for them, and for their families.

As they bowled along the familiar road to Hale House, people stood aside or halted their wagons to let them pass. But Celeste's gaze was directed out of the window, toward the sky. They had braved the Emperor in his palace, and in the skies they had prevailed. There was nothing they could not accomplish—discovering his spies among them, improving and developing advancements to the air ship, building a fleet.

Even, *le bon Dieu* willing, winning this war at last.

THE END

AFTERWORD

Thanks so much for reading the second book in our Regent's Devices series. If you missed the first, which tells how Celeste and Loveday began their collaboration, we invite you to read *The Emperor's Aeronaut*.

To make sure you know when the next book is out, sign up for Shelley Adina's mailing list and begin the adventure with "The Abduction of Lord Will." Sign up for Regina Scott's mailing list and learn what happened in France while Celeste was first in England.

Now, we invite you to read this little sneak peek at the next book in the series: *The Lady's Triumph*.

Fair winds!

Shelley and Regina

THE LADY'S TRIUMPH

Only one thing could be worse than Napoleon's invasion of England...

After their daring adventures behind enemy lines in France, Loveday Penhale and Celeste Blanchard cannot settle into everyday life at home. Has the Tinkering Prince forgotten them entirely? What of the prize he promised? Then, with the flourish of a royal messenger's hand, their lives are changed. Not only have they won the prize, they are to join the Prince's Own Engineers in London!

They must overcome many a stone in the path, however—leave all they love, find a suitable house, and worst of all, cope with a chaperone—before they can take their rightful places among the most intelligent and forward-thinking minds in the kingdom. Their goal? To develop an airborne fleet that will end Napoleon's dreams of conquering England forever.

But the saboteur who has been plaguing their efforts for months has not yet been caught. And along with battling for acceptance among the engineers, tiptoeing closer to falling in love, and receiving invitations to Almack's, they must discover the traitor's identity... before the Prince Regent steps forward to command the fleet and finds himself playing right into Napoleon's hands.

Find *The Lady's Triumph* at your favorite online retailer!

OTHER BOOKS BY SHELLEY ADINA

The Magnificent Devices series

Lady of Devices

Her Own Devices

Magnificent Devices

Brilliant Devices

A Lady of Resources

A Lady of Spirit

A Lady of Integrity

A Gentleman of Means

Devices Brightly Shining (Christmas novella)

Fields of Air

Fields of Iron

Fields of Gold

Carrick House (novella)

Selwyn Place (novella)

Holly Cottage (novella)

Gwynn Place (novella)

The Mysterious Devices series

The Bride Wore Constant White

The Dancer Wore Opera Rose

The Matchmaker Wore Mars Yellow

The Engineer Wore Venetian Red

The Judge Wore Lamp Black

The Professor Wore Prussian Blue

REGENCY ROMANCE as Charlotte Henry

The Rogue to Ruin

The Rogue Not Taken

One for the Rogue

A Rogue by Any Other Name

OTHER REGENCY-SET BOOKS BY
REGINA SCOTT

Grace-by-the-Sea Series

The Matchmaker's Rogue

The Heiress's Convenient Husband

The Artist's Healer

The Governess's Earl

The Lady's Second-Chance Suitor

The Siren's Captain

Fortune's Brides Series

Never Doubt a Duke

Never Borrow a Baronet

Never Envy an Earl

Never Vie for a Viscount

Never Kneel to a Knight

Never Marry a Marquess

Always Kiss at Christmas

Never Pursue a Prince

Never Court a Count

Never Romance a Rogue

Uncommon Courtships Series

The Unflappable Miss Fairchild

The Incomparable Miss Compton

ABOUT THE AUTHORS

SHELLEY ADINA

Shelley Adina is the author of more than 50 novels published by Harlequin, Warner, Hachette, and Moonshell Books, Inc., her own independent press. She writes steampunk adventure and mystery as Shelley Adina; as Charlotte Henry, writes classic Regency romance; and as Adina Senft, is the *USA Today* bestselling author of Amish women's fiction.

She holds a PhD in Creative Writing from Lancaster University in the UK, won RWA's RITA Award® in 2005, and was a finalist in 2006. She appeared in the 2016 documentary film *Love Between the Covers,* is a popular speaker and convention panelist, and has been a guest on many podcasts, including Worldshapers and Realm of Books.

When she's not writing, Shelley is usually quilting, sewing historical costumes, or enjoying the garden with her flock of rescued chickens.

Find her at shelleyadina.com.

R.E. SCOTT

R.E. (Regina) Scott started writing novels in the third grade. Thankfully for literature as we know it, she didn't sell her first novel until she learned a bit more about writing. Since her first book was published, her stories have traveled the globe, with translations in many languages, including Dutch, German, Italian, and Portuguese. She now has had published more than fifty works of warm, witty historical romance.

Regina and her husband of more than 30 years reside in the Puget Sound area of Washington State on the way to Mt Rainier. She has dressed as a Regency dandy, learned to fence, driven four-in-hand, and sailed on a tall ship, all in the name of research, of course.

Learn more about her at reginascott.com.

www.ingramcontent.com/pod-product-compliance
Lightning Source LLC
Chambersburg PA
CBHW060907190726
48286CB00002B/410

9 781950 854554